CHANGING MAJORS

by

Ana Hartnett Reichardt

2021

CHANGING MAJORS

ISBN 13: 978-1-63679-081-7

This Trade Paperback Original Is Published By
Bold Strokes Books, Inc.
P.O. Box 249
Valley Falls, NY 12185

First Edition: December 2021

CREDITS
EDITOR: BARBARA ANN WRIGHT
PRODUCTION DESIGN: SUSAN RAMUNDO
COVER DESIGN BY JEANINE HENNING

Acknowledgments

Thanks to all who helped me along the way. I am beyond grateful for the continual love and support in my life.

Barbara Ann Wright and my mom, I promise to learn how to use commas.

CHANGING MAJORS

Visit us at www.boldstrokesbooks.com

Dedication

For my Broun crew.
My family.
And my wife, Sarah.

CHAPTER ONE

I never thought this day would come. Could never envision myself past this point, past high school. Thought I was fated for an early death. Bailey Sullivan, gone before her time. Maybe it would be a tragic fall off the stage at graduation. *She could never walk in heels*, they'd whisper. Or maybe I'd choke on my last order of shrimp and grits from Barbara's. An aneurysm. Any of them. I am just pretty sure I am not supposed to be here.

When I thought about college before, I saw nothing: dark, vast, what the hell am I going to do nothingness. Now, we are about twenty miles out from Alder University. There is still time for fate to run its course. I press my forehead to the shotgun window. Maybe there is a deer out there in all those pines, just one deer with my name on it. I scan the blurry woods, waiting for it to leap out in front of our Astro.

My mom squeezes my wrist. "Hey, babygirl. You okay over there?"

I consider her skin against mine, dark and leathery. Not in an old-looking sort of way but in a "lived life well" kind of way, the kind of tan that is earned from gardening and swimming and watching her kids play whatever sports. Not the kind from the salon. We Sullivans don't do salons.

"Yeah. I'm okay. I just don't know what this will look like." I wave at the highway and watercolor trees, blinking back tears. Stupid. If I'd died young, as according to the plan of the universe, I would've gone out on top. All right grades, plenty of trophies, never did harm to anybody. I was in the clear.

I'd like to settle my tab now, please.

"How what will look like? Being in college?"

"Yeah. Being in college." *And my whole life.*

"Well, that's not surprising. No one can know what to expect. Freshman year is like throwing yourself into a blender and seeing what flavor smoothie you turn out to be. Sounds like you feel how everybody feels about going to college."

I tug at the hemline of my shorts, unable to shake the feeling that I am cosmically doomed. "Yeah. You're probably right." I gaze out the window again, watching the dashes of the highway blur into a white streak.

From my bench on the south side of campus, I have a clear view of the sun setting over the Blue Ridge Mountains. When the conditions are right, fog gathers and falls into the valleys, slithering through the mountains like a ghostly river. My family always rents the same cabin here, just ten miles north of Alder, on one of the smaller North Georgia lakes. That's how I knew I wanted to go to Alder University. There's just something about this place.

Our church in Savannah partners with Alder to fundraise within our community and offer two academically qualified youths a partial scholarship, one of those lucky youths being me. Though I couldn't be more grateful, the responsibility of representing Live Oak Catholic Church feels like God turned on "track location" on my phone. The whole congregation will know where I end up and what I do.

I tighten my fingers around my wrist, trying to mimic how it felt when my mom reached over the console and squeezed my arm this morning. She didn't understand why I wanted to go to college six hours away when I could have gone to Southern, just an hour down the road from our house in Savannah, but she helped me pack and drove me all the way up here.

I just need to get away, I could have told her. But how could I tell her that? She is freshly divorced from my stepdad, whose alcoholism escalated into something we couldn't ignore in the last couple of years. A blur of beer cans, Tucker Carlson, and bitterness is all that guy ended up being. I never understood the anger. When he threw an empty Bud Light at the TV and said, "Men can give birth now? You believe that, Bails? I hoped I'd be dead before this shit storm started."

I looked at my mom. She shook her head and shrugged as if to say, "Silly men will be silly men." That was before the last straw broke my mom's back, before I told her how I actually got the scar on my eyebrow. With my brother, Dave, off at UGA, it was just me and my mom dealing with John. A team.

How do I tell my teammate that I need space now?

I drop my wrist and think of Haley. Think of driving home together after basketball practice. Think of her fingers dragging over my open palm in her lap. How I felt so high. How she stopped hanging out with me after her mother read our texts, and I started hanging out with Greg, who only lasted a couple months.

I squint, try to watch the last bit of sun fall behind the mountains, now black and backlit like a negative. The need to see the point, the very exact point when the sun has officially set, fills me with a kind of pointless anxiety, and I try to burn every shade of orange and black into my memory along with whatever sun damage I've burned into my retinas. *Peach, carrot, tangerine with black mold.*

"Did you know they're a billion years old?" a boy asks. I abandon my color cataloging and try to discern his form from the growing darkness, but my eyes explode with fireworks.

I blink. Blue, white, pink.

Blink, blink, blink.

I rub my palm into my eyes as he sits next to me on the bench, knee knocking mine, and I shift my weight away from him. "A billion, huh?" My eyes finally adjust.

"A billion."

"I didn't know trees could live that long."

He knocks his knee against mine, this time on purpose. "The mountains." I can see his smile through the dusk; he must use White Strips or something.

"That's pretty wild. Almost as old as my nana," I say. He chuckles at my little joke.

I wasn't really expecting company, is what I really want to say, but it's my first night of freshman year, and surely, turning down this exchange would result in some kind of karmic social hell.

"You live in my dorm, Baker Hall, right? I'm Luke."

"Bailey." I shake his outstretched hand, a little clammy in the humid night. "How'd you know that?"

"I met your roommate, Priya, and saw your picture on the corkboard outside your door. Which I am now realizing must sound a little creepy." He shrugs. "Have you met her yet?"

"Priya? No, not yet." I look away, try to make out the fog settling in the valley, but it's not there. Not tonight.

"Ah, I get it. You're avoiding that awkward part of moving into the dorms where your family has already left, and now you gotta meet your roommate and their whole family and watch them fret over bedding and cry and fuss. All the while, you're just sitting on your bed trying to be polite."

I smile and wonder if my teeth are white enough for him to make them out in the night. "Interesting theory."

"She seems super chill and funny. Priya. I bet you'll like her."

He waits for me to say something. Maybe he's realized I've only said five words against his thousand. "And I happened to see her family leave, like, a half hour ago," he adds.

I sense his body swaying from side to side, growing antsy. He hops to his feet and reaches toward me for the second time tonight. For some reason, I grab his hand for the second time tonight and let him hoist me off the butt-numbing metal bench.

We check for cell phones in back pockets and adjust our clothes.

"I was about to come back," I say.

He just nods and smiles.

We walk in the general direction of Baker Hall. The air is still summertime humid and cloying, but being from Savannah, it feels like a security blanket. I breathe in the slurry of water and air and try to reset my attitude. Luke is nice. Luke is a boy. Luke is a nice boy. And that is what I want. Bailey wants a nice boy. Bailey does not want Haley.

Luke and I pass the old chapel. "Do you go to Mass?" he asks.

"Yeah. Not recently, though. You know, end of the summer was busy getting ready to come here."

"Yeah. I'm kinda off and on. My mom would definitely want me to go more. I don't know if I wanna go here, though. It's creepy as hell in there." He nods to the big oak double doors under the stone entryway. All of the buildings at Alder University resemble the chapel: old gray stone and domed windows that beg for ghosts to stare through them. I wouldn't be surprised to glimpse a ghost at a Catholic college from 1850 nestled in the North Georgia mountains, elevated, hidden from society among all these pines and maples.

"Is she pretty religious?"

"My mom goes to church every Sunday, but she's not very involved. Moderately religious, I guess. But I have two younger sisters, and they're both in the choir, so we go to see them sing, too."

"Oh, really? If I could pick any talent, it'd be the ability to sing."

"I bet you're not that bad."

"I'd prove it to you, but I don't want to scare off the birds."

He smiles at me and starts to angle across the quad, away from the dorms. "Can we stop in the dining hall? I'm starving."

I guess I'm hanging out with this guy now. "Okay."

The dining hall resembles an old European beer hall. Wooden benches and tables that run at least twenty feet are scattered over the dark floor. Alder University has dragged its feet on most updates, but the old candelabra and woodburning fireplaces must have violated code because gas fireplaces and electric bulbs with flicker flames take their place in almost every common area. It toes the line of tacky, but a warm glow is a warm glow.

A few old leather couches and chairs sit in the far corner of the dining hall, so I sink into an armchair and watch the fire while Luke acquires some macaroni and cheese. Somehow, I knew he would go for mac 'n cheese.

"Nice choice." I grin at him as he approaches. He nods at his hot to-go plate.

"You wanna head to Baker? Meet Priya?"

I cross a leg and consider his offer. *No.* "Don't you want to eat while it's hot? I'll sit with you."

He must understand because he shrugs and heads to the nearest table. I settle on the bench next to him, and when he takes the plastic top off his dinner, a warm cheesy waft hits me, and I regret leaving my student card in my dorm room.

Luke catches me eyeing his meal. "Why don't you get something?"

"I left my lion card in the dorm."

"Oh."

"What?"

"You locked yourself out. That's why you were outside this whole time."

"Yeah, I wasn't trying to avoid meeting my roommate. I mean, sure, I'm a little nervous, but I gotta bite the bullet sooner or later." It's not a complete lie. I did get locked out, but I was avoiding meeting Priya, too. When I meet her, this whole college thing becomes real. I'll have to hit the gas pedal, and I'm scared of where I'll take myself.

"You shoulda told me I was wrong."

"That's no way to make friends." In my experience, it pays to keep the boat steady. He knocks my shoulder with his, takes another big bite, then hands his fork to me. Saliva shines on the black plastic in little beads. It feels too intimate, but I smile at him and shovel the cheesy goodness into my mouth. We pass the fork back and forth, making slow progress through the mound of mac.

"Where ya from?" I ask through a mouthful of food, shooting a hand in front of my mouth to preserve some semblance of being a lady.

Luke doesn't seem to notice. Or doesn't care. "Chattanooga. And you?"

"Savannah."

"Mmm. Love Savannah. It's haunted, right?"

"Supposedly the most haunted city in America." I throw a victorious fist in the air as if that's a fact to be proud of. I think it could be, if you take the time to honor the pain there, too.

"I heard this campus is haunted."

"I think anywhere as old as this place is haunted somehow. I mean, this campus is from the 1850s? Just think about what people went through back then." What women went through back then. What people like me went through back then. An icicle fist tightens around my spine at the thought.

He passes me the fork, offering the last bite. "I guess you're right. I'll keep my eyes peeled for ghosts."

"Why did you pick Alder?" I ask.

"Love this place. The mountains. And I got an engineering scholarship. Plus, I didn't want to go to a giant school."

"Yeah. That's how I felt about Southern and UGA. And my family used to vacation here. Always had a thing for the mountain towns. Have you always wanted to be an engineer?"

"Since I got my first set of Legos, yeah. And my dad is an engineer, so you know."

"Gotcha." I stare at my hands for a beat. "Hey. Thanks for sharing your food and whatever diseases you may be carrying." I pat him on the back. His dark brown eyes crinkle with warmth. They look like my eyes. "We kinda look alike. Like we could be siblings." Freckles dot his cheeks, but his features are almost as dark as mine. Almost.

His smile falters for a split second, but he recovers. "Meant to be, I guess." He throws away his trash.

"Ready?" he asks.

"Ready."

❖

The common room of Baker Hall sports the same roaring gas fireplace as the dining hall and the same worn leather couches and armchairs. A thick wooden coffee table sits on a burgundy and navy rug that somehow has remained unstained through the last decade.

Alder's coat of arms hangs over the fireplace, and a crucifix is mounted on the wall above the couch. I avert my eyes from the cross.

"This is you," Luke says as we approach 107. I stare at me and Priya on our corkboard, our faces huddled under a *Welcome Freshmen of 2021* banner.

"I'm aware." This boy annoys me but only because I want what he has. I want his confidence and steadiness. I am loath to admit that having him next to me makes me feel safe, and I'm glad he found me. I hesitate for a moment, my hand on our doorknob. *I should knock.* I knock on the door at the same time I realize that knocking on my own door is ridiculous. The questioning look on Luke's face confirms this. I open the door in tandem with Priya's, "Come in."

"Bailey." She crosses the room to embrace me. Her thick black hair smells like honeycrisp apples. "I'm Priya."

Most of her things are pink—bedding, notebooks, posters—but her side of the room looks tidy and warm, while mine still needs some finishing touches. The dorms at Alder are all original, which has afforded them the privilege of remaining large, with hardwood floors and giant windows that overlook campus. Baker is only three stories; the first two floors are for women, and the top floor is for men. The heated debate over coed dorms almost tore the university apart five years ago, but a strict curfew of 10 p.m. quelled the anxiety of the traditionalists.

I have a feeling Luke and I will be testing the strictness of our RA.

"Hey. It's great to finally meet you." I raise a hand toward Luke to relieve myself of the attention. "This is my friend, Luke."

She smiles and waves. "Oh yeah, we met in the common room earlier. Hi, again." She turns back to me and grabs both my hands. "Where have you been?"

I squeeze her hands so it's less abrupt when I pull mine away to grab my lion card off my bed for evidence. "I accidentally locked myself out, so I went exploring until Luke found me and let me back in the building." Luke sits next to me on my bed while I explain. And it feels so natural.

Priya plops down on my other side. "Ah, yeah, it's gonna be hard to get in the habit of always having our lion card on us."

And now I'm sandwiched by two people who really want to be my friend. It makes me nervous to be so seen. Normally, I find lying low to be an asset, but I guess there's no more hiding.

Priya claps, walks to her desk, and opens her laptop. Soon, the Alabama Shakes flood our room. "Is this okay? Why have a quiet room when we have all the world's music at our fingertips?"

"I love the Shakes." I smile and let the comfort of these two people and Brittany Howard ease me.

Luke pops off his shoes and scoots farther onto my bed until his back rests against the maroon wall. I may be stuck with this guy forever. Every time I think he should leave, he settles in more. I shuffle backward, our shoulders pressing against each other, and I realize I'd be disappointed if he left. We watch as Priya continues to unpack random knickknacks.

She holds a framed picture as she contemplates her desk, the real estate of which is reaching capacity, but she rearranges a few current tenants and places the last picture with triumph. She turns to us and smiles, hands on hips. I giggle at her overcrowded desk.

"Where are you supposed to do all of your schoolwork?" I ask.

She stares at me for a moment, eyes narrowed, then considers her desk. Her shoulders relax, and a self-deprecating smile breaks across her face. "Shit. I think I'm going to have to become a library person." She crosses the room and jumps on my bed, sidling up next to me, again sandwiching me. These people have no concept of personal space.

I didn't think I would find such intimacy here. At least not on night one. I'd been so used to holding my tongue around John that it feels unnatural to allow myself the space to be me. But this is why I left Savannah. This moment is mine. These friends are mine.

"Knock knock."

A girl with curly blond hair appears in the door frame of our bathroom, which connects to our suitemates' room. We respond with a chorus of greetings, Priya's being the loudest and warmest. The girl walks into our room, looking over Priya's pink explosion, and

I wonder what she thinks about my side of the room. I have an old sage green quilt that has been mine since my mother traded out my baby blanket. My laptop is the only thing that lives on my desk, and my coffee maker reigns over my dresser. I have a family photo in my desk drawer. My mom, John, Dave, and me. I'll display it tomorrow.

"I'm Cassie, y'alls' suitemate. My roommate, Noelle, ran to the dining hall to grab food," she says. "Loving the pink." She makes a point to look over all of Priya's things.

"Just trying to spice it up in here. I'm Priya. This is Bailey, my roommate, and Luke, our friend. He lives upstairs." It's funny how quickly we claim each other in situations like these. Yes, Luke, our old friend from upstairs, whom we just met.

"Nice to meet you," I say. "The view of Priya's pink paradise is actually best from over here." I lean over Luke and pat the open space next to him. "Wanna join us?"

She smiles and sits on the edge of the bed, feet planted on the ground. After what I assume is some deliberation about how close to Luke she should sit, she shifts backward to match our posture but leaves a couple of inches between her and Luke while the rest of our shoulders and thighs press together.

"Where y'all from?" Luke asks.

"Huntsville," says Priya.

"Knoxville. Both Noelle and I. We went to the same church there, so when we saw each other on the Facebook page, we were like, yeah, we should definitely be roommates," Cassie says.

"Everyone is pretty close. That's great," I say. I feel like my home is not only the farthest from Alder but the farthest from the experiences of my new friends.

"Where are you from, Bailey?" Priya asks.

"Savannah."

"That makes you the farthest," Cassie says.

"But the only one from Georgia." I wink. Then I realize my friends must be very wealthy or very smart because full tuition at Alder isn't cheap, and being a private university, there's no in-state tuition. I shift my weight, realizing I'm probably the only one who isn't here on a strictly academic scholarship. I'm here because I had just good enough grades and the sympathy of our church. It was a big deal in the community when my mom left John, and I used that in my essay about why I would benefit from attending Alder University. Broken family and all.

My stomach growls, and I shift until I give up and slide off the bed. "I'm going to grab some food. That mac was the only thing I've eaten all day."

Luke scoots toward the edge of my bed. "I'll come with you."

"No, no, you stay. Keep my seat warm. I'll be back soon." I need a moment to myself. I've never had a crew before, and though it's lovely, I need to take a breather. I slip on my Nikes and head for the door.

There are only a couple other people in the dining hall when I arrive. I take stock of my food options. I'm half tempted to get a full serving of the mac 'n cheese, but I know I need to eat something real, so I head toward the southern kitchen bar and eye the options. Shrimp and grits, baked chicken and green beans, barbeque and cornbread. The chicken and green beans smell fresh and savory and feels like the closest thing to my mom's cooking, so I grab a plate and reach for the tongs.

"I wouldn't. Not as good as it looks."

I turn to find a girl sitting at the nearest table, watching me over a plate of chicken and green beans with only a couple bites missing. I replace the tongs and take a couple steps toward her.

I throw a thumb over my shoulder. "But it smells so good."

She shrugs.

"How do I know I can trust you, anyway?" I ask because something in my gut pulls me toward her, and something in my gut tells me to run.

A grin forms on her lips as she pats the bench next to her. I sit, not bothering to swing my legs over. She opens her shoulders to me, long dimples cutting her cheeks. "Well, I'd argue that you can't trust anyone."

Her eyes are a kind of gray green, and her hair is dirty blond, but looking at her makes the term feel crude. In reality, it's gold and blond and honey brown all at once, her brows matching the darkest shade of gold in her hair.

"That's bleak."

She smirks and holds up her fork. "Try mine."

Again, I consider the shimmering beads of saliva and the intimacy of the act. I take her fork and swing my legs over the bench. I feel her eyes on me as I fork a bite of chicken and stab a green bean. The chicken is tender and juicy, and the green bean is not mushy but perfectly cooked, retaining just the right amount of crunch. I sigh with the pleasure of eating a home-cooked meal in a strange place and return her fork to her plate. Her eyes brighten and dimples deepen.

"Liar," I say through a smile.

She overflows into soft chuckles. "I told you. You can't trust anyone." She picks up her fork to continue her meal, and I wipe at the corner of my mouth.

"It's so good." I swing my legs over the bench to grab myself a plate.

"You should eat with me. You know, in the spirit of making friends and all that," she calls after me.

I take a few small steps backward, holding her eye contact. "All right. But I'll never forget that this beautiful friendship started with a lie." Even more so than Luke, I want to be next to this girl.

I reach for the biggest chicken breast, spoon the juices over the top, then fill the rest of my plate with green beans and spoon the chicken drippings over those, too. An older gentleman with the kind of furious eyebrows that cannot be contained eyes my plate and arches one of his brows as he swipes my lion card. I thank him and hope that none of his hairs fell in my food. I take my plate and settle on the bench across from the girl with dirty blond hair and gray-green eyes.

She laughs when she sees my overflowing plate. "Jesus."

I look around in mock horror and do a quick sign of the cross. "Easy with the J-bombs. I hear there's a dungeon full of students who use his name in vain." I dig into my food, feel her watching me again. "Growing girl," I mutter.

"What's your name?" she asks.

I put down my fork and take an awkwardly long time to swallow, embarrassed I hadn't introduced myself already. I wipe my hand on my jeans and reach across the table. "Bailey Sullivan." I attempt a smile, hoping I don't have green beans stuck in my teeth.

She leaves my hand alone in the wind and leans on her elbows, closing some of the space between us. "Sullivan? Sullivan, like, you're Irish?"

"Uh-oh. Is this the one Catholic college in America that doesn't allow the Irish?" I tuck my hand back in my lap, unbothered by her lack of reciprocation. I like that she colors outside of the lines. "'Cause, they definitely didn't mention that in the brochure."

Her eyes brighten, and her shoulders shake. She lowers her head and peeks at me from under her golden brows. "Yep. You shoulda gone to Notre Dame."

I shrug and pop a bite of chicken in my mouth.

"You just look, I don't know, not very Irish. You know, with your dark eyes and hair and all," she says, eyes downcast as if she's aware she may offend me.

"You know loads of Irish people have dark hair, right? Anyway, I'm only half-Irish."

"And the other half?"

"Cuban," I say between bites of chicken and beans.

"I'm guessing your mom is the Cuban one, given your last name."

I narrow my eyes and point my fork at her. "Nothing gets by you."

"Your scar is pretty." Her gaze flicks up to my left eyebrow. *Pretty.* I've only ever attributed pain and lies to that thing. It's not a huge scar, maybe an inch, but it interrupts the dark hair of my brow right where it naturally arches, drawing attention to itself. I finger the raised line of skin. It's almost six years old now, but it still itches sometimes.

"Um, thank you. Caught a stray elbow playing pick-up basketball." It's my standard line, but it tastes a little sour when I recite it to—"What's your name?"

"Noelle Parker." She reaches across the table as if I didn't just offer a handshake literally one minute ago. I take her hand. Warm, firm shake.

"Noelle. Were you born in December?"

"Nope. October nineteenth."

"Your parents should've named you *Hallow* or something. Doesn't *Noelle* mean Christmas?"

She shrugs. "I think they just wanted to name me something joyous. Besides, *Noelle* has Latin roots from the verb 'to be born.' So I guess it's technically a name for anyone."

"You've researched it."

She grins. "I've researched it."

"*Noelle*, that sounds so familiar. Oh, are you Cassie's roommate?"

"Yeah. How did you—"

"I'm your suitemate. I just met Cassie before I came here," I say, pleased with the coincidence. "Your name is really beautiful," I mumble, staring at my plate, mostly empty now. Heat floods my cheeks because even though her name *is* beautiful, what I really meant is, *you* are beautiful.

"Bailey." I look at Noelle, who watches me with something like affection in her eyes. Amusement, more likely. I wait for her to continue, too embarrassed to reply to my own name. "Do you want to head back together? Since we're headed the same way."

"Yeah. Sure."

We walk across the quad, shoulders skimming, pace slow. The chapel comes into view, and I steal Luke's conversation starter.

"Are you religious?"

"Um, yeah. My family is really involved in our church in Knoxville, and I've gone to Catholic school my whole life." For some reason, this shocks me, disappoints me. "Are you?"

"Religious? Sure. I mean, we're Catholic and go to Mass, I just don't know." Accepting the scholarship from my church felt like doubling down on my religion, but the truth is that I've never been more confused.

"It's okay to not know. Sometimes, I find myself questioning, too." She shakes her head as if she didn't mean to share that. "Not a lot, just sometimes."

"I get it. I think everyone has an ebb and flow in their relationship to religion. To anything."

We climb the steps to the front door. She turns to me before she swipes her lion card through the reader. Grabs my elbow. "Ready?"

I flinch.

Not because her dimples make me woozy, but because I know there's a pressure point right there, under her two fingers, that can bring me to my knees and make the backs of my eyeballs burn if she squeezes it, just like John used to. He never hit us because he didn't have to. He had a way of making me believe that, one day, he just might cross the line. That, combined with his pressure point trick, kept me on my toes.

She pops an eyebrow and pulls her hand from my arm as if it shocked her. "Sorry," she mumbles.

"Oh. No. It's just that, you probably don't know this, but there's a pressure point there. Here." I push lightly against the inside of her elbow. "My stepdad used to do it to me all the time." Concern flashes over her face. "Oh, no. Not like that." *Exactly like that.* "He just knew I was particularly affected by it. It was kinda like a joke."

She blinks at me.

"Um. Anyways. That's why I flinched. It hurts like a son of a bitch. And I'm rambling."

"Noted." She swipes us into the dorm. We walk up to our respective doors and stop.

"Everyone was in our room before I left. Do you want to come over? Or *in*. I mean, do you want to come *in*?"

"Yeah. I'm going to change real quick, and I'll pop through the bathroom."

"Okay."

"Bailey?"

I pause, hand on the doorknob. "Yeah?"

"It was really nice to meet you."

I get lost. Forget to speak. I want to stay in this hallway where it's only me and her.

"I mean, I'm really glad we got to meet the way we did," she explains.

"Me, too."

I open my door to find everyone where I had left them, plus one more guy sitting on the ground, his back against my bed. The Alabama Shakes has morphed into Beyoncé, and the volume level of the group's conversation has risen significantly.

"Y'all didn't miss me at all." I pull my sweater off and kick my shoes into the closet. I crack a window for some fresh air and take a seat on Priya's bed.

"Aw. I missed you, Bailey," Priya yells across the room.

I ignore her and wave at the newcomer. "Hey. I'm Bailey, Priya's roommate."

He waves back and runs a hand through his shaggy blond hair. "I'm Matt, that guy's roommate." He points to Luke. If I hadn't known any better, I would've guessed they'd been drinking. All rosy cheeks and smiles. I take a deep breath and let this crew surround me like air, let myself need them like air.

Noelle walks into the room wearing red and black flannel pajama pants and a gray tank top. I look her over and quickly avert my gaze. I think I notice Matt do the same exact thing, but I can't blame him. Noelle is the most beautiful girl I've ever seen.

"This is Noelle, our suitemate," I announce to the room. Noelle waves to everyone and sits next to me on Priya's bed. She elbows me in the rib.

"Didn't peg you for a pink fanatic," she says, eyeing Priya's decor.

"This is Priya's side. They're on my side."

Noelle studies my quilt, my desk, my lack of anything and everything. "I was going to say the pink suits you."

"Shut up." I push her away, and she bounces right back.

"What? You aren't the manicured boy-crazy cheerleader?" Something about the way she stares at me makes me feel like her questions are an expedition. An intimate exploration of me.

"I think you already know that I'm not."

She nods. "Who are you, then?"

Who am I? The loud chatting from the rest of our group saves me from an awkward silence. "Um. I like basketball and soccer."

She grins and looks at my lips like the stupidest thing in the world just crawled out of them, then considers the rest of the room. She clears her throat. "This is our crew, huh?"

I join in her observation of the others. "Yup. I think so."

She looks at me. "Well. I'd say we're pretty lucky." Her stare moves from my right eye, to my left, then back to my right. Talking to Noelle feels like playing chess. She moves her rook, a normal enough move, but what's her play?

"I'd say so."

"What's your major, Bailey?" Matt asks from the floor.

I tear my gaze from Noelle to respond. "Um. Well, I put a different major on every application I sent in. This one happened to have education marked on it, so I guess I'll do that." I scratch at Priya's comforter. My personal resume includes playing basketball and eating. I love food. But in terms of big dreams? I don't have much to add to the conversation. My mom is a teacher, my aunt is a teacher, and I reckon I'll be a teacher.

"Ah, you don't have to know right now," he says.

Generous. But what if I never know? I turn to Noelle and catch her studying my face, but she doesn't flinch. I pose the same question to her.

"Pre-med," she says plainly, her stare still prying into me.

I turn away first. "Cassie?" I ask.

"Engineering. Well, chemical engineering. Are you civil?" she asks Luke.

"Better believe it."

"What's your major, Priya?" Cassie asks.

"Animal Science. I want to be a vet."

"I hear that's even harder than med school," Cassie says.

"Noelle and I will have to compare notes at our ten-year reunion and let you know," Priya says. We all look at Matt. "You're next," Priya says.

"I round out the engineering trifecta. Software."

All of my friends are passionate about something, and I'm maybe going to be a teacher one day. Being a teacher is a great career; it just gets my gears cranking as much as a tepid bath. "Hey." Noelle lays a hand over mine, smothering my scratching. "No one really knows what they want to do. We're all just guessing and hoping that we picked right."

"Yeah." It's all I can say. I pull my hand away and look at Matt. "What about y'alls' suitemates? Why are you holding out on us?"

Luke and Matt exchange a look, and Luke scratches at the stubble on his chin. "They, uh, you wouldn't like them. They're obsessed with *Call of Duty* and never leave their room," Luke explains.

"Yeah, they've hardly acknowledged our existence," Matt says.

"Sound like jerks," says Priya.

Our collective intimacy becomes palpable as we abandon our vertical seats for more horizontal ones, all of us touching some part of another person. The three on my bed slump to one side, and Matt leans against Priya's legs. I sprawl across Priya's bed, back resting against the wall while Noelle lies on her side, head in my lap and hand resting on the curve of my thigh.

I look across the room at Luke, trying to ignore the accordion in my gut.

Trying to ignore her hand on my thigh.

CHAPTER TWO

The gurgling and spitting of my coffee maker wakes me at 7:30. God bless the automatic brew feature. The sun peeks through our blinds and surfs the coffee's hazy steam. Snores come from Priya's bed, light and feminine, like somehow, she snores in pink, too, and I can hear birds singing and flitting about outside our window. I stretch in the cozy mess of my sheets and slip out of bed to hunt for my coffee mug.

I wipe the dust out of my Alder Lion mug and jump at a knock on our door. I stride over, wishing we had a peephole, and open the door to find Luke grinning at me, wearing sunglasses, swim trunks, and trail shoes. I plant a hand on his chest and push him into the hallway, closing the door softly behind us. He makes it easy to focus on him, even though I was up half the night thinking about someone else's hand on my thigh.

"It's too early, dude. Priya's still sleeping," I whisper, groggy and confused. I run a hand through my hair, tug at my shorts, pull at the T-shirt clinging to my braless breasts, suddenly aware of my appearance.

"It's our last day of true freedom before classes start tomorrow. It's sunny and warm. Get your bathing suit on, wake everyone up. Matt and I are ready."

He pulls off his sunglasses and flashes me his charming smile. A smile that I'm sure would get him out of any trouble if he were the kind of guy to get in trouble. Luke's joy is palpable. It radiates off him like it's his purest, most natural state. His brown eyes are warm, and he pops his sunglasses back over them, breaking into another giant grin.

I want to be near him, want some of that easiness to wear off on me. It's simple between us. We're more like checkers as opposed to chess. I step closer and push him in the chest again. "Get outta here, loser."

He jogs backward, never letting the smile fade from his face.

"I'll meet you at the dining hall in an hour," I whisper-yell after him, hoping everyone will be awake by then.

When I walk back in our room, Priya is sitting in bed, stretching her arms high, her camisole riding up to her belly button, something I'd normally turn away from, but with her, it's just nothing. "Who was that?" She yawns.

I finally pour myself a cup of coffee and sit in her desk chair, noticing a pink coffee mug that has a graphic of a bullet leaving a gun. I didn't take Priya for the republican gun-toting type, but then, I did sign up to go to a private Catholic college, so I should have seen this coming.

"Mugshot," she murmurs, like it's the most obvious thing in the world. "Turn it around."

I spin the mug and find the second graphic: a single shot glass and lime. *Mugshot.* "I see. Coffee?"

She rubs her eyes and squints at me. "Do we have cream?"

"We don't even have a minifridge."

"We gotta fix that. No cream, no coffee. Thanks, though."

"That was Luke. He wants to wrangle the gang and go swimming. He and Matt are already dressed and ready to go. I said we'd meet him at the dining hall in an hour."

"Okay, I'm going to shower to wake myself up. I'll wake up the girls."

I sip my coffee in her chair and try to tame my eagerness. I get to see Noelle today. I get to see her every day.

❖

Students mill around the dining hall drinking coffee, chatting with new friends, and filling their plates with pancakes and eggs. I grab a banana from the breakfast bar. And one more cup of coffee. Luke and Matt are polishing off some waffles at one of the long tables.

"Morning," I say.

Luke finishes chewing a bite of syrup-soaked waffle. "Morning, Bailey. Ready for a swim?"

"Ready."

The rest of the girls walk in together. The pink strings of Priya's bikini are a bright pop of color under her thick black ponytail. I'd kill for her hair.

Noelle drops her plate on the table and settles onto the bench beside me, her hair still wet from her shower. Orange blossom. Her hands and arms are vascular-wiry but smooth. She places a hand between my shoulder blades and smiles at me, her eyes fixed on mine. "Hey, you," she says.

I offer a smile and stare at my banana peel, stomach aching. It could be the last cup of coffee. Or it could be that I have it bad.

Priya steals a blueberry off Matt's plate. "Where are we going?" she asks.

"Lake Carter."

"It's only an hour hike from here, and the trails are easy. Plus, the lake's small, so perfect for just swimming around. No motor boats or anything," Luke adds.

"Yeah, got a rope swing, too." Matt rubs his hands together.

"How do y'all know about this?" I ask.

"My brother went here. Told me about all the hidden gems," Matt says.

"What else is there around here?" Noelle asks.

"In good time." He winks at her. And I want to stab him in the eye with his fork.

Cassie pushes off the bench and gathers her trash. "Let's get going. We gotta be back by four to get ready for Mass, since we're obviously not going to make the morning services."

I blink at her, then look at our crew to see who protests being lumped into the category of *churchgoers*. Matt clears his throat. "Actually, I'm an atheist. No church for me."

Thank you, Matt. Testing the waters for all of us. I feel guilty not wanting to go to church, especially when it's why I was able to afford Alder, but I need space from it. It has never really sat well with me, even though it's part of me.

Cassie just blinks at him for a second, then recovers. "Oh, right. I shouldn't assume. Well, does anyone want to join me?" she asks the group again, and I'm right back in the same position. Priya and Luke politely decline.

"Of course," Noelle says.

"I haven't been to Mass in a couple of weeks, but I'll check it out," I say. Shit. This is the last thing I want to do, but I'm finding I'd do a lot to be on Noelle's team.

After an hour of mild hiking, the forest spits us out onto an earthy beach overlooking Lake Carter. The day is warm and bright, and the water is calm enough to hold the reflections of the pines. A cool breeze rustles through the leaves, but the sunlight heats our skin as we peel off layers of clothing. Noelle pulls off her T-shirt and shimmies out of her shorts, revealing a somehow modest green bikini. I swallow and look away, try to forget the image of her. It isn't for me.

Luke and Matt run to the old, craggy maple, a rope hanging from its farthest-reaching branch. Within five seconds, Luke flies through the air and splashes into the dark blue water. We apply our sunscreen while we watch Matt plunge in without giving Luke enough time to clear the landing zone.

"Boys." Priya sighs.

I can hear the adoration in her voice, though. And it hits me, too, for a second. Adoring them. Their carefree, screw sunscreen, run ahead and jump attitudes. Matt, not caring that his ass crack is in the breeze for all to see. *Boys.* My chest tightens. Dave was never home. He did what he wanted, which was to avoid John and hang out with his friends every night until he could escape to Athens. It felt like he abandoned me and my mom. He didn't; I was just jealous, because he felt entitled to protect himself. It's hard not to think of all men as entitled. Entitled to be "just so carefree and charming." It was only when my mom finalized her divorce that I saw leaving as a possibility.

Luke runs up to me and breathlessly encourages me to jump in. "You're next."

"Go on. I'll be there in a second. Not quite ready yet." I peel off my shirt and let the breeze tickle my skin. The briefest goose bumps, then sun.

The lake is warmer than I expected, still holding on to the heat that it has garnered all summer. The water is clearer than the lakes in the lowlands and lacks the murky shimmer of algae and silt. Even so, when a hand tightens around my ankle and pulls me under the water's surface, I panic, but it's just Luke. When I reach the surface, I brush the water out of my eyes and splash him in the face for retribution.

We spend the next half hour trying to drown each other. Grabbing, tackling, dunking. I have my eyes set on Luke because he's the strongest, and he knows it. Nothing would be better than to take him down a peg. I lock eyes on him. I've never been close with a guy. Most of the men in my life have been an intimidating presence, and something inside me wants to dominate Luke. Even if it's just dunking him in this lake. He makes me feel like I could be powerful, too.

He throws his hands in the air and slowly backs away from me. "Oh no you don't."

"Mmm. But, I think I'm gonna." I stay the course. At least I'm intimidating. But his face shifts, and he stops his retreat as if my threat has been neutralized. I abandon my crouch and straighten, confused.

Arms lasso around my shoulders with all of the force of someone's body crashing into me. I stumble, going under for a second before the lasso loosens. I wipe my eyes and turn in Noelle's slippery arms. She wipes some wet hair off her forehead, a smirk on her lips. Her legs wrap around my hips, smooth in the lake water, and tighten around me. My stomach tightens, too. I wrap my arms around her waist for lack of anywhere else to put them.

"If you take me down right now, there's no way you're not coming with me." Her eyes are lasers. Absolutely right. But would it be so bad? I could think of worse ways to go.

"Don't see any other option." Some things are inevitable. I lock my arms behind her waist, and pull her hard against me, displacing the water between our bodies in a wake. Noelle's eyes go wide, and her breath catches on her surprise. I pull her into a gator roll, and we corkscrew together to the bottom of the lake. When my back hits the clay, I release her. Dave taught me that move, something rugby players do in a ruck. He also taught me what it feels like to think you're drowning. Brotherly, sure, but Dave panicked me one too many times in that neighborhood pool. We would often walk home in silence, me pissed at him for not understanding that in those moments, he stole my consent. He scared me. Even if just for a moment, the feeling is too terrifying to impart on anyone, so I'm quick in my release.

We take a break from swimming to lie on our towels and let the sun dry our skin. I turn from belly to back every couple of minutes, then give up, never one to be able to *lay out*. I pull on my shorts. "I'm going to go pee somewhere."

Noelle sits up, watches me button my shorts and reapply sunscreen to my shoulders. "I'll come with you."

We walk straight back into the woods behind the beach, parallel to the trail we took to get here. Noelle looks like a woodland creature, born of the forest in all of her green and golden glory. I daydream that we've run away together in these woods, and we're searching for a place to camp together. I almost run into her when she stops walking and looks up.

"Whoa. This is perfect," she says.

"What?"

"This tree. We gotta climb it. It's so good."

It is perfect. The hardest limb is the first one, but it's doable with two people. Above the first branch, the limbs jut out every couple of feet like a stairwell to the top. I drop to one knee, offering my Captain Morgan stance as a boost.

"Don't you have to pee?"

"Nah, I just hate laying out. Needed to go do something." I pat my knee, eager to be of service.

She plants a foot on me and pulls herself up. I think I can manage on my own, but she lowers her hand to me. The bark bites at the skin of my thigh as I climb up and sit in front of her.

"You're a pro," I say. I wish I'd climbed every tree with her growing up instead of hiding in private nooks with *Robinson Crusoe* and *The Chronicles of Narnia*. I wish I'd had *someone*.

The sun scatters through the trees and illuminates our summer skin in bands. Noelle's eyes leave mine; she looks at the rest of me. It feels like an appraisal. I look at her, too. A couple of freckles nip at her shoulders. Her stomach is tight like her arms. She narrows an eye at me and grabs the branch above her head.

"Beat you to the top." She swings up through the branches, and I chase her.

❖

The hike back to Alder is arduous. Wet clothes cling to me in all the wrong places, and the seams of my sleeves and shorts chafe my skin into angry raw patches. I can tell from the group's silence that everyone feels the same way: drained from the sun, uncomfortable in our wet clothes, tired. The plus side, not even Cassie has the energy for Mass tonight. Though, I needed this hike to be over half a mile ago, I think I'd walk through the night just to be next to these people. It has only been two days, but having them in my life makes me feel like somehow there are more possibilities for me.

My shower is painful. The hot water scorches the tender, rubbed raw skin under my arms and on my inner thighs, but I'm rewarded with the sweetest feeling in the world when I jump into sweats and pull a warm dry hoodie over myself. I poke my head into Cassie and Noelle's room.

"Shower's free," I announce. It's just Cassie, though. Noelle went to grab a bunch of food from the dining hall with Priya. I think their plan is to have a makeshift picnic in Cassie and Noelle's room for our last dinner of summer, which will also happen to be our first dinner together. It hits me that I haven't been in their room yet, and I let my eyes roam over their space. Cassie shares Priya's affinity for pink but in a milder way. She breaks up the sharpness of it with blues and purples. There's a crucifix hanging over her bed and a Bible on her desk.

"Thanks, Bails. I'll hop in."

Bails.

That is the quickest I've ever gotten to nickname status with new people. Only my family calls me that. I glance at Noelle's side of the room before I turn to leave. White sheets. Gray comforter. Peach pillows. I want to check the title of the book on her desk. I want to catalogue every object that she owns. I blink at the empty space of their room, then bolt back to safety, knocking the door frame on my way. I sit on the edge of my bed and smooth my hands over my thighs. Over my face.

Noelle is not for me. The same way that Haley was not for me. Her mom's reaction to our texts was like she thought I was corrupting her daughter. Even though Haley reached and crossed that razor thin line first, I half believe her mom. I can't help but feel guilty. I cut my losses with Haley and decided to be grateful that her mom was probably too embarrassed to call mine. The last thing I needed was John finding out.

I don't want to have a negative impact on anyone, especially Noelle. She's a nice Catholic girl who will bring home a nice Catholic boy, not me. I need to focus on my own nice Catholic boy.

Matt opens the door on my third knock.

"Hey."

"Oh. Hey, Bailey. Come in. Luke's almost done showering, then we were going to head down to you guys." He steps aside to welcome me into their room. Their navy blue walls are trimmed with Luke's Arsenal flag and a Pink Floyd album cover poster that I assume is Matt's. Dirty clothes already litter their floor, but the room still smells fresh. Well, boy fresh.

I sit on his bed and riffle through his schedule for this term. "Priya and Noelle were taking forever, so I thought I'd come hang with you guys while I waited."

"Sweet. We share any classes?" He points to his schedule in my hands.

"Yeah, actually. Lit. Tomorrow. That's it, though." I place the schedule back on his desk and notice a photo of him with his older sister. She smiles proudly at him draped in his graduation robes as he beams at the camera.

"Awesome. Well, save me a seat if you beat me there," he says.

"You, too."

The bathroom door opens, and steam bellows into the room. Luke takes a couple of steps, then locks eyes with me.

"Bailey. Hey." I stare at him. Stand to clear out of his space. His towel is cinched around his waist, and beads of water run down his skin to disappear into the cotton. I'd just seen him more exposed at the lake, only a few hours ago, but something about the smell of his body wash hanging in the steam and the way his skin is reddened from the heat makes me stammer. No boy has ever made me stammer. But no boy has ever been so nice to me or given me so much attention as Luke has.

I walk backward to their door. "Sorry, Luke."

His face shifts into an amused smile as he watches me make my retreat. He runs a hand through his dark wet hair.

"I'll see ya down there," he says.

I grasp for the doorknob behind me. "Yeah. See you guys down there."

CHAPTER THREE

Rain pelts at our window in an incessant *tap tap tap*. The first week of classes has been drenched in summer storms, the kind of southern downpours that no umbrella or raincoat can save you from.

I change from my wet raincoat and jeans into shorts, a T-shirt, and flip-flops. "There's no point in even trying to be dry. I'm just accepting it. Bring on the rain."

Priya laughs at my grudging determination. "You're going to freeze your ass off."

"It's literally ninety-five degrees outside. I think I'll live."

Wrong.

I burst through the classroom door, barely on time, and collapse into my desk. My clothes are soaked through, and the aggressive air-conditioning sends shivers down my body. Water drips down my goose bumped legs to form a little puddle around my feet. Lake Bailey. Priya was right. I'm going to freeze to death.

A tap on my shoulder interrupts my self-pity session. "Hey, you look like you could use this."

I meet the gaze of a boy with dusty blond hair and blue eyes. He holds up his very warm-looking sweatshirt and smiles at me. I mouth a *thank you* through my chattering teeth. His sweatshirt swallows me whole and brings me some much-needed warmth. It's well-worn, and my cheeks warm at the hint of aftershave and cologne still tangled in the cotton.

I open my binder and flip through the papers until I get to the syllabus. Intro to Ed is a pass-fail class, meaning minimal effort is required. Yes, yes, but where is the attendance section? How much attendance is required? I flip over two more pages and find the section I'm looking for.

Attendance is mandatory. This class only tolerates two absences. Anything in excess of two absences results in a failing grade.

It's not a ton, but I'll take it. I just want to get my degree and spend as much time with my friends as possible, so I'll skip as many classes as I'm allowed. I shade in the empty space of all the *o's* in my syllabus while I wait for class to end. The professor continues to drone. The thing I'm learning about college classes is that they're just like high school. I am not somehow more interested in academics now that I dwell on a nineteenth century gothic campus. I enjoy the agency of my independence, but while others' agency is leading them toward lofty goals, mine is leading me to this epic doodle of an ice cream cone on today's Intro to Education handout.

It's strange to me that we are always asking kids what they want to be when they grow up. When did our careers start defining our lives? I don't know what I want to do. I just want to be happy. Is it so crazy that nothing at the job fair turns me on?

"Women have always found themselves drawn to becoming educators. It's the natural caretaking tendencies we're born with. While this is wonderful, we need more men to join our forces to help mold young boys into strong men," I hear the teacher say.

What the fuck? There are probably so many reasons why teachers are historically women, and I'm positive it's not just because women are *randomly* so good at caretaking. I'm sure it has *nothing* to do with women being forced to stay at home for all of history. I also wasn't aware that dangling genitals was what made for a *strong* role model to help shape *strong young men*. What would they say about two women raising a son together? I want to vomit.

I don't want to be a teacher. I just want to feel free in my own life. I wish I knew what I should do or if I belong at Alder at all. Listening to my professor talk about teaching has energized me in the worst way. The opposite way than I was hoping.

When class ends, I reluctantly peel off my borrowed sweatshirt. "You, sir, saved my life. I was sure this was my end, freezing to death while reading an Intro to Ed handout. Not how I want to go." This is new to me, fun and flirty Bailey Sullivan. I tried it on with Greg in high school, but that was just a knee-jerk reaction to Haley. I'd never put forth any real effort toward a guy. Not until Luke forced himself through that closed door in my mind. Not until he offered me a glimmer of possibility. "I'm Bailey, by the way."

"Bailey. I'm Hunter." He holds out his hand, skin burned white from some kind of acid. My manners shout at me to shake his hand, but I just stare at it, wondering if the bleached skin will slough off at my touch.

"Won't it hurt?"

"Naw. It only hurt when it first happened. The acid burns white, so it looks worse than it actually is."

I give him the worst handshake ever. "How'd you do that?"

"Chemical safety class."

I break out into laughter. He just watches me until I silence myself. "Oh, you weren't kidding." I cover my mouth in apology.

At last, he grins and releases me from my awkwardness. "No. I want to be a chemistry teacher. It's part of the curriculum. And I, being a dummy, knocked over the phosphoric acid."

"Ah, that makes sense. Well, I'd better run. Thanks again, Hunter."

"No problem. I'll see ya around."

As I walk back to Baker, the rain slows to a drizzle and Hunter, Luke, and Noelle race through my head in dizzying circles.

The first week of class is uneventful, mostly reviewing syllabi and expectations for the semester. Workload is low, and overall responsibilities are minimal. I've done some studying. I know exactly how many days of each class I can skip without it negatively affecting my grades. I smile at this thought while I whip my hair back and forth over my head, trying to air dry it a little as I get ready to go to Mass with Cassie and Noelle.

I don't have a lot of formal clothes, so I pick the one dress I wear to everything: church, funerals, weddings, whatever. It's comfortable in familiarity, but every time I wear it, it feels a little more out of place in my life. I throw it over my head and try to make my hair fall right.

I wait for Noelle and Cassie in the common room, enjoying the warmth from the fire while a hustle and bustle of students leave together for the service. They all look lovely, I notice as I tug at the hem of my dress again. It may be the last time I wear this thing. Noelle rounds the corner, and I stand when she enters the room. She wears a dress, too. A light purple sundress.

I must let my gaze hang for too long because she smiles at me and asks, "You like it?"

"Oh, uh, yeah. Good dress."

Her eyes scan me over. "You look beautiful."

Just being polite, I'm sure. Cassie walks into the common room and smiles at us both. "Aw, look at us. I can't wait to meet Father Kyle. Let's go," she says, and leads us out of the dorm to the chapel.

I hold open the big oak door and let the girls pass. I dip my fingertips into the holy water, make the sign of the cross, and follow Noelle and Cassie into the church. I'm hit with the familiar feeling of being hungry, of not quite belonging, of nausea building from the incense. But the dark coolness of the church eases my stomach. Color-soaked light pours from a stained-glass window, illuminating the stations of the cross and a wall-mounted Joshua tree sculpture hanging behind the altar.

I try to forget about the last time I went to church. It was Mother's Day, and Dave was home from college. We were listening to a harmless homily about all the different kinds of love, then the priest started talking about the *unclean* kinds of love. On Mother's Day. John would've nodded with fervor had he been there. My mom stiffened and took her purse with her to communion, which meant we were leaving right after Eucharist, something we never did. When we got to the car, she said, "I think it's time for a cocktail." We went home and had drinks around the firepit. No one mentioned what the priest had said.

"You okay?" Noelle wraps her arm through mine.

"Oh yeah. Just haven't been in a while. All good." I smile and step back so she and Cassie can sit first. She drops to one knee and makes the sign of the cross before she slides into the pew. Cassie does the same. It's these small personal rituals that set me on edge. Am I the kind of person who takes a knee before I sit? No. I shuffle into the pew behind them. Am I the kind of person who kneels to pray before Mass begins? No. I lean back while Cassie and Noelle settle onto their knees and close their eyes. Am I the kind of person who refuses to sit until the Eucharist is all locked up in the tabernacle? No.

It's not that I don't want it. Well, it's not that I *didn't* want it. I'm pretty well over it at this point. I used to envy them, the Noelle and Cassie types. The kind of person who is so sure about their faith. Or even if they're not, they're so sure about *trying* to be faithful. I can see that people are here in earnest, that they're not self-conscious when they kneel before the altar because they need something; they are something. Meanwhile, I accepted help from a church I'm not even sure I want to be a part of. I am a fake. I close my eyes when they close their eyes, hope my face reflects their same devotion.

It can't end quickly enough.

When we finally step outside, the sun burns my eyes, and the fresh air lightens me. I didn't even get to hold Noelle's hand during the *Our Father*, but I do get to walk into the dining hall with them, and this time, I make sure to sit next to Noelle. The pancakes and eggs feel earned, and the coffee is heaven. Noelle's dress is as short as mine, and her thigh is warm against my thigh. I guess I could be convinced to go to church again. But then, maybe I could just meet them for breakfast afterward.

After breakfast, we spend the afternoon on blankets, lying out in the quad, Priya's phone wedged in a glass cup as our portable speaker. We listen to Leon Bridges and let the sun freckle our faces. Cassie braids Priya's hair while the boys kick around a soccer ball, and I rest my head on Noelle's stomach. She holds a book in one hand and absentmindedly runs her fingers through my hair with the other. I don't believe anything has ever felt so warm.

After our sunny quad hangout, Luke knocks on my door. "Hey, what's up?" I ask.

"Matt said the café in the library is having a cupcake explosion. Two for a dollar. All kinds of flavors. Come with me?" His eyes are wide with anticipation.

"Of course. Priya? You in?"

Luke looks over my shoulder to Priya. "Oh yeah, you should come, too, Priya."

"Hah. No, thanks. Tricycles aren't my thing."

"What?" Luke's eyebrows scrunch up.

I grab my lion card and push us out of my room. "I think she means like being the third wheel, you know, like a tricycle." I get whiplash between Luke and Noelle. They're two personifications of my opposing desires. Luke offers me simplicity, the ability to keep my scholarship and not having to deal with what I really want—Noelle.

"Oh. *Oh*."

We buy ten cupcakes, even though I really only wanted one flavor—peanut butter and jelly—and go sit on the porch swing on Decker Hall. I push us into a steady rock while Luke pops open the box of cupcakes and reaches for the peanut butter and jelly one.

"You'll break my heart if you eat that one."

He stops, cupcake suspended halfway to his mouth. "You're joking, right?"

I stare at him. "Absolutely not. It's my favorite flavor."

He grins. "It's *my* favorite flavor."

"Rock, paper, scissors?"

I have a magical connection with the rock, paper, scissors gods in which they've graced me with an unstoppable winning streak. I crush Luke's scissors with my rock and reach for my cupcake prize, but he smashes it into my mouth before I can grab it.

I shove him in the arm and wipe frosting from my nose before it can cake into sugar boogers. I gather a hand full of cakey shrapnel and smash it into his face. How does he make it so easy?

He licks around his lips as far as his tongue can reach. "Mmm. It's really good."

I side-eye him. "Yeah, I wish we could've enjoyed it more."

He runs a finger over my jaw, collecting peanut butter frosting, and pops it in his mouth. My stomach drops as I watch him swallow. "I don't know, I'm thoroughly enjoying myself," he says.

I want to kiss the sweet frosting off his lips. "Well, since you ruined my rightful prize, I get the Oreo cupcake."

"I'll allow it. Do you want to go grab some pizza after this?"

"I think we got the order of things backward, but some pepperoni grease to cut through the sugar sounds perfect," I say.

We drop the rest of the cupcakes at the dorm and walk together to the dining hall to gorge ourselves on pizza. Luke wipes grease from his mouth with the back of his hand. "This should be a Sunday tradition for us," he says.

"Cupcake fights?"

He chuckles and swallows his bite. "Dinner and dessert in reverse. Every Sunday. You and me."

I stare at him for a moment. I had the urge to kiss him just a minute ago, but do I want to be claimed like that by him? I wipe at the corner of my mouth with my now translucent napkin. "Yeah, I could do that." My stomach revolts, and I know it's not from the sugar or the grease. It's because I know that I, in fact, *can't* do that.

"How was Mass earlier? You looked really beautiful."

"Thank you." I clear my throat. "Oh, you know, it was pretty churchy. I couldn't help but notice you haven't patronized our lovely chapel."

"Eh. I don't much feel like it, I guess."

"And your parents don't care that you aren't going?"

"Nah. They don't care. As long as I do well in school and I'm happy and healthy, I can do whatever I want."

It must be nice to feel so free. I watch him finish his pizza. He's pretty likeable for a golden boy.

❖

"Psst. Psst. You awake, Sullivan?"

I'm not sure if I'm awake. I think I'm in the hallucinatory first five minutes of sleep, the kind where I imagine Noelle Parker whispering to me from our bathroom.

"Hmm?" I groan.

Noelle tiptoes into our room and sits on the edge of my bed. She must be wearing all black because I can barely discern her form from our night-soaked room, even with the help of the spattering of moonlight that our blinds fail to block.

She puts a hand on my shoulder. A gentle nudge. "Listen up, Sullivan," she whispers. "I want something. In the arboretum. And I need your help."

"What?" I wipe the corner of my mouth and begin to touch everything, smooth hair, wipe eyes, swallow sleep mouth. The building lucidity of Noelle's presence activates my brain.

A squeeze on my shoulder. I push up onto an elbow. "There she is. Meet me in the common room in five."

Noelle disappears through our bathroom, and I take one more second to wrap my head around what just happened. I blind myself with the home screen of my phone—half-past midnight—slip out of my bed and pull on some jeans and my Alder sweatshirt. I tie my Nikes, anticipating some kind of running, then creep through our door, my exit masked by Priya's snoring. Anticipation of a nighttime adventure with Noelle wakes up my limbs as I walk to the lobby.

Noelle sits by the fire, dressed in black. She breaks into all teeth and dimples when she spots me. She grabs my hand and pulls me through the front door of Baker, into the night. "I'm not going to lie, I'm pretty disappointed you didn't wear black."

"Um. I, wait. Are we doing something illegal?"

She stops and looks at me. "Illegal? What? No. No, not illegal. More like not allowed." I bite my lip. "Hey. Trust me."

"Okay. What's the plan?"

"We're going to the arboretum. There's this little sign at the end of the path that is *exceptional*. And I want it. Let's go."

We speed walk through campus, a streetlamp every hundred feet bringing me bright images of her. During the day, campus is a beautiful hue of stone and wood, but at night, things are highlighted, lowlighted, curves of windows and depths of awnings juxtaposed. Alder is a little more magical at night.

"Come on." She turns into the small mouth of the arboretum and leads the way onto the path.

The small trail runs between a thick wall of trees and is veined with bulging roots. Decaying leaves and pine needles muffle the sound of our footsteps as we pass through the sleeping trees.

My eyes flit back and forth from Noelle to the trail, both too dark to fully see. While my eyes are on Noelle's back, I catch the toe of my shoe on a gnarly root and stumble a couple paces forward.

"Careful." She steadies me, then turns to continue through the trail. "Almost there."

The end of the trail lacks any frills. Instead of a streetlight, a safety post with an emergency call button stands next to the small information board. Noelle waves for me to join her.

"This." She points to a small metal sign bolted to the right side of the shadow box filled with info sheets and flyers. "This is what I want."

I follow her point and squint to make out the print on the small sign.

Property of Alder University
Do not steal

I shake my head as she nods.

"Isn't it perfect? Why does this sign even exist? It's like its sole purpose is for us to steal it."

"It feels like a trap."

"It feels like destiny." Some things can feel like both.

"How are we even supposed to get it off?" I ask.

Noelle switches on her phone flashlight and shines it on the sign. It's secured to the metal bracket by two square bolts. "Do you have a wrench?" she asks.

"What? Why would I have a wrench? I live in a dorm. Also, you didn't tell me to bring anything."

"Can we just rip it off?"

I take her phone and shine the light over the bolts. They're shiny under a minimal dusting of rust. "No way. These look pretty new. I doubt they'd fail just from us pulling on them."

I hand her back her phone, the light passing over her face. Her eyes catch mine. "Well, I really enjoyed our adventure, sign or no sign." She sighs and starts back into the trail.

"Wait. Let me think for a second." There's no way I'm disappointing this girl.

"Okay."

"We just need something to grip the edges of the bolt. Doesn't need to be a wrench. Something flattish. Like a rock. Like a rock you'd want to skip in the lake. If we got two, maybe we could sandwich them over the bolt and turn it."

She switches her phone light back on and crouches over the ground. "Okay two rocks that I'd want to skip. I'm on it." She runs her hand over the earth, picking through mostly small pebbles and sticks. "Will this work?"

I take the smooth rock out of her hand, and she illuminates it for me. It's flat and long. Perfect. "Yeah. Yeah, I think this will work. Just need one more."

She drops to her knees and continues to sort through the leaves and rocks. She hands me her next selection. "Here."

"Not as good. But it could work." I sandwich the two stones over opposite faces of the bolt. Twist. After a second of effort, the bolt creaks to life and whines as it gives in to the torque. The threads release rusty crumbs as the bolt pushes out of the metal. Noelle steps close behind me and grips my shoulders, shines her light on my project. Pride swells in my chest.

"It's working," she whispers. Her words tickle the nape of my neck, urging me on. The little metal bolt pops free, and I stash it in my pocket.

"There's one," I say.

I'm almost done with the second when we spot a flashlight about fifty yards away.

"Shit, shit, shit. Campus security is out." Noelle cuts the light on her phone, and I continue to coax the bolt out of the metal until it pops into my hand. I tuck the sign, a little smaller than a license plate, into the back of my jeans and pull my sweatshirt over it as the flashlight nears us.

"Got it. Run," I say.

I don't know what would happen if we got caught defacing university property, but I have never so ostentatiously broken a rule, and judging by how fast Noelle is running, I'd guess that this is her first time, too. I keep pace with her, her hair occasionally whipping my face like the overhanging branches. With every stride, the rough metal edges of the sign claw at the skin of my lower back until I find myself worrying about when my last tetanus shot was. But if we get caught, we can't let campus security know we have the sign.

We don't stop running until we reach the basement door of Baker, and Noelle swipes us in. She sucks in air, hands on her knees. "Holy shit, I haven't run like that since high school track."

With the adrenaline and endorphins tapering out of my system, the pain of the little devil eating away at my back screams at me, and I shift my weight from left foot to right. "I—" I tenderly peel off my sweatshirt, touch a hand to my lower back and wince. "I think the sign—"

"Oh shit." Noelle steps behind me, fingers pressed to her lips. "You bled through your shirt. Cassie may be able to get the blood out, but—"

"I don't care about that right now. Can you get the sign?"

She lifts my T-shirt and hisses a breath between her teeth. "Jesus, Bailey. Why didn't you just hold it?"

"It was uncomfortable, but I didn't know it was like Jaws bit my ass. Not until we stopped running."

Noelle tugs at the sign.

"Stop, stop, stop. Please. Just one second." I fumble with the button on my jeans and unzip them, pull them down an inch. The sign falls limp into her hands.

"Let's get you cleaned up. Come on."

Maybe this wasn't worth it, after all.

The fluorescent bathroom light assaults my eyes, too aggressive for almost two in the morning. Noelle pats a soapy rag over my lower back and clears her throat. "Um. Can you pull down your pants? Just a little. I can't clean the other half of it."

I nod, keep my eyes glued to the off-white tile of the wall and push my jeans halfway down my hips. This is the least romantic thing I think I've ever done with someone. And it's with her.

"Okay. That's better, thanks," she mumbles. I know what's coming next. I shoved a piece of jagged metal down the back of my pants, and it tore up my ass. Noelle exhales and tucks a finger into the waistband of my underwear, plucks it from my skin, and tugs it down to meet my jeans. I wince. Sure, it hurts, but I'm not even wearing my nice underwear, just some shabby pair I've had for far too long because I've never had anyone to impress. Now, Noelle is examining my ass like a pediatrician.

"Sorry," she says. "We gotta get this clean." She continues to dab the soapy towel over my tender skin. I plant my hands on the wall, hoping the cold of it will travel up into my face and extinguish the fire there.

"You're not going to like the next part."

I crane my neck to peer over my shoulder and let out a little maniacal chuckle. "But I've been having such a lovely time so far."

"Hey, it's not my fault you tried to give yourself butt tetanus."

I bury my head into my arm, smile against the salty heat of my skin. "You commanded this operation. I'd argue that *my ass was in your hands.*"

Noelle's bellowing laugh pings off the crisp tiles and echoes into the vents, rattles the bones of the old dorm. She grips my hips to steady herself through her laughing fit, and I start to relax. The worst is over.

"Shh. You're going to wake everyone up."

She wipes her eye. "I think you're going to be the one to wake everyone up." She opens the medicine cabinet and produces a little brown spray bottle of hydrogen peroxide. My body tenses, and I root my feet to the floor, fighting the seven-year-old in me who's trying to jump out of my skin and run away from the brown bottle of doom.

"Oh shit," I mutter into my arm.

"I hope you still like me after this."

I raise an eyebrow and look back at her, at the bottle she wields and the little grin playing tug-a-war on her lips. "Never said I liked ya."

"Nothing to lose, then." She shrugs and douses my skin with kerosene, then torches my ass.

I ball my fists with the kind of force that could make diamonds of the sweat and grime stuck in my palms, grind my teeth into sawdust, squeeze my eyes shut until my eyeballs burst into goop. Anything to stay quiet. It's a point of pride.

"Wow," she says once the stinging flames of hell subside. "You didn't make a sound. Pretty impressive, Sullivan." She dabs at me with a dry towel, then blows gentle drafts of her aloe breath over my skin, turning my body into a menthol jelly. The joking stops with the burning, and I'm left wanting more of her touch and more of her attention. It feels good to be taken care of by her.

"Okay," she breathes. "I think we're done."

I hitch up my underwear and jeans.

"Maybe don't do that." She puts a hand on mine to stop me. "Just go put on something loose. Like your sweats. I'll come make sure you're okay after I change."

"Thank you, Dr. Parker." I change and slide into my bed. After I've settled in and relived the bathroom experience in my head a couple times, Noelle tiptoes through my room.

"Scoot over," she whispers.

I scoot as far as I can without my back hitting the wall.

Noelle lifts my quilt and shimmies in next to me, her body heat flooding my pores. My whole body hums at her nearness. Sharing a bed has never felt quite so intense. "Thank you for my sign. I'll cherish it forever."

"You'd better."

"Does she always snore like this?"

"Yes. From the second she falls asleep. I love it. Not too loud, not too soft. She's like my personal white noise machine."

"I wonder if I snore." Noelle lies flat on her back, gaze to the ceiling. I stare at the shades of black that form the curves of her features. "Are you okay? Comfortable?" she asks.

"Yeah, enough. Thanks for cleaning me up. I know it wasn't a very glamorous job. Not my best look." I blink back the image of what I assume was my most unflattering moment.

She rolls onto her side to face me, her breath tickling my eyelashes. "You were adorable. Are you always so cute?"

"Um. I guess that's in the eye of the beholder."

"Whenever I'm around, then."

I stay silent. Attempt to roll on my back. *Ouch.* This can't be real. I can't be reading her right.

"Did I embarrass you?"

I swallow sticky hesitation and return to my side. "No."

She stares for a beat. "Are you sure?"

"Yeah, just trying to get comfortable."

"Okay." Another beat. "Where does Bailey Sullivan come from, anyway?"

Her minty breath reminds me that I forgot to brush my teeth. I throw a casual hand on my pillow, blocking the stream of my breath from reaching her. "Savannah," I say, disappointed that she didn't remember.

"No, no, I know that. That's not what I meant. I mean like what was your life like then? Okay, how about this, name five things that feel like home to you."

"Okay." I scratch at my brow and consider my world of options. There's so much good, so much love, and some bad. How do you wrap all of that into five words? I have to pick the perfect things. "Our firepit."

"Oh, that's a good one. You have a firepit in your backyard?"

My mom always has Mr. and Mrs. Taylor over on the weekends. They're my favorite people in the world. I would sit with them and sip some wine while they all smoked cigars and chatted. It would be a dream until John had one too many. Then it always played out the same way. Everyone would get embarrassed, except for him. Mr. Taylor would yawn and say that it was way past their bedtime. And the night would be over. But since my mom left him, those nights have gotten even better. "Yeah, our backyard is kind of this magical place in my mind. I'd tell you all about it, but I only have four more things."

"Better use them wisely."

The last four pop into my head in rapid-fire. "Spanish moss. Cigars. Citronella. Kisses." I might have left out a few keywords like *Bud Light, cynicism, anger.* But I don't want to kill the vibe.

"Kisses?"

"Yeah. We're Cuban. We greet everyone with a kiss on the cheek. That's how we say good-bye, too." We can focus on the fun bits tonight.

"I love all of your homey things. I feel like I'm in your backyard with you right now."

"What are your five?"

She turns onto her back and rubs the heel of her hand against her temple. After a minute she whispers, "They won't be as nice as yours."

"All they have to be is true."

"Frankincense. Roasted chicken. Trophies." She taps her teeth. "Fox News. Service."

"My stepdad was a Fox News junkie. I feel that. What do you mean by 'service'?"

"For church. It wasn't from the kindness of our hearts, though. It was so my parents could be seen in the community. Like punching their charitable clock for all to see. It's how we keep our prestige. The Parkers are a pillar of the St. Francis community, don't you know?"

I guess we all have something pressuring us into one thing or another. "Sounds intense."

"Yeah. It is. But it's what I'm used to."

"But do you like it? Being so visible in your church community and having all the pressure on your family?"

She rolls back over and finds my arm under the quilt, gives it a quick squeeze above my elbow. "Don't worry, I remember your weird elbow pressure point thing," she says. "You only get the five things. I can't spill all of my secrets, even if we are thick as thieves." She slips out of my bed.

"Wait," I say.

She stops at the bathroom door.

I struggle out of bed and pick up the sign from my desk, the red of my blood still streaked across its dusty metal. I hand it to her. "After all this, you almost forgot your sign."

"*Our* sign." She leaves me in the darkness of my room. The full force of my wounds scream in her absence, and I spend the rest of the night aching.

CHAPTER FOUR

I have a fake ID courtesy of one of Dave's more entrepreneurial friends. It's Friday night, and our Baker crew is up to our usual half lounging, half studying. Matt feels like the best option for this mission. He'll keep his cool, and he has a car, so I make him drive me to the grocery store about five miles down the mountain roads, back into civilization.

Matt ponders the snack options while I make my way to the wine and beer, doing my best to keep a natural gait, a casual face. I run my hand over all the different labels. I know my way around the wine section. *Drinking age* is not a term my family is familiar with. I pick a pinot and a grenache, hoping the lighter styles will win over my friends. Matt follows his instructions and clears out of the store with a bag full of snacks.

I bite my lip while the cashier observes my counterfeit.

"What's your birthday, hon?" she asks me in her tobacco-dipped voice.

I clear my throat and totally blank on the year. "January third."

"Year?"

Shit. My stomach drops, and I can see myself sitting in the dean's office surrendering my scholarship. That will be quite the phone call to have to make to my mom and quite the explaining she'll have to do to the Live Oak community. But everyone drinks. It would be expected, really.

I spot the little yellow sign hanging on the side of the POS: *No alcohol sold to persons born after today's date in 1995.* The sign seems like it hasn't been replaced in a year or so. Hopefully, just like my fake.

"1995."

"Just a baby," she muses but rings up the wine.

I grab the paper bag before she can change her mind and meet Matt in his car.

Back on campus, Priya and I open the bottles with our plastic corkscrew and switch on our twinkly lights. With the main light off, they cast the perfect mellow glow across our room, like a thousand contraband candles.

Priya opens up her laptop. "The Shakes?"

"Definitely."

I curl up in our big faded blue chair that we procured from Harvest Thrift, and Priya pours me some grenache in my Alder Lions mug. I sip it, letting the warmth pool through me and fill me until it floats me.

A faint knock, and the girls pop through the bathroom. One more knock, and Luke and Matt walk in. Luke grabs the Cheshire Cat mug, crosses the room, and plops right in my lap. I receive him with an *umpff* and wrap my arms around him. He sips his wine through a Twizzler straw, bending all of my perceptions of childhood and adulthood, landing me right in the space where they bleed into each other. We're all just kids, jumping into the deep together, hoping we can swim. It's not so bad when you don't have to jump alone.

"Aren't you two just adorable?" Priya says.

"All right, all right, pass that bad boy." Matt grabs Priya's laptop and cracks his knuckles. And on comes "Songbird."

I tighten my arms around Luke and press my face into the back of his shoulder. He smells notably like boy but in the nice kind of boy way, like Tide and Old Spice. Always warm. Luke is the first guy who has made me feel this comfortable. He can touch me or hold me, and I don't recoil. I lean in. I don't know if it's our friendship that shields me from that certain anxiety, but I don't care to analyze it. I'm grateful and hopeful for our intimacy. Maybe I could be happy and satisfied with him.

I almost don't care that Matt is lounging on my bed with Noelle. I almost don't care that her head is on his shoulder.

Almost.

Priya does some kind of soulful shuffle in the middle of the room while the laptop makes its rounds, each of us building upon the warmth of the last song until we get into Iron and Wine territory.

"I love you, but you're getting a little heavy for me. Also, I need a refill." I push Luke off my lap and hand him my empty mug. "Please." I give him my most winning grin. He relents and pours me more grenache, garnishing it with a Twizzler straw.

"Thank you, sir."

"You're welcome, m'lady."

Noelle stands to refill her own mug and dances with Priya for half a song. I watch her shamelessly, the wine and our laughing friends shielding me. Their dancing is for all of us. She twirls Priya and bows her thanks before she walks my way and drops into my lap like it's an empty seat waiting to be filled. She's much lighter than Luke, but even if she wasn't, I would let my legs go numb and fall off before I asked her to move.

"Does no one see the human in this chair?" I ask.

Noelle turns in my lap and drapes an arm around my shoulder. "Oh. I didn't see you there. Hi, Bailey." Her smile is so close to mine. The heat of it fills my lungs and tickles my lips.

"I hope you're comfortable," I say.

"Oh, I am." She sips her wine, gazing at me over her mug. A mischievous glint plays in her green eyes. I keep my hands safely glued to the arms of the chair. And she notices.

"What? Don't you love me as much as Luke?" She pulls my arm around her waist, mimicking the previous cuddling. The others continue their own banter and singing and dancing. The conversation between Noelle and me is ours, alone. I want to collect these moments between us, the ones that are private and hidden away, because the words meant for only my ears are different than the ones she gives to everyone else. She has a way with the words that are for me.

"You know I do."

"I know." Two words is all it takes to slay me. She pulls my arms tighter around her. My fingers rest in the curves between her ribs. I don't press my face into her like I did to Luke or hug her with the same familiarity because Luke and I are safe, but Noelle and I could explode. I drink my wine and concentrate on the weight of her on my thighs.

"Did anyone notice if Ryan was still at the front desk?" Cassie asks.

I saw him clearing his post for the evening but can't find the words to answer because Noelle's thumb begins to windshield wipe my shoulder.

"Ah, he doesn't care about curfew. We got lucky with the RA," Matt says.

"What time is it?" I whisper to Noelle.

She glances at her watch. "Half-past midnight," she mumbles and nuzzles into my neck. My fingers twitch against her ribs until I decide more pressure is better than revealing that I tremble at her contact. I steady my hands against her body and let her bones absorb my tremors. "I'm exhausted, guys. Time for y'all to sneak out of here," she says to Matt and Luke.

The boys pout at her dismissal but leave us girls to listen to one more song together before we go to bed. I look around at them, rosy-cheeked and sleepy, and deem our first wine night a success.

After lit the next Wednesday, we all make our way to the dorm common room to shake off the day's tedium together, making a plan to buy frozen pizzas and OJ at Walmart.

Alder is a small town, so Walmart doesn't just serve as a hotly debated department store. Walmart is our Mall of America, more of a destination than a means to an end. We walk into its air-conditioned foyer and are greeted with suspicion, like we're walking into a five-star hotel in ripped jeans and stained T-shirts. I'll hand it to him, the greeter has us pegged. We're about to be obnoxious customers. Obnoxious customers who refuse to spend more than twenty bucks in this establishment.

Once we clear the entrance and the McDonalds lobby, Cassie wheels around on a heel and slaps a palm on Matt's chest. "You're it," she shouts, already jogging backward away from the group.

"But I wasn't ready," Matt tries to protest, but the rest of us are already twenty paces away at that point.

Luke yells over his shoulder, "Remember, one full minute."

The Rules of Walmart Tag:

The person deemed "it" waits one minute to try to tag other players.

Players are "safe" and have officially won once they have purchased an item without being tagged.

The "it" player must tag at least one person to win.

The person who is "it" can't camp. No waiting at the registers for their prey.

I sprint past electronics, then hook a sharp right into women's clothing, finding a nice rack of weird lingerie to take cover in. I pull out my phone, realizing that Luke and I never planned on who was going to buy the pizza. An important detail. Timing is everything in this game.

Me: *Who's buying pizza?*

Luke: *Me. You're juice and Twizzlers.*

I make my way toward the candy aisle first, thinking the freezer section would be too risky right now with everyone trying to buy dinner. I see the empty aisle before me. Safe. I snag the Twizzlers, only momentarily distracted by every other candy in the world, and take off at a sprint before I slam into something broad and solid at the end of the aisle. I hit the cold tile floor with a thud. Luke extends a hand toward me and yanks me off the ground.

"Easy there, Bails. You okay?" He checks over his shoulder every couple of seconds, two family-size frozen pizzas under one arm.

"My bones hurt. It's like you're made of solid oak or something."

He grins his boyish grin and grabs my hand like it's the most natural thing in the world.

And it may be.

"We gotta move." He pulls me through the store, sending me special ops signals, trying to get us to safety. I follow him, my hand still in his, trusting him with our adrenaline-spiked pseudo-mission. Right now, I want to be on his team. I gravitate toward him in her absence.

"Cassie got juice so we're good to check out." We catch a glimpse of Priya making her way to register one, closest to the exit. I gesture toward her. "Bold move."

"Yeah. You go to self-checkout. I'll go to customer service. There's no line."

"Okay, go." We break off to our respective check-outs. When my register prompts me to *please follow the instructions on the keypad*, I spot Matt sprinting toward the self-checkout station. He must not have seen Priya and runs right past her. *Shit.* I jam my card into the reader, painfully aware of how slow this stupid system is. I'm not technically safe until I have a receipt in hand.

Matt runs toward me, weaving through annoyed customers and side-stepping shopping carts. He tries to avoid a woman who juts out from the cleaning supply aisle cart-first. He lunges to his right and catches the edge of a Bud Light display, sending a cardboard cutout of a bikini-clad woman and bottles flying across the floor like grenades, exploding into a foamy mess of beer and broken glass. He pushes himself off the ground and shakes beer from his hands, careful to avoid the shards of glass all around him. His face pales as two managers jog toward him.

The machine spits out my receipt, and I snag it. I catch Matt's eye and shrug, flashing my receipt for him to see. Remorse escapes me when it comes to him, for the moment at least, because the way he flirts with Noelle is starting to annoy the shit out of me. I walk the other way to meet up with Luke and Priya in the McDonald's.

"Not only did you lose but you also got banned from the store. You know what that means?" Luke teases Matt through a mouth full of an M&M McFlurry, pale white oozing from the corner or his mouth.

"Please, enlighten me."

"You are the forever loser of Walmart tag. You can never redeem yourself. Ever."

"You're such an ass." Matt focuses on his ice cream.

"You would've gotten me if you hadn't wiped out." I throw an arm around his shoulders and give him a squeeze. It turns out that I might feel a tiny bit bad about how the game ended.

"We'll never know," he says.

"It's not all bad, you got to touch that cardboard lady. That's probably the most action you've ever gotten," Luke says.

"Come on, man," Matt whines. "I'm pretty sure I was the only one to show up to Alder with a girlfriend."

Our collective jaw drops.

"What? How did you not tell us that?" Noelle asks.

"When did you break up? Or wait, are you still together?" Cassie asks.

Priya looks from Matt to Luke and back to Matt. "I don't understand," she says.

"Nobody asked. Y'all don't have to know every single little thing about me. And for the record, yes, we broke up."

"Who—" Priya starts.

"She broke up with me a couple of weeks ago." Matt's brows fall out of their furrow, and he stares at his ice cream. Cassie wraps her arms around him.

"I'm sorry, Matt. I only wish we would've known so we could've been there for you," she says.

"Did you know?" I ask Luke. He nods. "Well, shoot, I definitely would've let you catch me if I had known," I tell Matt.

"It's okay, the fresh pain of being the forever loser of Walmart tag will take his mind off it," Luke says.

We lounge in the basement of Baker when we get back and feast on the frozen pizza, even though most of us are full from our McFlurrys.

"First kiss?" Matt asks Priya.

"First grade. Mikey McDaniel. During story time in Ms. Dillard's class. It was beautiful." She declares it with the kind of faraway look that tells you Mikey McDaniel was the one that got away. Must have had more wild oats to sow.

"Oh my God, Priya." Noelle laughs. "Are you still pining over your first-grade crush?"

"No, he turned out to be gay. Damn shame, too. He was so hot."

Gay. The word stings me. I want to swat it away like it's a wasp coming to ruin my picnic.

"Ew. Are we still talking about a first-grader?" Cassie chimes in. I know Cassie is grossed out by Priya referring to first-grade Mikey as hot, but all I register is "ew" and "gay."

"He was beyond his years," Priya says.

"I want to hear about Bailey's," Noelle says.

"Oh God. Well, I was at a Bob Dylan concert with my friend's family, and me and her snuck off to meet our classmate and his older brother. His older brother kissed me when Dylan started playing 'Hurricane.' I was fifteen, I think."

"Yes, I love it. Did you see him again?" Priya asks.

"No, I, uh, I didn't really want to."

"Why not?" Luke asks.

"I don't know. I guess you don't feel a spark with everyone, you know?" Also, I forgot to mention the tiny insignificant fact that when a guy touches me, it feels like a cockroach meandering over my body, and I can't do anything but squirm and panic. They've always reached for too much, too fast. But not Luke. He makes me feel like he would wait for me forever. No pressure. He's just here where I want him for when I want him. Which will be any day now.

"Luke?" I ask. "What was yours?"

"It was with my middle-school girlfriend. After soccer practice. It was nice."

Of course.

"You're such an old man," Noelle says.

"Eh, he's definitely still got a lot of little boy in there," I say.

"I will defenestrate both of you right now," he says.

Cassie claps. "Oh, good word."

"The hell does that mean?" I ask.

"It means I'm going to throw both of you out of this window on the count of ten." Noelle and I erupt into giggles, shielding each other from big bad Luke.

"One." His lips curl into a smile.

"Oh, come on," Noelle yells.

"Two."

Noelle and I look at each other.

"Three. Four." Luke pops his knuckles.

"Run," I yell. Noelle lets out a short, high-pitched yelp, and we tear out of the basement, laughing and breathless, thudding barefoot down the hallway to the staircase. We throw open the door to the first floor and skid to a halt at 107. Noelle and I bust through the door as Luke appears down the hall. We slam it shut behind us, fumbling to latch the lock.

I try to catch my breath.

Noelle laughs, her cheeks red from the narrow escape. "That was close. He would have tickled us for eternity."

Luke pounds on my door. "Hey, let me in." But his shouts are muted by the thick wood. Noelle and I shake our heads, smile at each other and take a seat on the edge of my bed. Another moment just for me.

"I'm sorry you didn't like your first kiss," she says.

"I didn't say I didn't like it."

"You didn't have to." She looks at me like she's trying to figure something out. Her attention makes me feel special and a little vulnerable.

"It was fine. It was just a first kiss. Most of them suck. What was yours? We never made it to you."

"Haven't had it yet."

My brain melts with confusion, but I try not to look too astonished. "What?"

"Yeah, just had never met anyone I wanted to smash my lips against."

I look at her lips.

"Bailey. It's all good, really."

I snap out of whatever trance I'm under, snatch my hand back from her leg. "Yeah, no. All good. You deserve an awesome first kiss with an awesome person." I try to gain back my composure. "I just can't believe no one has caught your eye."

"Well, I didn't say that."

My eyes fix on a beauty mark in the hollow of her throat. I watch it beat with her pulse.

Knock, knock.

We both jump at Luke's loud banging. "Can you open now? I miss you guys."

"Coming," Noelle yells back, then looks at me. "You ready?"

No. I don't want to give up this moment. But maybe it's for the best that I don't find out who has caught her eye. Because what would I do if it wasn't me?

What would I do if it was? "Yeah. Yup. Ready."

Some nights aren't meant to end, so we cuddle in the common room and tell stories by the fire, determined to catch the sunrise over the mountains. Matt and Priya had faded to bed by four in the morning, not able to survive the entirety of what we deemed our first Wakeful Wednesday. The only survivors left are me, Cassie, Noelle, and Luke, but Cassie's eyes droop a little more every minute.

"Okay. I give in." She yawns.

"Dropping out?" Luke asks.

"Yeah. I'll make it to the end next time," Cassie says and pushes herself off the couch, stretching her arms high over her head.

"We can definitely make it to sunrise. Anyone want tea?" Noelle asks.

"Yeah. That sounds great. I'll help," I say.

Noelle and I walk to her room and boil some water in her electric kettle. Cassie rustles around in the bathroom, probably brushing her teeth. I catch Noelle's gaze getting stuck on her bed.

"Noelle. Come on, you can't go to bed now. We're so close."

"But it's warm and nice in there. And it's where I do my sleeping."

"Please stay up with me." I pull her into a feigned desperate hug.

"You still have Luke. You guys got this."

"But I want to watch the sunrise with *you*."

"When it's just you and me left." She's right. That's what I really want, too. Luke, Noelle, and I are a bit of an awkward trio, and it's because of me. I'm trapped under a spotlight when it's just the three of us. I have to choose between them, and I think they can feel it. I end up going quiet, waiting for someone else to bring the energy to the group.

I release her from my grasp. "Okay. Hey, can I borrow your coat? It's getting chilly out there."

"What? You don't have a coat?"

I shrug. "Honestly, most of my clothes are linen. From Savannah, remember? It only hits the sixties in winter."

She shuffles around her closet and pulls out a navy coat. "Here. I got a new coat this summer. You can have my old one."

I pull it around my body, slip my arms through it. "It's perfect. Thank you." I walk into the lobby with two mugs of honey mint tea. Luke smiles when he sees me approaching, then frowns at Noelle's absence.

"Lost another, huh?"

"She caught sight of her bed."

We have about thirty minutes until sunrise. The night sky softens and glows at its edges, giving way to the morning. Luke and I finish our tea, and he puts on his jacket. I press the inside of my coat collar to my nose. Smells like her. We walk in silence toward the parking deck where there's a clear view east, over the pines and oaks. We climb to the top level and stand shoulder to shoulder, looking out over the sleepy valleys. I feel like we're the only ones in on a secret.

His warmth reaches me through our jackets, and I let it take me. I wrap my arm through his and nuzzle into his shoulder for more heat. He tightens me against his body. When the sun pushes its way into the sky, I look at Luke and see the beams of gold radiate off his freckles, off his dark brown eyes, off his curly hair. I look at his lips, and see being with Luke as a path I could choose. Maybe it can be that easy, just choose. What difference would it actually make? His skin against me instead of hers. It's all just flesh and bone. Just another human. Does it actually matter which?

He notices my appraisal, pulls me in tighter to his chest, and lowers his head to mine, but the breeze stirs through the trees, carrying to me the scent of my hand-me-down coat. And all I can see is her. I duck my head into Luke's chest and squeeze him while the regret washes through me.

CHAPTER FIVE

The last week of classes has been easy, except for calculus. I hate calculus. But Luke has taken pity on me and started tutoring me in the basement of Baker, which I pay him for in pizza and good company. He's patient with me, and I adore him for that. Love him for that. I feel like I am his number one, and that carries a lot of weight for how I feel about him.

All of my friends have their books splayed across the tables as I curse under my breath, failing again to solve the derivative that Luke has written for me. I know I'm out of my league when it comes to my friends. They're all pre-med, engineering, biochem, or whatever other brilliant majors. I appreciate that about them but can't help but feel self-conscious sometimes. An education major with literally no interest in becoming a teacher, that's all I am. Everyone has an immense goal, but my goal is just to be with them. But I won't be in the basement of Baker with them forever. When I graduate, I'll graduate into nothing unless I can figure out what calls to me.

"Come on, Bails, I know you can do this. It's just like the last one we did." Luke gives me a pat on the back. Such an older brother move. I cringe under his hand, hoping that he hasn't categorized me as a little sister after our missed kiss. He's patient, but I guess everyone has an expiration date, and mine might be on the horizon. "Try one more time, then we can do it together."

I sigh and erase my previous proof with a smudge from my palm. I stare hard at the derivative for a minute or two and scribble down my next best guess.

Luke grimaces.

"Shit. I'm going to fail this test." I can't help but frown at the whiteboard. I don't belong here with them. Don't have the grades. Don't have the drive.

"Okay, Luke. I'm stealing her. She needs a break." Noelle comes up behind me and tugs at the sleeve of my sweatshirt. "Come grab a coffee with me." Her hand trails down the remainder of my arm, and she interlaces her fingers with mine, pulling me away from the evil derivatives. Once outside in the cool night air, she squeezes my hand, sending a shiver down my spine. I drop her hand.

"Are you okay?"

"I just forgot my coat. Your coat."

"*Your* coat. Go grab it. I'll wait here."

I return as fast as I can. "Okay. Ready," I say, then a gaping sigh flies out of my lungs. I'm scattered. Between people. Between my present and future. Between being an education major and being something else. I have no idea how to pull myself together.

"Bails. What's wrong?"

A lot.

A lot feels wrong.

"Sorry. Calculus is just really frustrating. And I'm pretty convinced I'm going to fail my test on Thursday." I look at my shoes as we walk across the quad to the campus Starbucks.

"Calculus is notoriously terrible. For a lot of people. Besides, being good at calculus, or not, is so irrelevant in the scheme of things." We pause to buy coffee and walk back out into the night, warm cups in hand.

"It's not all about calculus. I just feel a little lost. In general. Y'all have these big dreams. You know what you want and—"

Noelle stops walking and pulls me around to face her. "You think I know what I want?"

"I'm sorry, I just—"

She takes a step toward me and cuts me off again. "I mean, yeah, I know I want to be a doctor. But so what? There are so many other things to figure out." She pulls me to a nearby bench.

I struggle to respond, burn my mouth on my steaming hot coffee instead.

"Do you think if someone knew everything about you, I mean every terrible little thing, that anybody could actually love one another? Like, what if you knew everything?" She taps the plastic lid on her coffee.

"I wish I could know everything about you," I say, shocked at how quickly those words crawled out of my throat. Being alone with her is the closest I've ever felt to being whole, but she doesn't need to know that.

"No, you don't, trust me."

I stare at her, and for the first time, she breaks the connection first. "Aren't we just the physical manifestation of all those terrible little things? And all the great things, too. So when I look at you, I see the sum of everything you are. I see my favorite person."

She grins. "You just casually used 'sum' in a sentence. Luke must be a good tutor."

"A miracle worker, hopefully."

She studies my face and reaches a hand out. Her thumb brushes over my scar. The contact makes my body hum. "What happened here?"

I swallow. "Pick-up basketball, remember?" The lie feels tired and lazy at this point. I try not to close my eyes and lean into her touch. She smooths my brow one more time before she drops her hand to rest between us on the bench. Next to mine.

"What really happened?"

"It was a dumb accident. It was my fault." I don't know I'm going to tell her until the words are already out.

"It's okay." She squeezes my knee, then returns her hand to the bench. I can feel it there. "It's me, Bails. Just you and me."

I bite my lip. "When I was twelve, me and my friends met for burgers near Forsyth Park. He was supposed to pick me up. My stepdad, John. Everyone had gotten a ride already, and it was getting dark. He wasn't answering his phone, so I knew he was drunk somewhere and forgot about me. John struggled with that. He always had this cloud over him, and I think it was just too heavy, you know? Like there was just a little more darkness than light in him."

She nods. "What about your mom? Where was she?"

"She was at a science teachers' conference in Vegas. Anyway, I started walking home. It was about an hour's walk. But I got spooked by some noise in an alley and started running. I looked over my shoulder to make sure no one was following me, and when I turned around, I clipped my face on the side of a bus line sign."

"Jesus, Bailey."

"He asked me to say I got the stitches from a pick-up game of basketball. Which, you know, kinda benefitted both of us. It's a weird thing to have given the scar to myself while he held the true blame. It confused me. So I agreed. I lied to the doctor, to my brother, even to my mom. I only told her what really happened last year. John was being a complete asshole, per usual, and had already passed out. My mom was making some lame excuse for him." I shake my head at the memory. "What makes amazing women like my mom fight so hard for men like him? It's like a fucking tale as old as time. She clung on to the 'truth' that John never actually hurt us. I was tired of it, so I told her. And when she found out that he, in fact, had hurt me and made me lie about it, she left him. After all we'd been through with the guy, and me telling the truth is all it took."

Noelle stares at me, making me wish I'd stuck with the basketball story. "It wasn't your fault. He abandoned you in the city when you were twelve. *He* scarred you."

"I don't know. I should've been paying attention to where I was running. It's so dumb."

"He should've picked up his twelve-year-old daughter from downtown Savannah so she didn't have to walk home alone at night." Her voice creeps up in volume and pitch.

We're both quiet for a beat.

"I was so relieved when my mom left him, but I feel guilty, too, because I caused it. She's happier, I know, but I can also tell that she's lonely. And the weirdest part is that I kinda miss him, too. It's all so fucked-up." I squint into the night.

"First of all, you didn't cause a damn thing. Your mom left him because of his actions, not yours. And human connection is a whole mess of different kinds of attachment. He's been a part of your life for a long time, it's okay to miss him. Have you heard from him since?"

"No. Don't even know where he's living." I take a deep breath.

"And your biological father?"

"He died when I was two. Prostate cancer. I don't remember him. But that old Eddie Bauer sweater I have is his. He had a bunch of them. My mom says he wore them every day." I feel her fingers come to a rest on top of my hand. I close my eyes and turn my palm up. Her fingers interlace with mine. We sit in silence and listen to the wind shake dead leaves from the maples. "You owe me something now."

"What do I owe you?"

"A bit of me for a bit of you. Tell me something that no one else knows."

She stares at me as if trying to judge how much she should say, then studies her lap. I rub my thumb over her knuckles. "I want to believe in God." She looks up, and I follow her gaze to the chapel. "But it feels like I've been faking it lately. Feels like I've been faking a lot lately."

"What do you mean? What have you been faking?"

She shakes her head. "I don't know. I don't know how I feel about my religion. I only know how my family feels about it. And I know I'm supposed to become a doctor and give them grandchildren and all that. It's just a lot. You know?"

"A lot of pressure?"

"Yeah. But it's not just pressure. There are real consequences for me. I can either choose my family and what they expect of me, or I can choose something else and lose them."

"They would do that to you? Just drop you?"

"Maybe not disown me but close enough. My family hosts our parish's priests for holiday dinners. We are the portrait of Christianity in our community, or at least what my parents believe Christianity looks like. Our bookshelves are full of Focus on the Family books, and my parents regularly donate to everything conservative: the NRA, National Right to Life, you name it. Oh my God, you should hear my dad praise Chik-fil-A." She shakes her head. "The older I get, the more I want to run from this shit. It's not me. I don't think it's necessarily the Catholic church, either. But I don't know."

I blow out a breath. "Sounds intense. My mom's not like that at all. She's religious, but in the truest form, you know? She prays the rosary but also sees immigrants seeking asylum as the real people that they are. You know, like a Christian would."

"Yes. It is so bizarre to me that Christianity is so tied to the conservative right. Like, do they really think that's the party of Jesus?"

"Right?" I laugh with the relief of her understanding. "But I got my scholarship through our church, and it feels like I owe them something now."

"What do you mean?"

"Like, since I accepted their help, I should be indebted to them. You know, be a good Catholic girl. Whatever that means."

"I think Alder expects that of us, too."

"What else would you choose if not staying in the mold of your family?"

She smirks. "I'd probably run away and join the circus."

"I'd run away w...with, shit." My cheeks flush at my stutter, and I study my Nikes. "I'm sorry. Sometimes I get stuck in a word."

She squeezes my hand. "Were you trying to say you'd run away with me?"

I nod, not trusting my ability to speak with her hand holding mine.

"Is that a promise?"

"Yeah. It is." I don't let go of her hand, and she doesn't let go of mine. They anchor us together along with everything we've admitted to each other. Noelle Parker is my best friend.

CHAPTER SIX

"You're insufferable," Noelle says. I meet her eyes. She hunches over her notebook, staring over her shoulder at me. The rest of our history class shuffles through their notes and textbooks, probably trying to find where we left off on Tuesday.

"Come on. What're friends for, anyway? Priya always hooks me up in chem," I say.

It's only the first semester of my college career, and I have already slipped into my bad student habits. Number one being that I seem to never bring a writing utensil to any of my classes. Which is impressive because I just bought a ten-pack of pens from the student shop on Monday. I have no idea where they go. I think there may be a troll living in my backpack that eats them.

She opens her notebook to a fresh page. "Well, that's not surprising. Priya would give you anything."

Dr. James clears her throat and walks to the center of the room in front of the projector screen. I take one more shot before she begins class. "Please. I swear, I'll give it back. Even pay you interest, somehow." She ignores me, but I know she heard me.

"Okay, everybody. We'll begin with chapter seventeen today," Dr. James says, her voice cracking. "But, as you can hear, my voice has escaped me. Instead of lecturing, I'm going to let you get started outlining the chapter in class. This will not require talking. Feel free to come ask questions." Her hand rests on the base of her throat. She nods at our silence and walks to her desk in the corner of the room.

I startle when Noelle slaps a pen down on my textbook. I peek over at her desk and see she has already outlined most of the chapter. Probably did it last night while we were all at the library together. I tear a bit of paper off the corner of my notebook and scribble a quick *thanks*, then start reading about the end of the Mayan civilization. My mind is already wandering when Noelle slips a piece of paper onto my textbook.

I grab it as soon as her hand pulls away: *How will you pay me interest?*

I feel my lips tug up at the corners. I tear another bit of paper and tap the pen against my teeth: *I guess I'll help you study for our exam.*

I can hear her smother a chuckle as she reads my note and writes another. *Hah, I think I'll set the terms of interest. I already outlined this chapter, so entertain me with that pen I let you borrow.*

My heart rate quickens, and I turn to a fresh page in my notebook. Entertain her. I write, *Would you rather Luke or Matt?* I don't know why I ask it. It's just what pops into my head. And I'm curious how she'll respond.

Neither. You?

Luke, for sure.

She studies my note. Then scribbles a response. *You should go for it. It's pretty obvious you like each other.*

What? No. Not like that. He's just Luke. He's one of my best friends.

A line cuts vertically between her brows, and her finger taps on her desk. I wait until she finally slides a note on my desk. *Just like me, then?*

Heat creeps up my neck. *No. You know you're different.*

I watch Dr. James write something on her calendar as I slip Noelle my note. She hesitates to read it, as if my answer could change something between us. She tears another piece and delivers her response. *What am I to you?*

How do I explain to her that she is something else? That *sister* feels wrong, and *best friend* falls flat. That it makes my palms sweat to think about what she means to me. I pick up my pen: *You're my*

Noelle. I pass her the note before I can change my mind. What am I even trying to say to her? She's everything. She's everything that I'm not willing to write on a torn piece of paper.

She places her response on my desk, and I stare at it, feel her eyes on me. I swallow, lick my lips, try to get the moisture back in my mouth. *You're my Bailey.*

I turn away from her, hoping she can't see the burning in my cheeks. I just did something—opened a door—and I don't know if I'll be able to close it again. I tuck her note in my pocket.

Hope it bursts into flames.

Hope I never lose it.

"All right. Y'all can head out. I know it's early, but I won't tell if you don't," Dr. James tries to announce from her desk.

Laughter and shouts fill the concourse. At this point in the afternoon, most people have just finished their last Friday class and are headed back to their dorms to get ready for whatever the night will bring. Priya and I catch the current of the concourse and float toward the student center, passing a group of yelling religious zealots.

A guy heckles us with, "Leviticus twenty thirteen."

"Homosexuality is an abomination in the eyes of our Lord! Come clean with your unnatural sin and bathe in the light of the Lord or suffer with the devil."

He can't know.

I feel like he's looking right at me. I pull at my backpack straps, tightening the bag against my back, steeling myself. Shame chokes me, a slow burning hand tightening around my throat. What have I been doing with Noelle?

It's not worth it. Not worth losing my scholarship. John's disgusted face flashes in my mind. The beer cans. Fucking Tucker Carlson. The MAGA bumper sticker on his Chevy. My mom's fingers tangled in her rosary. The worry in her eyes.

"Someone needs to get laid," Priya yells at him as we're about to turn off the concourse.

"Priya."

"Don't scold me. He's the one spreading hatred and lies."

"You don't believe in that stuff?"

"I may be Catholic, but, no, I don't believe in that archaic shit. Wait, do you?"

"What? No. No, I definitely don't." I white-knuckle my backpack strap.

"Why do you look like you're about to vomit, then? Hello?"

I want to throw-up because that crazy asshole saw me for who I am. I don't know if I believe in God, but I believe in people's capacity to hate. I believe in this university's capacity to throw me out.

"Earth to Bailey."

"What? Oh, I'm, uh, going to pick up my calculus test from Dr. Lawrence. And I'm dreading it. Because I know I failed." I drop my hands, shake them out.

Priya stares at me for a beat. "Okay, weirdo."

I know Priya wouldn't care. But it's easy for her to be open and "so chilled" about queer shit when it has nothing to do with her. It's not scary to be an ally. It's scary to be queer.

My calculus test could have gone worse. I lean against Luke's open door and dangle my test in the air. He pauses his game of FIFA with Matt and looks at me. "Whatcha got there, Bails?"

I rush over to him and present my first calculus test. He jumps off the bed and sweeps me up into a huge bear hug, spinning me dizzy. It's nice to be literally swept off my feet every once in a while.

"A seventy-five. You passed." He slides past Matt to his mini fridge and hangs my passing grade with a novelty magnet from Mt. Rushmore. I can't help but grin. I plop on the bed next to Matt and call dibs to play the winner of their game.

"What do y'all wanna do tonight?" Luke asks, never taking his eyes off the TV.

"Pizza and soccer in the quad?" I suggest.

"Nah," Matt says, then jumps off the bed and flings his arms in the air, startling me. "*Goal*!"

"Shit. Goddamn Neymar is so overpowered in this stupid game." Luke's brows meet in a vee.

"Move over, Luke. My turn. I call Tottenham." I wiggle between them and set up my roster.

"Kappa Sig is throwing their Autumn rave tonight. We should all go," Matt says.

"A rave? I don't know." I don't feel ready for my first real frat party.

"I'm in," Luke says. I suspect he has some wicked "dad" dance moves he's itching to break out.

It's decided. I guess this is the part where we party like college kids. But I'd rather it just be us.

All the girls pile into Cassie and Noelle's room to get ready for the party. It seems like the entire contents of our four closets are strewn across Cassie's bed. I've never been great with makeup or clothes, which makes me grateful for the army of fashionable friends to get ready with. It's not my most comfortable situation, but I trust them.

Priya throws me a little black dress. "Try this, boo."

"Oh. Uh. No, thanks. I hate wearing dresses."

Noelle grabs the dress and holds it over her tank top and boxers, studying herself in the mirror. I try not to look at her, but the waistband of her boxers is rolled one too many times, leaving a visible expanse of smooth skin and thigh and muscle. When she grabs the hemline of her tank top and begins to pull it up and off, I turn and rifle through Priya's makeup bag.

Priya catches me sorting through five different tubes of mascara. "I'll do your makeup," she offers.

"I'm doing her makeup," Noelle says. She pulls her tank top back on. "Totally wearing this later, thanks, Priya. Bails, come sit." She points at the floor next to her bed. I grab the makeup bag and sit against her bed frame, stretching my legs out in front of me.

Noelle stands over me, a leg on either side of my thighs. She hikes up her boxers and lowers herself to her knees, settling her weight in my lap. It's all I can do to keep my hands from holding her there, from gripping her hips. Her face is only inches from mine. She sweeps a thumb over my scar, just like in the quad.

"I'll keep it natural, don't worry. I know you don't want much."

I can't respond. All I can focus on is her lips, slightly parted in concentration, her hand brushing over my face, the warmth of her breath on my skin.

The Kappa Sig frat house looks like an underground rave club, its black walls wild with graffiti and paint splattered everywhere. Even most of the people have covered their bodies with the glowing electric paint, like they're in the dark, deep part of the ocean where anglerfish abound. Blue and white beams streak through the haze of sweat, cutting through the dankness. And the music is a lot. The baseline shakes through my body with every beat; the vibrations chatter my teeth and tickle my bones.

"Let's get drinks," the boys seem to yell in unison.

"Yes, please," I try to yell back through the pounding music. My eyes pass over Noelle. An instant chemical reaction ignites in my body, like vinegar and baking soda.

I just want an off switch.

Our Baker crew stops in front of the open coolers on the back porch and falls into an impromptu emergency meeting.

"Y'all, we cannot drink that." Concern drips from every word Priya speaks.

"Yeah, that literally screams date rape," Noelle says. She touches my elbow. "Are you sure about this?" I nod and step out of her reach. "All right. Well, I'm going to go find a beer." She turns and leaves the rest of us to determine our fates.

We stand together on the precipice of reason and stare into the bright red liquid. The cocktail, presumably fruit punch and a high concentration of Everclear, has been mixed straight into the coolers. A tower of Solo cups stands sentry on the table next to it. Hundreds of dirty hands have been dipped into the nasty cocktail, though I doubt any type of bacteria can survive in what is sure to be an extremely high alcohol content.

"Screw it." I grab a cup and scoop myself a generous serving of the Kappa Sig sweetwater.

"Hell, yeah," The guys are right behind me, but Cassie and Priya decide to hunt down the Coors Light with Noelle.

The boys and I form a small triangle, holding up our Solo cups. Every cautionary health class video that I have ever seen plays on a loop through my mind.

But I don't care. I press the edge of the Solo cup to my lip.

I'm fucked-up.

"Let's get fucked-up," I mutter. Can't shake the urge to throw myself away. Down in one. We all reload together and make our way inside to the glowing masses.

The Everclear makes quick work of me. It's a far cry from a glass of wine. Way more potent than I'm used to. Sharp lights bend and soften at the edges, my focus narrows, like I'm peering down a long tunnel. Anything outside of my telescope view is hazy, muted, beyond the realm of existence. Beyond my care.

The Baker crew has scattered, and I can't recognize anyone who's jumping violently around me. I didn't even want to come here, and now I'm alone. Paint-splattered limbs thrash through the air, and I feel like I'm in a haunted house instead of at a party. A rave zombie crashes into me and spills my drink, coating my hand in a sticky mess of the sweet punch. I do my best to shake it off when I notice Hunter. He wiggles through the dance floor to reach me.

"Hunter, long time no—" A wide-framed frat boy slams into my back before I can finish my greeting. Hunter catches my arm and steadies me while my drink trickles down the front of his Polo. The bright red stain looks like a rave zombie sliced open his chest.

"Oh my God, I'm so sorry." I press my sticky fingers to his button-down. He just chuckles and keeps his grip on my arm.

"It's good to run into you outside of class," he yells into my ear. "Let me refill this for you. Stay here." He grabs my empty Solo cup and disappears.

I forget what number drink this will be. Four? Definitely four. Five? It doesn't matter anymore.

My counting is interrupted when I spot Noelle leaning against the far wall, entertaining some dude I don't know. Without any consideration for Hunter's imminent return, I start toward her.

Noelle trumps everything. She's spades.

She spots me and gives an encouraging smile. Reels me in. She looks stunning in Priya's black dress, the waves of her hair fall onto her shoulders, and I want nothing more than to run my fingers through it, to push my mouth into her neck and breathe in her warmth.

"There you are." Noelle rewards my valiant journey across the dance floor with a grin and squeezes my hand. She turns her attention back to the stranger. "Tom, right? It was nice to meet you, but I'm going to talk to my friend now." He cuts his losses and leaves us to it. *Scram, asshole.*

"Thought I might have to brave this night without you." She loosens her grip, but I catch her fingertips before her hand falls out of mine. The music pounds, and the lights strobe over her face. A thousand snapshots of Noelle. I try my hardest to burn them into my memory. The look on her face, like she wouldn't trade my presence for anyone else's. Like I light her up.

The tips of our fingers stay hooked, and I stare at our joined hands. Search Noelle's eyes. Her eyes. Green eyes. There's something there. No clue what it is, but she leaves her hand in mine. I lean forward, probably sway, and put my mouth against her ear. Want her to feel me there.

"Noelle." My lips press her name to her skin. I just want to say it out loud for her. There's no way she could know how beautiful it sounds, how sweet it feels to form the two syllables. She turns into me, and her lips meet my ear. The contact is stronger than the Everclear.

"Yes, Bailey?" Her breath carries heat from my name, a brush of her mouth, and warm lips on my ear.

"I think. I think you're so beautiful." I pull back, and my lips graze her cheek. Did I mean to do that? Yes. I don't know. I can taste the salt from her skin. Even through my haziness, I can see her blush, a shy smile. She pulls me back to her.

"Then dance with me." She presses a small, easy kiss to my cheek, like that's what friends do. I pull away, follow her eyes as they scan my face and pause on my lips.

My stomach drops. What the fuck am I doing?

Noelle's stare darts back to meet my eyes, and concern floods her face. I drop her hand. She winces. "Are you okay?" She cocks her head and examines my face. I blink a couple times. Say nothing. I'm drowning. All I have to do is ask for help. Just open my mouth and scream. But I just can't. I can't. I'm saved from further scrutiny when Matt appears with two cold beers and hands one to Noelle.

"Hey, Bails." He cracks his beer and takes a long pull, his Adam's apple bobbing with the beat of the music. He wipes the foam from his lip with the back of his hand and turns to Noelle. He leans toward her and whispers something; his hand falls to her hip, rests there with unearned confidence. Noelle laughs in response to whatever dumb thing he whispers.

I turn and disappear back into the sea of strobe lights.

"Ah, there you are." Hunter hands me a fresh cup of cheer. I take a hearty gulp and let the liquid ease my dry throat. I take his free hand and start moving with him to the beat. We dance together for a couple of minutes before he spins me away from him and pulls my hips back into his. He holds me there and loops his thumb into the waistband of my jeans. I feel him start to venture farther down my hip, his hot breath tickling my neck.

I hate you. Not even sure who I'm thinking about: myself, Noelle, Matt, or everybody. I turn into Hunter's chest and grasp the back of his neck, pulling him down to me. I close my eyes and press my lips against his. Hunter pushes his tongue into my mouth. Tastes like hot and sour soup. Makes me nauseous, but I couldn't care less. This is what I'm doing tonight. This is what is expected of me. Fuck up, but fuck up inside the lines.

Hunter slides his hand into my back pocket and pulls me into his body so that our thighs interlock. We grind like middle schoolers. I feel his erection push against my inner thigh as he tightens his grip on me. The nausea builds. The image of Matt's hand on Noelle's hip burns in my mind. When I feel tears begin to well, I swallow hard and move my hand down to Hunter's waistband. I squeeze my eyes shut and push into his boxers.

He gasps. "Let's get out of here."

His dorm room looks like Luke's. I lift his shirt and work on unbuttoning his jeans. Success. I nail the zipper. Easy. He sighs, maybe moans. Well, no going back now. He shimmies off his jeans and boxers.

"Just tell me if I hurt you. I've never done this before." Probably the sexiest thing I could've said. I lean over him and take him into my mouth. He pushes to the back of my throat, and a riptide of fear rushes through me, pulls me under. Should he be wearing a condom? What if he has an STD? What do I do if he comes in my mouth? I can't handle the anxiety. I withdraw and hand his penis back to him, wiping my mouth with the back of my hand.

"I'm sorry, I just—" I pull off my shirt and offer it to him, feeling so naked all of a sudden. "Can you finish yourself?"

"What? I'm not going to cum in your shirt." He throws it to the side and grabs a Kleenex from the drawer of his dresser. One discarded tissue later, Hunter is on top of me, kissing me. He reaches for the clasp of my bra, but I can't be that naked in front of him.

"Leave it. Please." I bring his hands back to my chest. Over the bra is fine, for now, but he pushes his hand under the fabric. I shiver, and he seems to take my fear for excitement.

He peels off my jeans in one quick yank and tosses them on the floor next to my shirt. The boy is skilled in the art of passing by moments of consent. But I *am* consenting, aren't I? I kiss him back, run my hands down his back and dig my nails into him. He doesn't take off my underwear, just pushes it to the side with no warning before he thrusts his calloused fingers into me. But I'm not wet. I bite my lip to keep from crying out. Try to push past the pain, but he seems to mistake my labored breathing for pleasure and pushes into me with more force. Rips through me.

"Hunter, I can't. Please." I say, out of breath. He pulls his fingers out, and I try to calm myself, relief filling me, but he pulls at my underwear in a weird trance, as if he didn't just hear me. I shove hard against his chest. *Get the fuck off me.*

"Stop!"

I roll out of his bed and gather my clothes. I have my hand on the doorknob before I realize I'm about to burst into the hallway in only my bra and underwear. I pull on my clothes and fly out of his room without saying good-bye.

I can't escape fast enough.

I break into the night, and half walk, half jog to a bench behind the physics building. I sit, shifting my weight from one butt cheek to the other, trying to avoid the raw sensitivity of my center. I wrap my arms around myself, dig my nails into my biceps. Dig. Dig. I wish I didn't bite my nails so that I could excavate through my skin, tear into an artery. Bleed out, maybe.

My contacts burn into my eyes as tears scrape over the lenses. My heart flutters in my chest. In a faint way. In a way that makes me feel like it could just stop. Quick breaths overwhelm my nose, overflow through my mouth. I close my eyes. Breathe. It's too much. This is too much.

Come clean with your sin and bathe in the light of the Lord.

Trying to *bathe in the light of the Lord* apparently makes me want to kill myself.

I'd rather fucking burn. I'd rather be thrown out of this school than ever let a man touch me like that again. I'd rather stand in front of my parish and tell them I'm falling in love with a girl than keep feeling this shame. It might not be tonight, might not be tomorrow, but I will be okay. I will never put myself through this again. I choose to love myself.

Chapter Seven

Noelle laughs over her cup of tea. "Okay, but if he says 'penetrate' one more time, all respect is lost," she says. I take in the warmth of my friends and try to push last night out of my thoughts. The library holds a light hum of activity as we sit around a table and finish our homework for the weekend.

"Dr. Simon? Oh my gosh, for real." I laugh. "Penetrate the idea of the 'other.' Penetrate this, penetrate that, penetrate your mom."

"*So* original, Bailey," Matt says.

"Shut up, Matt," Noelle says.

"Ugh. Gross. Why is he obsessed with the word 'penetrate'?" Cassie asks.

"I think he's trying to penetrate our boredom," Luke says.

I look at Noelle across the table. I need her. After last night, I just need to feel her near me. I pull out my phone to text her: *Meet me in my room.* I stand and grab my backpack. "I told my mom I'd call her. I'm going to head back." I know Noelle will make something up and come meet me.

In my room, I throw my backpack on my bed and turn on the twinkle lights, play "Harvest Moon" on repeat, and try to calm my nerves. There's a soft knock at my door, then Noelle.

"What's this?" she asks.

"I'm sorry we didn't get to dance last night, but would you dance with me now?" I'm done trying to trick myself. I'm not ready to talk about it. But she doesn't need me to.

She grabs my hand and pulls herself into me. No words could describe this feeling, anyway.

"You may have to show me," I say.

"Here." She guides my hand to the small of her back, and we dance slowly together, laughing at ourselves at first, then settling into mutual comfort. Left, one-two, back, one-two. The song repeats, and it feels natural to desert our rigid form. Noelle rests her head on my shoulder, and I wrap my arms around her waist. My fingers trace her lower back where her muscles dip to meet her spine in a gentle valley. She feels so good in my arms. This is right. This is safe.

She turns her head into me, brushes her lips against my collarbone. I close my eyes and imagine we're in a different dimension, an alternate universe, Middle Earth, a place where Noelle is shamelessly mine. One day.

Her lips bring me back, traveling up to the spot where shoulder meets neck. Teeth brush over my skin, and I feel a surge, low in my stomach. A heat between my legs. She nips, sucks at my flesh. I shudder in her arms, dig my fingers into her back. Her lips pull back from me, and she releases a quiet breath.

My door flies open.

"Y'all are obsessed with each other. It's kinda cute, actually."

I stiffen and lift my mouth out of Noelle's hair. She's a board in my arms, seemingly too shocked to jump away. I release her, wonder if I'll ever get to hold her like that again. Priya leans in the doorway, grinning at us. I hate her right now.

I clear my throat. "Noelle was teaching me how to dance." I slap my hand over where Noelle had been kissing me. *Kissing me.* I want to grab her hand and run away to California. Where no one cares. Where she wouldn't care. Where no one knows us.

Priya laughs. "Oh yeah, prom is coming up, right?"

"It's these damn twinkle lights. How can you *not* dance in here?" Noelle adds, eyes breaking from Priya's too many times. I wonder if Priya can feel the heat in here, if she can see our flushed faces and know.

"Well, don't let me interrupt. I'm just grabbing my Microbio book." Priya grabs the textbook, then leaves for the library again, stealing our moment as she goes.

"Um, do you want to head back, too?" I ask Noelle, trying to give her an out. The energy in the room has faded anyway. Back to stifling reality we go.

"Yeah. I have a lot more to get done today." We grab our bags and head back to the library. I can't stand how heavy the air is between us.

"Noelle?" I slow my pace, and she matches it.

"Yeah?"

"How do you feel about us?" We both stop. I point to her, then me, then her, then me. I give my finger a surprised look, as if I can't gain control over it. Her, me, her, me. Panic.

"We're best friends. You know that."

"I know. But what if nothing else in the whole world mattered? What if nothing existed except you and me? Just you and me."

"We'd be best friends. I don't understand what you're asking me." Her eyes are hard, but she clamps her lip between her teeth when she finishes speaking. This is the line she won't cross with me.

"I guess I don't know what I'm asking, either." I look at my feet.

"Hey," she says. I meet her eyes again. "You know you're my favorite person."

But I want so much more from her. Metaphors. Metaphors are the only way we can touch this right now, like two kids poking at some peculiar thing with a tree branch. Don't get too close.

"You know that feeling you get when you see something, like the most beautiful something in the world?" I fling my arms out to encompass the night around us. "Like a Blue Ridge sunset or that shooting star we saw in September? And it's painfully sweet to observe that beauty, but it's like you can't get your hands on it. You can't obtain it. All you can do is long for it, you know? Do you ever feel frustrated with it, the longing?"

She seems to consider all the words that I unloaded on her, taking each of them, weighing them, trying them on for fit. She looks into my eyes, opens her mouth to speak but bites her lip instead.

"Yes."

Her voice startles me. The clarity of the single word startles me. Her admission startles me. I stand blinking at her, off-balance and unsure of what the word admits to exactly. She reaches for my face, changes course, and lands on my backpack strap. She grips it, pulls a little, pushes a little, guiding me into a soft rock, back and forth on my heels. Then she steadies me, both hands gripping a strap.

"Yes. I do," she says. My chest bursts into flames.

"Me, too."

To know that I'm not alone in this is all I need from her tonight.

❖

The next day, I wait for Priya to leave for the library, and when the door closes behind her, I pull out my phone to call my mom.

"Babygirl, hi." Her voice is warm and loud.

My eyes prickle with tears, an instant thing. I flash back to my almost kiss with Luke, to Hunter's fingers tearing into me, to Noelle in my arms. "Mom." My voice cracks from the dam about to burst in my eyes.

"Bailey, what's wrong, honey?"

"Nothing. Nothing. I don't know." I notice salt in my mouth and a constant stream of tears down my cheeks. I've totally lost it. Composure down the drain. "I'm sorry. I don't know why I'm crying."

"Hey. It's okay. It's okay," she coos.

"I'm having the best time here. I don't know why this is happening."

"Breathe, Bailey. Just breathe. Shh." I shut up for a minute and concentrate on breathing. In, out. In, out. Just breathe. "You've always been like this. Something gets inside you that cracks you a little, and sometimes you get flooded. It's okay to not know what it is. It's just life, baby." I know what it is that cracked me. And I know, in the deepest part of me, that she wouldn't care, but there are so many layers on top of that truth. There are so many moments from Mass, from John, just from living in the south that have cemented doubt over the beautiful fact that it's okay to be gay. I'm trying to excavate through that doubt. But right now, I just need my mom.

In, out. In, out. "I miss you," I say.

"I miss you so much. You know you can come home whenever you want. The Taylors are coming over tonight, and you know what that means."

I ease at the thought of our house on the weekends. The Taylors in our backyard, around the fire, whiskey and wine flowing while the crickets chirp, cigar smoke thick in the air. "I wish I could be there."

"We'll toast to you. It's not the same without you. Who will pick out the wine?"

I laugh. "We all know you only drink chardonnay these days. Hey, do you think you could send me a family picture? Um, one without John?"

"Of course, sweetie. I know just the one. I'll get it in the mail tomorrow."

"Thanks, Mom." I wipe at my sore eyes. "Listen, I actually have to get going. I'll call you soon. I promise."

"You sure? We just started talking."

"I know. I just needed to hear your voice. But honestly, I don't feel like talking right now. I'll call you next week." I collapse into my pillow, exhausted, but I can feel something building in me.

"I understand. I love you, Bailey."

"Love you, Mom."

CHAPTER EIGHT

L eaves have fallen and crisped, the air has sharpened and dropped its lazy humidity. Students fill the concourse, shuffling by each other, trying to make it to their next class in time. Ten minutes from the end of one class to the beginning of another is barely enough time to speed walk across campus. I rush from lit to history, dodging other students in fall sweaters. I stop at a safety call post that has been flyered over.

Halloween Party in the Clearing
Bring Your Tents
And a Will to Survive

I snap a picture and send it out in a group text to everyone, knowing they'll be all about it: *Figured out what we're doing for Halloween.*

Matt: *Hell yeah.*

Cassie: *I've got a tent.*

Priya: *Me, too.*

Luke: *Me three. And some sick costume ideas.*

A girl in a mad dash clips my arm, and I drop my phone screen-down on the concrete. A new fracture creeps across the glass. *Shit.* Still works, though.

Another flyer for a music festival in Atlanta catches my eye. Pride flags decorate the paper, making it clear that it's a queer music festival, but the actual LGBTQ+ letters have been torn off the top. Kind of like me. I rip it from the post and shove it in my backpack, notice the time, and get back to my speed walking, barely making it to history before Dr. James begins her lecture.

I pull out the censored flyer and place it over a blank page in my notebook, put the tip of my pencil where the flyer is torn. Faintly write the letters.

LGBTQ+

I stare at the now complete flyer. It's better now. Whole. Noelle slides a note on top of it, and I erase at the letters so she doesn't see them.

I've been thinking a lot about you. About what you'll do one day.

I'd like to think that I'm on her mind even half as much as she's on mine. I write, *Oh yeah? What do you see?* I press my response into her open hand. She reads it and writes a word or two. Something small, apparently.

An eighty-year comet.

I roll my eyes, crumple her note and toss it at her when Dr. James isn't looking. She mimes a scoff then gets to work on the next note:

I'm serious. You're full of light and tether other people to you. Maybe you can find a major that helps you do that instead of molding yourself to a career that isn't you. Major in you.

I roll around the thought in my head. Would if I could. *I wish I knew how to do that.*

You'll figure it out.

Her words poke at me the rest of class. Maybe she's right. Majoring in education would pigeonhole me into something I'm almost positive I don't want to do. There are other options like business or liberal arts that would give me the flexibility and freedom to do whatever I want. Unless you want to be a doctor or something specific, it's just the fact that you graduated college that matters to employers, not so much what you studied.

Noelle and I walk out of class together. The day is bright and sunny.

❖

The rest of the week is a blur of studying and tests. We just finished midterms, and even though none of us feels like we did great, it's beyond our control at this point. Matt and Luke's room has become an outdoor trading post: tents lie over every inch of floor, sleeping bags hang over bedposts, and piles of stakes litter desktops.

Cassie sorts through the stakes, making sure there are enough for three tents. We're short two because Luke smashed them with a rock last time he went camping with his buddies in Chattanooga. At first, they were just bent but still usable. We watch him try to straighten them, but the metal gives, and he ends up snapping them in half.

Priya sits on Matt's bed with me, checking off our list as we go. Tents. Stakes, most of them, at least. Water bottles. Sleeping bags. Lantern. Flashlight. Pocketknives. Check. Check. Check.

"What about our costumes?" I ask.

"We should be the Power Rangers. And be like park rangers at the same time because we're camping," Matt says.

"Aren't there only five Power Rangers?" I ask.

"Naw, someone can be the white one," Matt says.

"Scooby-Doo gang?" Luke asks.

"Again, only five," Noelle says.

"How about the *Clue* characters? There are six of them," Cassie says.

"Yeah. I'd be into that," Luke chimes in.

"Y'all wanna be wearing dresses in the woods? I'm not doing that," I say, ready to fight this one.

"Good point," Priya says.

"How about we be zombie park rangers? Simple, topical, fun," I say.

"Okay, I kinda like it," Luke says. And everyone agrees because no one can come up with anything better.

We spend the evening sorting the rest of our camping supplies. It's pretty bleak. Most of the gear is the old, worn-out supply that our parents have long since replaced, leaving us with the originals. Which means we won't be pitching the new *throw it in the air and it puts itself together* type of tent. We'll be pitching the dinosaurs.

The kind of tents that have twenty different poles that lack any type of distinguishing feature.

It will be good team building. There's a hum of energy in our group, and I can't wait for whatever tomorrow brings.

Matt and I are in charge of beverages. He buys a Styrofoam cooler and ice while I push my luck with the same cashier as last time. I grow panicky, knowing I'm making a risky move buying a flat of Bud Light and a fifth of Bulleit rye. Nobody cares if we get caught listening to Joni Mitchell and sipping red wine. People care if we get caught wasted on rye, shot-gunning beers in the woods.

"You again," she says to me.

"Yes, ma'am." I try to maintain eye contact.

She eyes my selection of booze. "What's all this for?"

"We're going camping for Halloween tomorrow. All of us in my senior thesis class. 'Bout twenty of us."

She laughs at me. Hands me back my fake. "We're in the mountains. Ain't no liquor control ever been up this far, hon. Y'all be safe. Don't be actin' fools just because you got a little whiskey in your blood."

"Yes, ma'am."

Matt and I throw the ice in the freezer in the basement and leave the rest of the goods in his car, not wanting to risk getting caught with it in the dorms. The girls rummage through dressers and closets, putting together costumes for everyone. Noelle smiles at me when we get back.

"Success?" she asks. Everyone looks to us in anticipation.

"Well, she knows my ID is fake, but she sold to me anyway."

"What?" Noelle asks.

I shrug. "Yeah, I don't know. I guess she likes me."

"What's the state of the union?" Matt asks.

"I think we're ready," Cassie says. "We've pulled enough clothes and makeup together for everyone. Oh, and we're good on camping supplies."

"Awesome." Just one more sleep until we're all camping in the woods together.

❖

We spend the next afternoon packing bags and loading Matt's car. It's a tight fit with the cooler, all the gear, bags, and the six of us, but his old 4Runner is just big enough. The clearing is about forty-five minutes from Alder's campus, tucked away between County Road 7 and Whippoorwill Lane, right in the bosom of the Blue Ridge Mountains. Past Big Mama's Country Store, the road relaxes into a concrete dance through pine and maple. The air thickens, and a savory blend of wet earth and decaying leaves takes flight with the breeze, rushing through downed car windows and propelling us deeper into the mountains.

I try not to think about the winding roads that seem to lack guardrails in key places and keep my hand braced against the seat in front of me. Goose bumps pepper my skin, but the sun is shining, and it'd be a waste not to have the windows down for this short drive. Noelle's hair whips in my face, and Willie Nelson's voice fills the car as we all sit smiling with anticipation. Our costumes turned out terrible, but at least we're not in dresses.

Cars and tents litter the clearing. Every pickup's tailgate is down; every cooler's lid is up. Jack-o'-lanterns and bowls of candy guard all the tents, and I kick myself for not thinking to carve a pumpkin. All the girls are half-naked and seem to be freezing, already drunk, probably from trying to numb out the cold. The clearing buzzes with life and community, everyone happy to share their goods, everything from candy apples to cinnamon whiskey.

We find a spot big enough for our three tents on the periphery of the craziness, right at the edge of the woods. The first thing we do is pop the tab on a cold beer and toast each other.

"You can't set up camp without a beer," I say and grab one of the tents. Matt grabs another.

"I'll help ya. Reckon we should share one," Luke says to Matt. Cassie grabs the last tent and empties its contents onto the ground. Priya hunches over all the poles, then looks at me like she forgot something.

"Is it okay if I share a tent with Cassie? Just because, you know, why not switch it up?" she asks as if trying not to hurt my feelings, but when I look at her, she's smirking. I know Priya loves Cassie, but Priya is my ride or die, and I know I'm hers, too. She's up to something. Noelle steps toward me, and I wonder if her stomach is sinking the way mine is, if she's just as terrified and excited as I am.

"Oh yeah. Of course I don't mind," I say to Priya. I squint at her, trying to let her know that I'm on to her. "As long as you don't mind, Noelle."

Noelle takes the tent bag from my hand and loosens its drawstrings. "So long as you know how to put this thing together, I don't care who I share with." She takes a casual swig of beer. Her hair is tied into a French braid and a "blood" soaked bandana curls around her upper arm. She looks good, not like a zombie park ranger but a post-apocalyptic badass. Noelle empties the contents of the tent bag onto the ground, and I feel a ton of pressure to pitch this tent like a pro. I sort through the poles and organize them by length.

"Can you pick a spot and lay the tent flat on the ground?" I ask her.

She scans the ground. "Yeah. What kind of spot?"

I click two poles together. "You know, flattish, no big roots that will jab us when we're sleeping. Ground that will hold the stakes. It's a little windy."

"Okay." She bundles the tent in her arms and surveys the potential spots. The others have started setting up close to the car and each other, but Noelle picks a spot about ten yards away from everyone else, on the other side of Matt's car, close to the woods.

I walk over with the poles and lay them next to the tent. "Why'd you put us all the way over here?" The pit in my stomach begins to flood with the reality that we are sleeping in the same tent tonight. In a tent that Noelle wants to pitch away from the others.

"It's the flattest. And away from the chaos. It'll be quieter for sleeping."

I look around. "Okay, this works." I shrug and start clipping the tent to the poles. If I can't put this thing together, then there's no sharing it with Noelle.

She watches me with a grin. "It's a mess," she teases me.

"It only looks like a mess. I know what I'm doing." I clip the wrong poles to the door of the tent. "Shit."

"Mm-hmm. You know exactly what you're doing."

"Hey, I don't see you putting together a tent, so you're stuck with what I give you." I shake the mystery pole at her.

She puts her beer on the ground, grabs the pole, and clips it to the left side of the tent. "It's the same as that side. I should've camped with a boy." She winks.

"Then you'd still be arguing about which is the best spot to set up camp." We finish pitching the tent, stake it, and push on it to test our work.

She unzips the little flap door and crawls in. "It's nice. Come check it out."

The fading light filters through the green fabric, making the inside glow like algae. We stare at each other, the realization of our privacy settling on me. "It's a good tent," I say.

"Yep. Well, we should go see what the others are up to." She claps and crawls out. I linger for a moment, unsettled by Noelle's nervous energy. I should offer to stay with Priya. I sigh and crawl out to join the others.

The boys work on starting a fire with kindling they gathered from the woods. I watch them struggle to get even the smallest twig to do anything beyond smoke a little. "It's too wet."

"It'll work." Luke blows at the smoking mess of damp sticks. My stepdad was a scoutmaster who took us camping twice a month, but yeah, you know better, Luke. Who would listen to a girl about how to start a fire?

"It's not going to work," I whisper to Noelle.

She smiles at me. "Definitely not. But you know they won't give up."

"They'll be here all night." I turn to her. Her posture is relaxed, and the smile stays on her lips, but I need to be sure she's comfortable. "Hey. Are you sure you're cool with sharing a tent? Because it wouldn't be a big deal at all for me to bunk with Priya."

"No, I want to bunk with you."

"You're sure?"

She nods. "I promise." She sways into me and knocks my shoulder. "Let's go find Cassie and Priya."

I grab her hand and the bottle of rye and lead the way into the rest of the party to try to find the girls. A proper bonfire burns in the middle of the clearing; Lord knows why Luke and Matt are trying so hard when this fire is giant and roaring. I pull from the rye and hand the bottle to Noelle. My eyes are glued to the fire, the flames, mesmerizing against the darkening night. People dance to some dark-sounding rockabilly coming from the giant speaker system in the nearest tailgate.

"Hey, guys," Matt and Luke call to us.

"Do you want to go walk around together?" Matt asks Noelle. Her eyes flash to me. I just shrug like, *whatever, he's our friend.*

"Yeah, let's go get a candy apple," she says, and they disappear into the crowd together. Luke fills in next to me where Noelle used to be. The whole party dims, and disappointment clouds me.

"This is awesome." He lifts his beer toward the fire, and I remember to be present with my friend.

"Well, I'm sure it's not as good as yours," I tease.

He shoots me a challenging look, then just smiles. "It was too wet."

"Well, cheers to Halloween and all the spirits that came before us." I toast and lift the bottle of whiskey.

"Cheers." He knocks his can against it.

I pass him the bottle. "Where are Cassie and Priya?"

"They found a girl selling homemade jewelry out of her trunk, so they're making best friends with her."

"Seriously?"

He nods.

I laugh. "Oh my God, that is so typical."

"Yep. And Matt is trying to get with Noelle."

I keep my face neutral while every atom in my body combusts. She wouldn't go for him. Even if I'm totally wrong about us, she wouldn't go for him. No way. Though, we have all been drinking. I startle at Luke's hand on the small of my back.

"Well, good luck to him," I say.

He looks down at me as if trying to judge my vibe. "I, uh, told him he could use our tent if they need it later."

My chest tightens, and the frothy brew of whisky and beer creeps up my throat. The image of her with Matt makes me want to throw myself in the fire.

"And that would mean..." I look at him. I want him to say it.

"Maybe we could share a tent." His hand falls to my hip, guiding me closer to him.

No.

I can't let this go any further. Part of me used to want him. Part of me wanted to be the girl who is proud to be on his arm. If I could have done it with any man, it would have been Luke.

He pulls me closer, like he can hear my thoughts and is guiding me toward what he wants. What *he* wants. I step out of his arms.

What *I* want is Noelle. And she wants me, too. I know she does. *I'd rather fucking burn.* "Luke, I can't. I'm sorry."

"What?" He's surprised. I don't blame him.

"You can have my tent if Noelle and Matt hook up. There's space for me with Cassie and Priya." *If Noelle and Matt hook up.* I want to vomit. What if she feels for him what I felt for Luke? Some longing to be traditional. Love for a friend. Hope. And a lot of whiskey. What if they're already back at our camp? I can't let this happen. I have to at least let her know how I feel first.

"Bailey, I thought..." His expression is pained. People dance around us, and the party grows louder, louder.

"I did, too." I squeeze his hand. "I'm really sorry, Luke. Listen, can we talk about this later? It's so loud."

He nods.

"I'm going to go check on the girls, make sure they don't spend all their money on shitty jewelry," I say, but really, I need to find Noelle. I make my way back to the tents, pushing through gaggles of witches and zombies and some *Super Mario* characters. The buzz from the whiskey tickles my senses when I reach the tents. I call for Matt, not wanting it to seem like I'm desperately searching for Noelle.

"Matt," I call again. When I'm convinced no one is in our tents, I turn and head back to the bonfire.

"Bailey." Matt is a couple groups down, waving at me.

"Hey. I was just looking for you. Where's Noelle?"

"She took off to find you, said she was supposed to be your safety buddy tonight?"

I exhale a smile, loosen into my buzz. "Oh yeah, it's a girl thing."

Matt gives me a look like I'm being silly.

"Hey, that shit's for real," I say, then release him with a grin. "Luke is looking for you, by the way." They could both use the company. I'm not sure the extent of Matt's feelings for Noelle, but I might have broken Luke's heart tonight, and I just don't have the capacity to worry about it.

I'm worrying about myself and Noelle.

"All right, I'll go find him."

I have to find Noelle.

I grow frustrated after my second loop around the bonfire and sit on one of the logs scattered about. I drop the bottle by my feet, rest my chin in my palm, and stare at the flames. One of the Mario characters plops down next to me.

"Hey, sexy texy ranger," he slurs.

I smash a leaf under my boot. "Hey, Luigi."

He nods with enthusiasm. "Yeah, yeah. I'm Luigi. How'd ya know?" He slugs down his beer.

I point to his green trucker hat and the paper "L" taped to it. "It's not hard."

He scoots closer. Leans in. Breathes his beer breath in my face. "But it could be," he stage whispers.

I hop off the bench and knock over the whiskey bottle. "What the fuck is wrong with you?" I ask.

"Prissy bitch."

Someone behind me grabs my arm, and my adrenaline pours into my system. I'm ready to fight every fucking asshole in these woods.

Noelle yanks me back and steps in front me. "The fuck did you say to her?" She leans over him, her hand balled into a fist. I grab the whiskey as if I may go crazy and smash it over Luigi's head if things get out of hand, if he so much as touches her.

"Don't be mad, sweet'art. You can get it, too. Got plenty to share." He grabs his nuts and flicks his tongue at us. Noelle shoves his chest, and the next second, Luigi is flat on his back in the dirt, yelling a slew of profanities. I grab her hand and run, zigzagging through the monsters and Red Riding Hoods until we get to the far side of the clearing and slow to a walk. I let her hand go, breathless.

"That was incredible. You're, like, my personal hero," I say. But she doesn't smile. Her eyes are dark. "Hey, it's okay. He was just a stupid drunk guy. It's over."

She grabs my hand, pulls me through the crowd to our tent. She unzips the door, and I put down the whiskey. "Bring it." Her eyes are on the bottle, darkness still hanging on her features.

"Noelle, it's okay. We can go back and—"

She shuts her eyes, exhales through her nose. "Please. I just want to spend the rest of the night with you. That asshole is lucky he's still breathing, and I can still feel Matt's hand on my thigh. I can still see how Luke looks at you. And I can't take it anymore. I'm done for tonight. Please, Bailey, can we just hang out alone in this tent?"

It hits me for the first time that Noelle has been going through exactly the same thing as I have. And when I follow her, we'll both be done pretending. My blood drains and pools in a sporadic dance through my body. But I'm steady as I grab the bottle and crouch inside. Noelle follows, zips the door shut, then lights the lantern, setting our tent aglow. I study her features over the lantern. She takes a sip of whiskey, and quick bubbles run to the upturned bottom of the bottle.

"I thought you and Matt…" I take the whiskey, drink, pass it back.

"God, no." She takes the bottle back. Drinks. Sighs. "What do you think it is that draws two people together? Like, you and me were instant, you know?"

Instant what? For as long as I have pined for this girl, I'm afraid to cross the threshold first, even when she's holding the door open for me. I pick some lint off my sock while I think. "Maybe we're all magnetized somehow. Or like electrons. We just keep bouncing off one another, propelling one another, until someone makes you stick with them."

"Something inside me matches something inside you?"

I look at her, trying to gauge if we're walking hand in hand here. Because what I hope matches in us is love. "I think so. Or fits something inside me."

"Can I ask you something?"

"Yeah." I run a hand through my hair.

"Do you like me?" She pulls her knees to her chest and watches me.

"Of course I like you."

She picks up the bottle and shuffles next to me. Hands it to me. She rests her hand on the inside of my knee, and I try not to pass out. "I mean, more than a friend? Because I think I see something in the way you look at me. But sometimes, I see you give the same look to Luke."

There it is. Noelle is touching me and asking me if I want her. The answer has been yes since the day we met. And now I know, without doubt, that she wants me, too.

I look into her eyes with a confidence I've never felt before. "You're wrong. I've never looked at anyone the way I look at you."

Her shoulders relax. "Matt and I got candy apples. We ate one, watching the fire. I said I needed to go find you and he said, 'You should give someone else a chance to get to know you.' Then he put his hand right here." She slides her hand up my thigh.

I bite my lip to keep it from quivering. Her touch is dizzying. "What'd you say?"

"I said he'd forgotten a few steps before grabbing my thigh would be acceptable." She pulls her hand away and blushes.

"It's okay. You didn't skip any steps." We have trudged a thousand painful steps to get here. She can touch me however she pleases.

Her eyes flash, the small flame from the lantern dancing in her stormy green abyss.

"When you…" I pull my collar down to bare the skin she'd kissed. Bitten. "I couldn't stop replaying it in my head. Over and over and over."

Her eyes bore into the spot. She brushes her fingers over my collarbone. "You make me crazy."

Things fade in my periphery, and I lean into her, so sure I'm just going to hug her. And I do. But when arms loosen, I stay, forehead pressed to her temple. Her lips part, and a slow shaky breath escapes. It only takes the slightest effort, just inertia, really. She turns her head a bit, and I press my lips to hers. It feels like a storm. Our heavy breaths are thunder, and her tongue brushing over mine is lightning. She grabs a fistful of my shirt and pulls me closer.

"Bailey!"

I yank away from her and wipe my lips, try to cool my cheeks with the back of my hand, and grab the whiskey bottle. Noelle smooths her hair and takes a deep breath. Totally normal. Someone pulls the zipper at the door, and it feels like walking into the blinding daylight after sitting in a dark theater for hours.

"Noelle?" Priya pops her head through the little hole she's made.

"Hey." My voice croaks through a dry throat. I drink and pass. Can she feel it? That it stormed in here?

"There you guys are. Y'all turned in early." She unzips the rest of the door and crawls in, yelling over her shoulder for Cassie. "Girls' time." She smiles and drinks. Cassie is right behind her, settling across from me and Noelle.

"Hey, lovelies," Cassie says. "Nice and warm in here." It *was* nice and warm in here, but now it feels like the lantern is a garish fluorescent bulb.

I play ungrateful host until Cassie and Priya go to bed, then I turn out the lantern and lie on my back. Noelle lies next to me, keeping space between us. I stare at the ceiling of the tent. What now? Did we build something? Did we break something? Is Noelle lying next to me regretting it or reliving it in her head or wishing I'd leave? Wishing I'd touch her?

She rolls toward me and grabs my elbow. "Do you mind? It's pretty cold tonight." She tucks herself under my arm and rests her head on my chest. Faint chatter and music fills our silence.

"He almost hit me once," she mumbles into my shirt.

I tighten my arm around her body. "What? Who almost hit you?"

"My dad." She grabs my hand and interlaces our fingers over my stomach.

"What happened?"

She exhales into me. "God, I really don't want to tell you this."

"You know you can tell me anything. I mean, I kind of feel like our cards are pretty much on the table at this point."

She kisses me on the cheek and cuddles back into me. I stare at the dark canvas above us. "He walked in on me touching myself," she says.

"And he almost hit you? What the fuck?" I feel powerless. I would do anything to protect Noelle, but I can't protect her from her crazy family. Repression was forced on her by the man who is supposed to love her the most in the world. My heart breaks for her.

"He said if he ever caught me masturbating again, he'd hit me. Said it's not what ladies do. That's what a husband is for."

"I can't believe he shamed you like that. For the most natural thing in the world. I can't—"

"It's okay, Bailey."

I loosen my grip, realizing it's probably uncomfortably tight. She doesn't need me to be angry. There is nothing I can do for her but listen.

"I grew up with him, with my family. I'm used to being judged against an impossible ideal. That wasn't just a flash in the pan. It's how we live."

"And you accept that?"

"It's not like I stopped masturbating. I just made sure that there was never even a possibility of him walking in on me again. Do you see what I mean? I don't think he cares very much about who I am, just what I present to the world. I do my best to present how they want me to. They're my family. Do I have a choice? They feed me, clothe me, protect me. I owe them everything."

"You don't owe anyone anything, Noelle. Feeding you, clothing you, those are duties. Your life is yours, not theirs."

"I just wish I could be the daughter they want me to be. My brother is properly engaged. My younger sister is a perfect Catholic princess. And then there's me. Life would be so much easier if I wanted what I am supposed to want."

"That's exactly how I feel when I'm at Mass. What I pray for the most at church is to be filled with any kind of religious desire. But I'm just not. And I think that's okay, but I accepted a scholarship from my church, so it feels like I need to try."

"I understand. How can any person fit into these suffocating spaces? Is everyone faking it?"

"I don't want to fake it anymore." Her hand tightens over mine. "Do you even really want to be a doctor?"

"Yes. Thank God. I got lucky there. When things feel too out of place—when I feel too out of place—I focus on that. Being a doctor is the one big thing in my life that fits. I'm supposed to want it, and I want it so badly. But the rest is murky." She takes a deep breath. "Can I just join your family? Your mom sounds like a badass, and Dave seems chill. I could be a Sullivan."

"Noelle Sullivan." I'd give her my name in a heartbeat. "I don't know. It takes a lot to be a Sullivan. You'd have to drink more whiskey and smoke more cigars and break into brawls over spades games."

"A girl can hope."

It's a night that I wish could last forever, but my eyelids grow heavy, and our words grow sparse.

When the morning light pushes through our tent. I roll over, sit up, and shake out my stiff limbs.

Noelle is gone.

The memory of last night crashes into me, and I rub my palms into my eyes. When I walk out of this tent, I will have to face my new reality. For better or for worse, my world will never be the same. The one thing I hope doesn't change is Noelle's feelings about me. We can do this together.

CHAPTER NINE

We sleep away Sunday, and Monday crashes into us like a bus. I avoid Hunter in our Intro to Ed class, like always. We haven't spoken since rave night. I wonder if he's as ashamed of that night as I am, or if he thinks about that night at all. The professor is extra droney, so I spend the period replaying Saturday night in my head. Noelle and her lips on loop. I never knew it could be like that. I think of when my high school boyfriend touched me or when Hunter touched me and how they were always grabbing for too much. Overreaching, invading. But her touch opens and affirms. Warms me, loosens me.

"Being a teacher isn't so dissimilar from Jesus being a shepherd," I catch the professor saying.

I need to change majors.

And I need to talk to Luke.

I avoid all of these things the rest of the week. I don't know what major to pick, and I don't know what to say to Luke.

Noelle hasn't tried to hang out with me since Saturday, and I didn't go to Mass with them on Sunday. Something nags at me and keeps me from approaching her. Some part of me knows she needs space, and I'm terrified to find out why. A dull ache has taken permanent residence in my gut. We speak like acquaintances in history, in the dining hall, in our dorm rooms. *Hey. How's it going? Boring class, huh?* Closer and further apart than ever. She joined a new Bible study with Cassie on Wednesday nights, so I go find Luke when they leave for the library, Bibles in hand.

I take him down to the common room, and we sit on the couch near the fire. I warm my hands, gather my thoughts.

"Is this about Halloween? Because if it is, I'm sorry," he says.

I try to keep the guilt from taking me over. He has nothing to be sorry for. I led him to believe I wanted him. I was selfish. "What? You have nothing to be sorry for. I actually wanted to apologize to you. I feel like I've sent you a lot of confusing messages since we've met. A lot of those messages being that I'm into you."

"And you're not?"

I have an urge to abandon my resolve, but I love this guy, and he deserves the truth. Well, not the whole truth, just the part that is relevant to him. And even though I have no clue what Noelle and I are, or if we're anything, I'm committed to her. There's no more room for *maybe I could make it work with a guy*. I kissed Noelle, and now there's no turning back for me.

"I'm not going to pretend that we haven't had our moments. Because we have, and I have thought of you in that way. I love you. And think the world of you, but no, I don't feel that way anymore. I'm really sorry for confusing you, and myself, honestly," I say, rambling.

His eyebrows scrunch, and his cheeks redden. "It's okay. Look, our friendship is the most important thing to me. I just hope I didn't make you uncomfortable."

"You didn't make me uncomfortable. I know I led you to that point. I just can't pass it with you. I—"

"I get it." He gives me a weak thumbs-up. "We don't have to talk about it anymore. Just friends."

I can't tell if he has accepted that we will never be together or if he is just accepting that we won't be together right now. But I don't press the issue any further. Call it a win. I have too much on my emotional plate, and I can't handle this right now. I choose to take his words at face value and move on.

Noelle and Cassie walk through the door as Luke and I are hugging it out. We greet each other, and I ask how the new Bible study is. Noelle doesn't make eye contact with me, so when everyone heads down the hall, I tug her arm.

"Hey, can we talk?"

She looks down at her Bible and tucks it under her arm. "I don't have anything to say."

"I just miss you. I miss being your friend." I hate how I sound like I'm begging. I'm scared to know her feelings, but we can't just go on ignoring each other.

She stares at her feet. Drops her voice so I have to lean in to hear her. "What happened on Halloween—it was a mistake. And I don't want it to happen again."

I teeter on my heels, trying to string together neutral words to deliver to her. "I understand," is what I hear myself say. Deep down, I knew this is how she felt, and I've been avoiding it. Now it's confirmed. And now my heart is broken. I at least want her friendship in return. I can't take her avoidance anymore.

"Okay. Thanks." She starts to walk away.

"Wait." I grab her hand, then drop it like it's on fire and mumble an apology. "I understand if you don't want *that*, but I don't understand why we can't go back to being friends. You're kinda my partner in crime. I'm just bouncing off everyone, trying to find a Noelle."

Her dimples cut a little deeper. "Yeah. We can be friends."

I smile at her. "Well great. Friends it is. I'm going to grab some dinner, *pal*."

She rolls her eyes at me, but she should be grateful I didn't disintegrate into a puddle at her feet. I'm torn between feeling abandoned by her and wanting to be there for her. She wasn't lying to me on Saturday. She's lying to herself now. Knowing this makes it possible for me to set aside my disappointment and be her friend. There's still hope for us, just not right now.

"Hey, guys." I greet Priya, Noelle, and Cassie when I get back from the dining hall. The girls sit on Priya's bed with hot tea and Pop-Tarts. I make myself a cup of tea to shake off the mild Georgia cold, tug at my peppermint teabag, drown and float, drown and float.

"Daniel was talking about you the other day," Cassie says to Noelle. I pretend to be extremely busy with my tea operation. Drown, float, drown, float.

Noelle wipes a Pop-Tart crumb from the corner of her mouth. "Oh yeah?"

"He said he thinks you're cute." Cassie sips her tea with anticipation. I want to yell at her to mind her own fucking business.

"I've actually kinda been crushing on him for a while."

Noelle knocks the life out of me. Like I'm a *Mortal Kombat* player, swaying back and forth, an inch from the end. *Finish him.* And Noelle doesn't hesitate to deliver the final blow. KO. Bailey out.

"I'm going to give him a little hint that he should ask you out," Cassie says, so pleased with herself, so pleased with Noelle.

"Bailey, you're dripping," Priya says. All eyes are on me. I'm holding my wet teabag over my laptop. "Shit." I wipe the puddle with my sleeve, and harvest words from the searing rage in my throat. I can understand needing to hit pause on Noelle and me. It's a lot to process and figure out. But this is straight-up betrayal. This is cruel.

"Sorry. I'm, uh…I'm going to go get some fresh air."

I pull Noelle's coat around myself and walk down to the bench where I met Luke. I try to make it until sunset but only last about five minutes before I can't take the wind anymore.

I pass by the chapel on my way back, but something pulls me toward its giant oak door, the promise of warmth and real candles, I think. I take the thick metal handle and pull it open, always surprised that churches are just *unlocked.* Warmth rushes me, as if the glow from the candles and lights is its physical adaptation. I pass through the foyer and into the church, scanning its aisles, and find myself alone.

I toss Noelle's coat on the back pew and make my way to the stations of the cross. *Jesus falls a second time.* I see me there, in Catholic elementary school, memorizing each station, nervous for my first reconciliation. It's funny, confessing at eight years old; we were all so blameless. I touch the little sculptures, think of the rosary my mother carries in her pocket, and feel a familiar pang deep in my chest. I walk to the other side of the church, averting my eyes when I walk past the altar, past the particularly gruesome depiction of Jesus on the cross. Light a candle for my mother. Light one for Dave. Shit, light one for my stepdad. Because the funny thing is, I have love for him.

I think of my mom: her face dark from sunshine, wrinkled from laughing, eyes molten with love. I say a prayer for her because I know she's praying for me.

I pick a pew from the hundred or so available and quickly learn that the fourth from the front, on the left side of the altar, is my favorite. I drop to one knee, only aware I'm about to do so when it's an inch from the ground. *Father,* my hand moves to *Son,* and I feel like when this sign of the cross is over, I will have shaken on something. *Holy Spirit.* I wonder what I agreed to. I get up with a groan and slide to the middle of the pew and stare at the altar. At the Joshua tree. At Jesus on the cross.

It's been a while. Well, you know that.

I open my eyes. There's no pressure here. No making sure I'm doing everything right, no remembering the right words to respond with. No one here. Breathe. I look around at the empty pews, pull down the knee support, and kneel.

I think it's the people who fill this place on Sunday. I think it's the people who make me uncomfortable here. Does that yelling guy on the concourse piss you off? Saying all that hateful shit in your name? I'm also uncomfortable here because I'm gay.

I'm gay.

I rub my temple. Scratch at my scar. I whisper the word just to see how it feels in my throat, on my lips. No lightning bolt strikes me down.

And I'm just trying to figure it all out. If I was supposed to be with a guy, why do they make my skin crawl when they touch me? That can't be holy. Can't be right. I'm gay. And I know that it's okay. I just want to be a good person. Anyway, I don't really know what your deal is. Nobody does. But I hope you're not as terrible as everyone says you are. If you are anything at all.

Please help Noelle. She doesn't have to be mine. She just has to be whole. Please take care of my mom and Dave. And John.

I grab my coat from the back of the church and head home. The night doesn't feel as cold as it did before. The stars are bright. I look at them, and I realize I wasn't praying, I was talking myself through what I needed hear. I needed to set myself free from the expectations of anyone else. I'm not John. I'm not the church. I'm not Noelle. I'm me.

I don't know if I believe in God.

But I believe in myself.

My crew lounges with popcorn in the common room of Baker, watching *Lord of the Rings* on the projector. A chorus of greetings reaches me and fills me. I kick off my shoes and float toward the glow of the movie. There's an open seat on Noelle's left, which any other time would be mine; any other time, I would assume that she'd saved it for me. But I walk past her and sit next to Cassie, cuddle up to her, and eat from her popcorn stash. Noelle watches me, a polite smile on her face.

I'm thankful for arriving during the last few scenes of the movie. Otherwise, I would've been asleep within twenty minutes. When the movie ends, I tell my friends that I've never made it through awake.

"What do you mean you don't like *Lord of the Rings?*" Matt asks, incredulous.

"I don't know if I like it. I've never watched the whole movie. I've fallen asleep twice trying. And tonight, you guys were mostly done."

"It gets worse," Noelle says. And I know exactly what she's going to say. "Bailey hates *Star Wars.*" Matt and Cassie almost fall over with shock. Luke's mouth hangs open. Priya doesn't seem to care.

"How can you possibly hate *Star Wars*? I mean, it's *Star Wars*," Luke says.

"I'm sure the series is great. I've only seen the first one. Well, the fourth episode? I don't know. It's confusing. The main one, where they discover Luke Skywalker."

Matt nods. "Yeah, and it's awesome. What's the problem?" He raises his hands in question.

"I guess I had all these expectations. But it turns out that Luke Skywalker is a whiney, spoiled little boy who gets handed all his power without earning a damn thing. And it's annoying because is that really a good message to send?" I take a breath, surprised that I apparently feel so strongly about this topic. Everyone looks a little shocked, but Priya smiles at me and gives me a slow nod. I shrug. "I don't know, I guess it didn't make a lot of sense to me. Are we even supposed to like him?"

"Just because Luke Skywalker is a guy?" Matt asks.

"No, because he's an entitled guy. And he doesn't even realize it," I say.

Matt sneers. "What are you? Some head-shaving, feminist lesbian?"

"I'm not a lesbian." My face is on fire. What did I just say? Noelle stares at her phone.

"Sounded pretty man-hating to me," Matt says.

"Dude, you're being an asshole. You're making me feel pretty 'man-hating' right now." Luke punches him in the shoulder.

I grab Noelle's coat and start down the hallway. I go to the first private place I can think of, the bathroom. I crank on the shower. Strip. Get in. A surge of anger pulses through my body, to my fingers and my toes and the roots of my hair. I feel like a toddler about to erupt into a tantrum. Not at Matt, though he fucking deserves it. At myself. I tighten a fist until I feel my nails digging into my palm. *I'm not a lesbian.* I want to choke on the words and vomit. I just cowered in front of Matt like a scared dog. I scrub at my skin, leave it raw and angry, grateful for some kind of manifestation of my anger.

Enough.

I believe in me. I am a lesbian. I am a feminist.

I dry off. Jeans, shirt, Nikes, coat, lion card. Out of here.

"Bailey, wait," Priya calls after me.

I stop impatiently, but the concern on her face slackens my resolve. "I'm just going for a walk. I'll be back soon, I promise." I force a smile.

Priya crosses the room, grabbing her coat from her desk chair. "I'm coming." She doesn't leave any room for me to argue.

We're silent as we pass through the quad. The campus is mostly empty, save for a few stragglers making their ways back to the dorms. I pass the chapel and the dining hall, not quite sure where I'm headed, Priya on my heels. We turn right at the science building and pass the arboretum, finally arriving at the small amphitheater on the edge of campus. Big ledges carved out of the earth serve as stadium seating, and in the dark, it feels like great productions have been put on here, but in reality, it's best suited for Shakespeare in the Park. Priya sits next to me, and the surrounding pines hold us in their fortress, lending us some protection from the wind.

"Matt's right, you know," I say.

"You wanna shave your head? Because I'll do it for you."

"No, not yet, at least." I smile at her, and when she meets my eyes, I see how much she cares about me.

"Well, first off, I am a feminist," I say.

Priya chuckles softly and pats my knee. "Well, I'd sure as hell hope so, Bails. We all are. Matt's just an ignorant fuckhead who doesn't know what that word means yet."

My heart rate quickens, and a drying in my throat tickles my gag reflex. I have to tell her. *Three…two…one… Three, two, one.* My heartbeat wooshes in my ears. *Three, two, one.* I register a squeeze on my knee. I want to be free.

"And I'm gay." I spit the words out and immediately search Priya's face for a reaction. She squeezes my knee again and breaks into a warm grin. Wraps her arms around my shoulders and pulls me into her.

"And I love you. It's 2021, boo. It's cool to be gay." She kisses my head, and I melt into her body. The tears pool over my bottom lid and flow down my cheeks. I don't bother wiping at them. Just let them flow. Just let Priya hold me.

"Do you think everyone knows?" I ask. I want her to say no because I put so much pain into "being straight," and it would annoy me if it were for nothing, even if it is irrelevant now. On the other hand, as relieved as I am, coming out is physically and emotionally draining. And there's a lot of people to come out to.

She looks around the amphitheater, touches her nails to her teeth. Taps them. "I don't want to say I knew, but I strongly suspected. Although, I think I can speak for everyone when I say that we were all just waiting for the rule of Luke and Bailey. Does that make sense? I think multiple and slightly opposing truths can exist at once."

"Yes. That makes so much sense. This whole semester, I've known deep down that I'm gay. That's one truth. And the other truth is that I love Luke, and the boy made me feel something. Not something that could carry me through life with him forever, but something that made me consider trying." I take a deep breath. "God, I'm so glad it didn't happen. I came so close to fucking up our friendship." The consequences of me and Luke getting together finally settle on me, the damage I could've caused.

"You know rave night?" I start.

"Yeah, you made out with that dude. Hunter?"

"Yeah. I also gave him a hand job. On the dance floor. In front of everyone," I admit. And it feels so good.

"Ew. But okay. No one cares."

"I also went home with him, gave him a blow job for about ten seconds until I literally handed his penis back to him and made him finish himself."

Priya breaks into laughter. "Oh my God, that is hilarious."

I smile, too. In hindsight, it's kinda funny.

"I accidentally bit a dude's dick in high school. We all have dumb nights. We all have bad sex. It's all good, Bails."

"You're literally the best."

"Well, if not Luke, is there anyone else you have your eye on?"

I sway my knees from side to side, gathering Noelle's coat around me. I lower my face into its collar, breathe her in. She's still in the fabric for now but fades a little more every day. Coming out to Priya without her feels like a step away from her. All I can do is keep walking.

"No. No one."

She narrows her eyes at me. "You sure? You know I got you."

I know she would never tell anyone, but what happened between me and Noelle isn't just mine to share. "I'm sure. I think I want to keep this between us for now. I've just barely begun to process it myself. You know?"

"I totally get it. But in the meantime, you can always talk to me. About anything."

"Thank you. I feel like the patron saint of college freshmen must've handpicked you as my roommate. No one else could've done the job."

We walk back through campus, to the dorms.

I'm going to figure this out.

CHAPTER TEN

I study my plate, search for a couple square inches of space, fail. My pumpkin-shaped sugar cookie balances on top of my roasted potatoes, and I try to keep my hand steady so the cookie doesn't fall into my gravy. It's the good kind of sugar cookie, the kind that doesn't skimp. Give me the bright orange icing and sprinkles. And the pumpkin shape. This would turn some people off, but I am a shameless Fall enthusiast. Pumpkin everything, please. Cozy sweaters, mulled wine, apple pie.

I find a deserted corner of the dining hall, lay a napkin on the table, and set my cookie safely aside. I pop a potato in my mouth, all butter and rosemary and salt. A lightness fills the dining hall, one that only a Saturday afternoon could bring. Everyone has already partied hard on Friday, finals aren't for another month, and Thanksgiving plans are being made. The other scholarship recipient from my church is staying on campus during break to work with his research professor. And without a ride home or a car, it feels like too much trouble to get back to Savannah for Thanksgiving. But I'm looking forward to some quiet time on campus.

Meanwhile, Noelle and I have settled into a mild friendship. It's the worst, really. But I'm not sure what else to do or how one is supposed to navigate these strange waters. I chew and close my eyes, let the low hum of happy chatter clear her out of my head. Focus on the rosemary. On the way the butter coats my tongue, pierced by the salt.

"Hey."

I open my eyes, and Noelle sits next me, her plate resembling mine. I notice that I don't care all that much that she's here. Like, I could have it either way, take her or leave her.

I stab a potato. "Hey."

"I don't think I've ever seen anyone eat like that. No food is that good." She sorts through her own potatoes, searching until she finds the smallest, crispiest one.

"It's more than the food. It's the season. And the vibe in here right now." I scan the dining hall and wonder if our conversation adds to the contented white noise or dampens it.

"Fall really does it for you, huh?"

I look at her and wonder what her objective is here. It's not as if we've been close these last couple of weeks, even after our *friend truce*, because there's nothing to fall back on now. There's never been a time when interactions between us weren't magnetic and charged with something else. Meanwhile, we fumble around each other, trying not to get too close. Wouldn't want to get pulled in again.

"Yep. I love Fall."

I know that she deserves more than I'm giving her, so I snap my pumpkin cookie right in half, a sacrifice of which she'll never know the weight. I place the broken pumpkin on the edge of her plate, and she picks it up as if it were the matching part of a friendship necklace.

"I'm sorry. What I want most is to respect how you feel. It's just a little harder than I thought it would be," I say. What makes it so hard is how she reacted to me. She was the one who wanted the distance between us. It's like when Haley's mom found our texts. It made me feel dirty. Noelle shamed me. Unintentionally, but how am supposed to be around that energy? And, of course, I still have intense feelings for her. It hurts to be around her.

She shifts in her seat, averts her eyes, no doubt uncomfortable to be speaking about this at lunch, in the light of day. Or probably at all. She clears her throat quietly, like she's in a silent auditorium taking a midterm.

"Yeah. I know." She nibbles at the pumpkin's stem. "Look, I miss you, okay? Like, when you asked if we could at least be friends again. I feel that way now. You've been cold to me. And..." Her eyes water. She puts down the cookie and takes a deep breath, hand finding my knee under the table. Her thumb strokes at the fabric of my jeans. I close my eyes for just a second, imagining her thumb smoothing my brow. When I open my eyes, I find her pleading ones.

"And you're breaking my heart," she whispers. "I don't like Daniel. I never have. You know that."

I look at my food, take a moment before I respond because I feel the thrumming rise of my blood pressure. Anger prodding at my nerves. I want to lash out at her. Doesn't she get it? We were never just friends. I'm breaking her heart? That's rich. I'm vaguely aware that her thumb has stopped its rubbing, and I feel her staring at me.

I scratch at my scar. I think of how I responded to Matt, denying myself. Shaming myself. And it's not too hard to understand how Noelle feels. Even if she doesn't have feelings for me anymore, I value her. She is my friend. One of my Baker family members. I squeeze her hand, and in the most delicate way possible, remove it from my knee. I think I'm successful with the move because Noelle barely flinches. She wants words, so I hold up my half of the cookie.

"I know. It doesn't matter. I wouldn't have sacrificed half my cookie for anyone other than my best friend. Don't you know me at all?" I try for a warm smile, and it lands. Her face melts into relief, and she picks up her half of the cookie to tap against mine. We each take big bites to seal the deal, then turn back to our real food.

"We should make pumpkin muffins," Noelle suggests.

The idea rushes me with warmth, easing every nerve ending in my body. I turn toward her, eyes wide. "Today?" I am more excited than is reasonable. She gives me the smile that slays me, all cutting dimples, the smile that tells me I'm adored.

"Yes. Let's do it. We'll grab ingredients after lunch. We'll see if the student store has all the spices, but I definitely saw cans of pumpkin puree in there the other day."

"I'll text the group." I shift my weight to one side so I can fish my phone out of my back pocket.

"Actually"—she stops me—"maybe this could be just a you and me thing. If they come down to the kitchen or ask about it, let's just say we're making surprise treats for everyone." She looks at my arched brow and adds, "Don't worry, we'll make a double batch so there will be plenty to share." This time, there is no effort required in my smile. I get to make pumpkin muffins with one of my best friends. I've missed her.

❖

The kitchen in Baker is in a perpetual state of disgusting, but pretty much nothing could bother me right now, so I wipe the crumbs from the counter and spread out our ingredients. Noelle searches through the cabinets, trying to find a muffin tin and bowls. I turn when I feel a hand on my lower back.

"Hey, do you have any wine?"

"Yeah, I have a red in my closet."

"What if we broke it open?" She winks. It's funny how quickly the anger melts.

Just like that, I'm hers again. She's making me believe she might still be mine.

I run upstairs to my room, register that Priya has gone somewhere, and search through my closet until my hand hits the cool glass of a bottle. I open it too fast and break the cork in half. *Amateur.* After one attempt at salvaging it, I give up and push the second half of the cork into the wine. I fill two mugs almost to the brim, and run back downstairs.

Noelle beams when I hand her the mug. She brings it to her mouth, breathes it in, pauses. "Do you know any toasts?"

"I do." I raise my glass again and give a quick disclaimer. "We use it when we're a little further into the mayhem of the evening."

"I like the sound of this."

I clear my throat. Raise my mug again. "Here's to us, who's like us, damn few 'n they're all dead." I clink her mug again, and she breaks into laughter.

"Where is that from?"

"Some Scottish poet, I think."

She reaches a hand out and brushes a thumb over my scar. I try not to shudder as chills fall down my spine like dominoes. "It suits you."

I pull up the recipe that Noelle emailed me and shuffle an Iron and Wine playlist. She cracks the window so we can breathe the crisp Fall air, then we get to work opening the cans of puree and measuring out the dry ingredients. Noelle sways to the song, and it takes all of my strength to avoid placing my hands on the curve of her hips.

She turns to me and giggles. "Are you going to help, or are you just going to watch me?"

My cheeks burn, and I step into the spot at the counter next to her. If I'd known baking muffins was the answer to getting her back, I'd have opened a bakery at this point. It's like she's totally letting go of everything bad between us. I'll let go, too.

She hands me a bowl. "You start on wet ingredients." She wipes her hands on her jeans and scrolls through the recipe. She reads me my instructions. "Got it?"

"Got it." I crack the eggs into the bowl and wash my hands. Then scrape the puree out of the cans and throw in the coconut oil and vanilla extract.

"Now we combine them." She takes the bowl out of my hands and grabs a wooden spoon. "Okay, pour it slowly into my bowl while I stir."

I pour until she scrapes it clean. She hands me the spoon to finish stirring while she sips her wine and greases the cupcake tin.

She comes behind me and places a hand over mine. "Easy there. We don't want to beat it to death. Gently stir until it's just combined." She dips a finger into the batter and tastes it. Sighs with delight. All I want in the world is to kiss her again. I'm starting to feel like it's a possibility.

"Is it good?"

She dips her finger in the batter again. "Taste it."

I raise a brow, but she holds out her batter-covered finger in earnest. I lean against the counter and take hold of her hand, guide it to my mouth. She stumbles forward a couple steps until the fronts of our thighs press together. The batter is sticky and sweet. Her lips part as she watches me. I suck her finger hard, so that it comes out clean when she pulls it from my mouth. Her eyes widen, and I grin at her, wipe the corner of my mouth with my thumb. "It's sweet. But not too sweet. I like it." She stares at me for a beat. Fails to retrieve any words. *She's still mine.* "Shouldn't we get these in the oven?"

"Right. Um, let's spoon the batter into the tins, and I'll set a timer on my phone."

We both sit on the counter, feet dangling, drinking wine, while we wait for the muffins to bake. We joke and sing and tease each other, shamelessly bathing in this gray area of friends who flirt. Maybe it's our sweet spot. Or maybe it's just a stepping stone to what we both want: more.

Matt walks into the kitchen with Luke. "Smells awesome in here."

"Yeah, I didn't know this nasty kitchen could produce delicious baked goods," Luke says.

"Noelle helped me make pumpkin muffins."

"Well, they were supposed to be a surprise, but yeah. Wanted to help Bailey get in the Fall spirit."

I eye Matt. He at least has the wherewithal to look a little bashful in my presence. Luke jumps in before I can decide what to say to him. "I can help us get in the Fall spirit."

Noelle's phone timer rings, and she hops off the counter to check on the muffins. I hop off right behind her. When she opens the oven, I reach over her shoulder, trying to snag a muffin. She slaps it away.

"Excuse me. What was your plan there? Just stick your hand in a hot oven because it smells good?"

I open my mouth to answer, then realize there's no way to defend myself. Instead, I turn to Luke. "Sorry, got distracted." I throw a thumb over my shoulder at Noelle as she pulls out a tin to check if the muffins are done. "How can you help us get in the spirit? She set the bar pretty high."

Noelle pulls out the second tin, and the aroma of warm cinnamon pumpkin goodness fills the room.

"Is that wine? Y'all are like an old married couple," Matt says. I'm flattered, honestly.

Luke shakes his head at Matt. "Anyway, we should play flashlight tag tonight. Campus is perfect for it."

"Yes. We played that all the time growing up. I'm so down," I say.

Noelle slaps my hand away from a tin again. "What's flashlight tag?"

"Ouch."

"They have to cool, Bailey. Go on the other side with the boys." She pushes me out of the kitchen.

"Flashlight tag is basically tag, except at night, over a larger area, and you're tagged by the light of the flashlight, not by someone's hand," Luke explains. "It will be cold, and campus is pretty spooky at night. Ergo, Fall."

"It's true. I swear I saw a ghost in a window of Fisher Hall," Matt adds.

Luke socks his arm. "Shut up, dude."

"What?" Matt rubs his shoulder.

"Common room at ten? I'll bring the flashlight," Luke says.

"We'll be there," I say.

"With muffins," Noelle adds.

After the boys clear out, Noelle pops the muffins out of the tins and into a big Tupperware. I hop back onto the counter and watch her work. She's deft. Only breaks one muffin, sets it aside, and seals the container. She grabs the broken muffin and walks over to me to stand between my dangling legs.

"*Now* you get to try them. If you want." She puts a hand on my knee for balance as she holds up the muffin. I open my mouth like I want her to feed it to me, but when her hand gets close to my lips, I chomp down hard on nothing, making her jump with surprise. Hand over her heart, giggling, she smashes the muffin against my mostly closed mouth. I erupt in laughter and try to salvage as much of the muffin as possible.

"Delicious," I manage to say through a mouthful. I wet a rag and clean myself up, then start on the dishes.

Noelle hands me the last dirty bowl. "I'm glad you like them."

I nod and spray the remnants of batter down the drain. When all the dishes are dried and put away, I focus back on Noelle. "Are you okay? With this?" I ask. I make my vague question just as vague by motioning to both of us and the entire kitchen. But I know she knows what I'm asking.

She wraps me up in a tight hug. "Yes," she says against my ear. "I'm so sorry for everything. I've missed you so much." She pulls away and looks into my eyes. "Life is nothing but a dull ache without you."

"I've felt the exact same way."

The six of us huddle in the middle of the quad, breath hanging in the cold air like speech bubbles. A flashlight dangles in Luke's hand. Everyone fidgets, shifting their weight from one foot to another, trying to build some warmth.

"Okay. The entire campus is fair game. No woods. No buildings. I'm *it* first. If the light hits you, you're out. The first one out is *it* next round." Luke flashes the light on and off a couple of times, as if to show us *this is where the light comes from.*

The streetlamps scattered around campus are dim, a sore subject for the campus safety group and the budget committee, and a pale orange glow is all they can stand to emit, leaving endless dark nooks and crannies to hide in. I start mentally planning where I'll hide, but before I can decide on anything, Luke begins the game with a holler.

"Go! You have one minute."

We all abandon each other and take off into the night, *Hunger Games* style. I sprint to the science buildings. I know they have a few loading docks and weird alleys to hide in. My adrenaline spikes. Funny how we can trick our bodies into thinking that we're in danger. Matt runs in the direction of the amphitheater. He'll definitely get tagged there. I keep running, legs pumping, cold air burning my lungs, eyes on the loading dock.

"Psst. Bailey." I hear a whisper yell as I run by a dark, narrow alley of dumpsters. I stop, scan the distance for the glow of a flashlight, then duck into the alley. Noelle and Cassie are tucked behind one of the dumpsters, backs against the brick wall, panting like they had just arrived here a minute before I had.

"Nice spot," I whisper and try to catch my breath.

"Noelle thinks so," Cassie says.

"You should go to the arboretum if you want to so badly," Noelle says.

"I dunno," I say. "Who knows where he's at by now?"

Cassie peeks around the dumpster. "I'm going to go for it." She runs past me, and right when she turns out of the alley, the flashlight beam breaks out of the darkness.

Noelle grabs fistfuls of my coat and pulls me against her behind the dumpster. I throw a hand against the brick building to slow my momentum, afraid I'm going to crush her when she yanks me. She puts a finger to her lips, begging me to be quiet. I try to catch my breath, concentrate on slowing my lungs. I can see the glow of Luke's light hitting a dumpster, a wall. My heart rate quickens. Noelle pulls me tighter against her, and our chests rise and fall into each other. It feels so good to be this close to her.

"Come out, come out, wherever you are!"

Then, darkness. We stay still for a couple minutes, Noelle still gripping me tightly, me still trying not to pant in her ear until we're positive that Luke is gone.

I feel her grip loosen, and I use my leverage on the wall to push my weight off her. I sigh with relief. I stand on my tiptoes and peek over the dumpster, just to be positive the light is gone.

"That was close. Wonder if he caught Cassie," I whisper.

Noelle tightens her grip on my coat again and pulls me against her. She presses her lips to mine: soft, a little salty from running in the night. We breathe heavily through our noses, catching air between kisses. Her tongue is on mine. I push my hips into her. My world explodes, and all the pieces of it settle exactly where they're supposed to be. This is exactly where we're meant to be.

I breathe against her neck. "We can't do this here."

She ignores me.

"They could find us." Not that I'd care. Something about those words brings her back. She presses a kiss to my cheek, smooths my coat.

"You're right." She touches her lips. Presses her forehead to mine. "What are you doing to me, Bailey?"

I open my mouth to answer but think better of it. I wrap my arms around her instead and squeeze her body against mine. The strobe of Luke's flashlight returns, but this time, my focus is so far from tag. I step to Noelle's side, back against the rough brick, and await our fate.

I run a hand through my hair, wait for the erratic yellow light to hit us. Noelle grabs my hand and squeezes. Whispers, "It was nice knowing you, Bails."

She drops my hand right as Luke rounds the corner and blinds us.

We all warm up together in the common room. Rub hands in front of the fire, smooth down windswept hair, and wait for Cassie and Noelle to bring hot tea. Our cheeks are pink, highlighted by the orange glow of the flames. Sometimes, it feels like we live in a castle, at least when we're in the dorms or dining hall. The other buildings sport beautiful old courtyards and stunning exteriors while the inside is uninspiring and drab, like the interiors all got remodeled in the seventies.

I rest my head on Priya's shoulder, wishing I could telepathically tell her everything about me and Noelle. Maybe if I think about it hard enough, the information will travel from my head through her shoulder and into her brain. Everyone else gets to have friends' support through their dating wins and losses, but I'm just here, waiting for Noelle. Alone. I'm floating from our kiss tonight, but I'm also scared she'll wake up in the morning and change her mind again.

Cassie and Noelle round the corner with six mugs and a plastic bear of honey.

"Ah, yes. Thank you so much," Luke says.

Cassie sits on the couch next to him. "No problem, loves. Listen, Thanksgiving is just around the corner, and we haven't even discussed our plans. I think everyone is staying here, right? So we'll all be together."

"Everyone is staying?" I ask. I assumed I was the only one staying on campus.

Noelle clears her throat. "I, uh, might've mentioned that you weren't going home for Thanksgiving, and everyone wanted to stay on campus together."

I blink and sink back into the couch a little. "Wow," is all I can say. I might have underestimated how much I am loved.

"Yep, we'll all be here," Luke says.

"Great. Well, we should start planning. It's next Thursday. What do we want to eat?" Cassie asks.

"Bails and I are in charge of drinks and dessert," Matt says, like this was something we'd discussed. It's nice to feel wanted, but I'm annoyed to be snatched by Matt when all I want is to cook with Noelle again. I look at her and catch her smile at me with a shrug.

"Okay, yeah. We got it," I say.

"Are we doing a turkey?" I can almost see the drool forming at the corner of Luke's mouth when he turns to ask Cassie. She looks to Noelle for guidance.

"I don't know. I feel like the muffins were a feat for that kitchen. I can't imagine trying to properly roast a turkey in there," she says. And I think I actually see Luke's heart break inside his chest.

"What about pork chops? Or chicken? Something lower risk, easier to manage, quicker?" Priya suggests.

"Steak?" Matt asks hopefully.

"There's six of us. We could get six nice steaks for like forty bucks." Luke leans forward with his elbows on his knees, hope returning to his voice.

"Yeah. Sure. We could do steak, I guess," Priya says with a shrug.

Luke fist pumps into the air. "Okay, me and Cassie are on steaks."

"But if we're doing steaks, y'all gotta cook 'em right. I'm no well-done and ketchup type of girl. I'm a rare, no A1 type of girl," I say.

"Well, obviously," Luke says.

I point at him. "I'm going to keep my eye on you two."

"Okay, that leaves you and me for sides. Potatoes and green beans?" Noelle asks Priya.

"Definitely potatoes. Maybe a big salad. I don't know. Some kind of veggie. Let's just see what looks good at the store," Priya says.

"Decorations. Y'all got decoration duty, too," Matt chimes in.

Priya scoffs. "Why don't *you* do decoration duty?"

"Guys don't do that stuff." And just like when explaining to the crew why I hate *Star Wars*, my blood starts to heat again. I open my mouth to spill, but Priya beats me to the punch.

"Maybe boys weren't socialized to care about that stuff like girls were. And maybe some boys weren't socialized at all." She gives Matt a frigid stare.

"Geez." He throws up his arms in surrender. "I don't even know why this is such a big deal."

"I'm not trying to be a bitch, Matt. But you really need to learn about feminism. Like, yesterday."

Matt stares at the ground as if this is the first time in his life he has ever considered the word *feminism* beyond dykes and hippies. Some people just miss out on exposure to this stuff. Especially men.

"When I was little, I was in Brownies, and on the weekend that the Cub Scouts got to go camping, we had to learn how to make scrunchies in the school cafeteria," I say.

Matt's brows furrow. "Really? Sounds lame."

"Yeah, it was so lame. I wanted to go camping so badly. I quit after that. I know it doesn't sound like a big deal, but it's the same reason you think decorating is a *girl job*. I hate that stuff. You've seen my room. And at that age, we mostly do what we're told. A lot of those girls never got to find out if they like camping because an adult didn't prescribe it to their gender. And that's just the tip of the iceberg."

"I—" Matt starts, then looks down again. "I'm sorry. Especially to you, Bailey. For, you know, that one time." He looks at me, and I can see that he's sincere. And embarrassed. "That's why I called you for Thanksgiving prep. So we could spend some more time together and talk about it. I know I can be an ass. No excuses, I'm just sorry."

I throw an arm around his shoulder and squeeze him tight. Kiss his forehead quickly like I'm kissing a gator that may snap at me. This is just the first conversation of many and far from the last time Matt will piss us off with his ignorance. But it's worth it. Matt is one my friends. One of my best friends. And I love him.

"Water under the bridge. We can talk about feminism whenever you want. Because, well, I'm a feminist." *I am a feminist.* The words feel warm and strong and right.

CHAPTER ELEVEN

I drop the grocery bags on my desk and hang my coat. Priya is in the bathroom wielding a curling iron. The smell of burning hair and perfume fills our room.

"How fancy are you going? Don't you know Thanksgiving is supposed to be super casual?" I ask, hoping I'm not expected to put effort into how I look today.

"I just want to look nice. We're always lounging together in jeans and sweatshirts. It's a nice dinner we're making. I want it to feel special." She holds my eye contact through the mirror, and I exaggerate a sigh.

"Fine, I'll wear my nice clothes."

We can't openly drink alcohol because Alder is a dry campus, so instead of having the wine and beer in the basement, I set up the bar on my desk for people to discreetly serve themselves. I form the line up; Barolo, French Syrah, and pinot noir from Oregon. I finger the labels, fight the desire to hoard, and open all the bottles, wanting my friends to feel uninhibited in their indulging. Once I finish with my bar setup, I turn to my closet.

I slide my obligatory dress to the end of the railing. *No way.* Shuffle through the couple of linen button-downs. My dad's old Eddie Bauer sweater; not John's, my dad's. I never really have to dress up, which leaves me confused, staring at my clothes. Priya places a hand on my back.

"Promise me you'll never wear that dress again. It's just not you. Here, let me help you." Her words are gentle.

I step back from the closet and allow her to take over. "Thank you. First, I need a beer because it's Thanksgiving. Want one?"

"Actually, is it too early for wine?"

"It's Thanksgiving. It's not too early for anything. White?"

"White."

I grab a Solo cup and write her name on it, dotting the i with a heart.

Noelle and Cassie pop through the bathroom and wish us a happy Thanksgiving.

"Happy Thanksgiving. Y'all want a beer or anything? The bar is officially open," I say.

"What the hell, I'll take a beer," Noelle says. I pull out two beers and open the pinot. Priya steps away from the mirror on her closet door, hair done, makeup done, in her terry cloth robe. I hand her the wine.

"What are y'all wearing?" she asks the girls.

"Looks like we're going a step above casual, judging by your hair. Looks great, by the way," Noelle says.

"Thanks. I just want it to be nice, you know?"

"Yeah. Let's all dress nice but not like formal nice. Just nice, nice," Cassie says and disappears back into her room with Noelle.

"Okay, perfect." Priya grabs my hand and drags me to my closet. She shuffles through my clothes and pulls out a pair of navy pants. "Put these on. And black socks, please."

I put down my beer and shimmy into the pants. Tug on a pair of black socks which immediately bunch at the hem of my pant legs.

Priya sighs and drops to her knees to help. "You should put your socks on first with pants that have a narrow ankle." She hikes up my pant legs and tucks my socks under them. Then pulls them back down and cuffs them once. I smile down at her even though she can't see me. She's too busy playing at being bossy and making me feel ridiculously taken care of.

"Makes sense."

She turns back to my closet. "Okay, okay. We need a shirt." Hangers glide down the metal pole one by one, in quick succession. "You've got some good stuff in here. You should wear it more often." She snags a shirt off a hanger. "This one." She tosses me a short-sleeve, white, linen button-down. I hold it against me. I love this shirt. "With a nude bra, please."

I sip my beer. "Obviously." I sneer, but I would've worn a white bra. Who knew?

"Don't give me lip. You're going to love this."

I put on the shirt. Present it to her.

"Tuck it in. And let down your hair. Where are your belts?" I open my top dresser drawer and pull out my brown braided leather belt.

"This is my only belt."

"Perfect. Put it on. And these." She pulls out my matching brown loafers.

I slip on the shoes and present myself to Priya.

"Yes." She claps. "This is so you. You look hot. The ladies are going to be all over you soon." She grins. I press a finger to my lips to quiet her down. "Just one last thing." She undoes another button on my shirt and rolls my sleeves once. "Cause you're still kinda tan from summer."

We grab the shopping bags with the pumpkin pie, veggies, and potatoes, snag our drinks, and make our way to the basement to meet with everyone. The music flows through Matt's wireless speakers, and flameless candles and red streamers fill the eat-in kitchen. The dorms are pretty much empty—most students elected to travel home to be with family—so it feels like we rented a vacation home together.

Everyone has put some effort into their appearance. Matt is wearing his nicest plaid shirt and khakis. Luke is wearing a black button-down with dark jeans. Noelle is wearing a dark green jersey dress that hits at her knees and clings to her form. I can't help but stare because now I feel like she's mine to look at. She pulls me aside.

"Bailey. You…" She runs a hand down the length of my arm. I follow her eyes as they take me in. "Wow. You look so good."

"It's all thanks to Priya." I turn to the rest of our friends. "The bar is open. Our room on my desk. And their room in the minifridge. Everybody, go get a drink."

Everyone makes their way to the stairs. Priya looks in her cup and shyly follows in the bar pursuit.

I look at Noelle's empty cup. "Don't you want to go grab a drink?"

When Priya disappears around the corner, Noelle kisses me. "I just really wanted to do that."

"You look incredible tonight."

With Noelle looking at me that way, her dimples deep and my hand on her hip, it feels like we fit. Like we are hosting this night together. Partners.

"Maybe we can refill our drinks together after everyone gets back," I say.

"I'd like that."

Our crew returns, rowdy and happy, cups full of cheer. Noelle had warmed the leftover pumpkin muffins in the oven, filling the room with cinnamon and cloves. Everything is warm: the pumpkin aroma, the light from the candles, our cheeks from the booze. We empty all the shopping bags and start to sort through ingredients. Noelle disappears up the stairs, and I take the cue to drain my beer and follow.

"Empty already?" Luke says to me, smiling like a proud father.

I shrug. "Time for wine. Be right back." I take the stairs two at a time, open the door, and find Noelle pouring herself a glass of Syrah.

"It's good, right?" I ask.

She takes a sip, sets down her cup, and meets me in the middle of the room. "So good."

I pull her into me and kiss her. Her tongue tastes like red wine. "Can we just spend the night up here alone?" I breathe into her ear. I want her so badly. I lift the hem of her dress, run my fingers up the back of her thigh, her stuttering breaths encouraging me. Higher. Higher. Until I brush against the lace of her underwear. She pushes me away, and I stumble backward, breathing heavy. She steps to me and puts a hand on my cheek, making it clear that this isn't a rejection. I hate letting her go even for a second because I know how it feels to lose her the next.

"One day, we're going to find the time and space to do this." She points to me and herself. "And I want to wait until we have that freedom. Maybe we can stick to kissing until then. Everyone is downstairs waiting on us." She kisses me as if to show me our physical limit. "You look like you need a drink. What can I pour you?"

I look at her, wait for my pulse to return to normal. This is the first time she has referred to what we're doing in the future. A promise for more. *Can I get that in writing?*

"Yeah. I want that, too." I shake my head, try to focus on being a human in the world. "Uh. The Barolo, please."

Noelle pours me a hearty glass. "Drink up, love."

❖

"I don't know, man, I just don't see why'd you need the oven to cook steaks," Matt says to Luke. Luke shakes his head and tears the cellophane off the individual pieces of meat.

"It's a two-prong system. Start it in the oven, finish it on the pan," Luke says, failing to keep the annoyance out of his voice. Cassie and Priya season the potatoes while I help Noelle snap the tails off the green beans. The kitchen is thick with heat from the oven and the hum of a family cooking.

"Dude, just let Bailey do it. Please," I hear Matt beg.

I look over my shoulder and wink at him. I've cooked many steaks. John didn't fall into the *grillmaster* role in our family, so it's a hobby my mom and I picked up together. On Savannah summer nights, we'd host our family friends on the back porch, torchlights and citronella candles lit for bugs, cups full of wine or whiskey, and my mom and I seasoning and grilling the meat.

Luke washes his hands and literally throws in the towel. "Okay." He walks across the kitchen to me, taps me on the shoulder.

"What's up?"

"Well, Matt and I were hoping you could take over the steaks. You just have more experience, and we don't want to mess them up."

"Yeah, I'd love to." I walk over to the other counter to assess the steak situation. I generously pepper and salt them all, then walk away.

"That's it?" Luke asks.

"Yeah. The meat is the star. It's all about simplicity."

"Well, should we start the oven?"

Matt sighs and touches his forehead.

"Oven? Um, we could do it that way." I speak lightly, trying not to trample all over Luke's ideas. Actually, fuck that. It's not my fault men are fragile. "But if there's no grill, I normally just get a cast iron really hot with butter. It's quick, too, so we'll cook them when everything else is almost done."

"Yeah. *That's* how you do it." Matt smiles. And though I appreciate his trust in my skills, he's still being an ass.

To Luke's credit, he smiles at me and slaps his hands together. "All right. We got the easy job. More beer for me, then." He turns to go upstairs to the bar.

We all freshen our drinks and set one of the long tables in the study room, family style. The kitchen table is too small to hold all of us, so our beautiful Thanksgiving feast sits among whiteboards of derivatives and organic chemistry equations. We sit and raise a glass. Then, Matt shoots up off the bench.

"Sorry. One second." He rushes to the whiteboard and uses his palm to erase the schoolwork, leaving a faded blue smear in its place. It takes him a minute to erase it all, then he grabs a red Expo marker and starts writing.

Happy Thanksgiving, Baker.

He completes it with a hand turkey and walks back to the table with red and blue marker all over his skin.

"Had to get rid of that stuff. No school. Just us." He swings his legs back over the bench.

I lift my glass again. "Thanks, Matt." I wink at him, then turn my attention to everyone else. "I can't say what you all mean to me. Instead, let me just say that you light me up. And I am so full of gratitude." I close my eyes, try to think of the biggest words, words that encompass, fat words full of meaning. "I…ah screw it. I love you guys." I never expected these people to stomp into my life and make themselves at home in me. I never want them to leave.

Noelle smiles that smile at me, and I feel her foot tap my ankle. "How about you give us your family's toast?"

I look around at the table. Everyone is rosy and riding a steady hum of alcohol. This time, I stand. And everyone stands with me, Solo cups at attention. Thanks to the architecture and long banquet tables, it feels like I'm hosting a feast in my castle. I clear my throat.

"Here's to us. Who's like us. Damn few 'n they're all dead," I shout. It lands. Everyone hollers like we're at a football game, knocking cups and cheering for each other. Cheering for us. Cheering for this time of our lives.

❖

We all pitch in to make cleaning a little less painful; we destroyed the place. The music slows with our energy level, bellies weighed down with steak and pie and beer. Though we all want the evening to last forever, as soon as the countertops are wiped clean, we drag our heavy feet and sleepy eyes upstairs, wishing each other good dreams and asking each other for Tums.

I sit on my bed and wait for Priya to get out of the bathroom. I pull out my phone and respond to my mom's text: *Happy Thanksgiving. Wish I were there, too. I'll call you tomorrow.* My phone vibrates in my hand.

Noelle: *Don't go to bed. And don't change yet.*

Me: *But sweatpants.*

Noelle: *Please? Meet me in the common room in twenty minutes. Everyone will be out when their head hits the pillow.*

When I get there, Noelle pats the seat next to her on the leather couch, and I sit as close to her as I can. No more pretending. I kiss her on the cheek like it's my job. She takes my hand into her lap and strokes my wrist. We both stay quiet, enjoying the fire, enjoying being alone together on Thanksgiving.

Noelle turns to me. "What I'm most thankful for is you. The fact that you came into my life. I can't even." She pauses. Strokes my face with her thumb. "You were my first kiss. And since that night, you are all I can think about. Since before that night, really. I can't study. I can't pay attention to other people. It's all too tedious if it isn't you. I just want to be with you."

I open my mouth to respond and close it again. I need a second to breathe. Her words are everything I've been waiting for. She stares at me, waiting for me to say something. I want to hear her ask for exactly what she wants. I need her to be explicit. I need to trust her. "Why don't you, then?" I ask.

"What?"

"Be with me."

"Well, that's why I asked you to meet me down here. To ask you to be my girlfriend." So close.

I smile at her, squeeze her hand. "Ask me, then."

She clears her throat and turns her full body to me. "Will you be my girlfriend, Bailey?"

My whole body floats. This is what it feels like to be asked out by my first love. I hope she's my only love. "Yes. Of course." I press rapid small kisses to her lips.

"You're mine now."

"Since day one." Since day one, we've fought so hard to get here. We made it through all the craziness together.

"I can't believe this is real."

"Me neither. Can we tell everyone now? Now that there's something to tell?" I feel her tense up next to me.

"Bailey, I can't. I can't. I'm not ready for that. I—"

I squeeze her hand and cut her off. I don't want to ruin the night with the thing that's always hung over us. With me wanting more than she does. "Hey, it's okay. In good time. We'll figure it out later." She nuzzles under my arm, rests her head against my chest. I want to think about anything else besides the impending "later" and if we actually can figure it out together. I breathe in her hair and focus on how her breasts feel against my torso. No guilt. She's mine to touch. "Why couldn't I be in sweats for this?"

"I wanted us to look nice. So when we look back at this night, you'll remember me by the fire in my green dress. And I'll remember

you looking at me that way, in your linen shirt and those loafers."
She tucks my hair behind my ear and kisses me. Slips her tongue
past my lips like those loafers really turn her on. I feel her hand
starting to untuck my shirt, and I break our kiss.

"Nuh-uh. None of that, remember? Just kissing until we can get
some privacy."

She sighs and drops her head. "I wish you could feel what you
do to me."

"Well, you know, it's your rule. But I think it will be worth the
wait."

Post-Thanksgiving is a fast two weeks. Students walk from
class to the library, from the library to study group, and from study
group back to the library. They keep their heads down, not able to
afford the distractions of normal life, eyes bloodshot from a lack of
sleep and a steady overdose of caffeine. Because this week is finals'
week.

While I'm just amazed that I haven't dropped out yet, my
friends are among the half-dead masses. I bring them coffee,
pastries, a pat on the back. *You're going to kill this final*, I tell
them. Especially Noelle, who hasn't stopped studying since classes
resumed after Thanksgiving. It's something I really admire about
her, the dedication. Not even I can distract her from succeeding.
From getting the top grade in her classes. I know I'm superfluous
right now, but that's okay. She keeps me happy with the occasional
kiss and late-night text. Most nights, I sit next to her while she
studies, doing nothing, just to be near her.

"Bails," she says, eyes not leaving her chemistry book.

"Mm-hmm."

"You have to start studying. Doesn't matter how much you hate
your classes. You have to pass them."

"You're not my mom."

She breaks her stare into her textbook and looks at me. Puts a
hand on my thigh, which honestly stirs me at this point.

"Listen. You hate school, I get it. But you have to realize its worth. It's a means to an end. A tool that you can use to get to where you want to go. Don't waste it."

"I don't know where I want to go." I still haven't gotten around to changing my major. I've been too busy changing my sexuality. It's been easy to avoid the other problem in my life that needs fixing: I still have no idea what I want to do professionally. It's hard to have faith that I'll figure it out this year.

"That doesn't matter. You're going to figure it out." She leans in to whisper in my ear. "Plus, I've been thinking about how we can get some alone time. Real alone time. And it all goes to shit if you fail out."

I perk up a little. "I didn't know you had time to think about that stuff."

"I need something to take the edge off at night. Something to ease me out of my caffeinated stupor." She refocuses on her textbook. "Now, can you get lost? Because now my mind's there and not here, and all of a sudden, you are very distracting."

I stand and squeeze her shoulder. "Don't work too hard." I leave to find someone else to bother.

It's not that I'm not going to study. I am. But my finals aren't until Wednesday and Thursday. That means I'll start studying Tuesday night. Noelle was being dramatic; I'm not at risk of failing out. I'm not getting straight A's either, but I'm fine with that. I go back to the dorm, grab my calculus book, and head to the basement to pretend study with Luke and Matt. I last about ten minutes before I start looking around the room for anything more stimulating than calculus. I look from Matt to Luke, Luke to Matt, waiting for one of them to catch my eye.

"What's up, Bailey?" Luke asks, not breaking his attention from his notes, just like Noelle.

"Oh, Luke. Hey." I close my calc book as if he's interrupting my studying. "Phew. I think I need a break. Wanna play a quick game of FIFA?"

He looks at me. "My physics final is tomorrow. At eight in the morning. I'm a little busy."

I just look at him, heartbroken. He closes his book and sighs.
"Really?" I ask.
"One game. That's it."
"One game. I gotta get back to studying, too."
"Mm-hmm."

My finals go as expected. Though our grades won't post until halfway through break, everyone has a general sense of how they did. And I did well enough, thanks to some last-minute tutoring from Luke and Cassie. Everyone's last final was on Thursday, so we have today and Saturday to relax and hang out before we leave for winter break on Sunday.

"I can't believe I won't get to see you for three weeks," Noelle says.

I take a bite of pasta. The dining hall has mostly emptied by now, most students getting a head start on the holidays. I avoid thinking about it. About Noelle's imminent absence in my life. I'm so excited to see my mom and the Taylors, but it's going to hurt to be away from Noelle. I swallow and push noodles around my plate. "I don't want to think about it."

Her dad will pick up her and Cassie early Sunday morning. Wants to beat traffic. My ride, the other scholarship recipient from my church, leaves last.

Noelle riffles through her backpack, pulls out books and notes, no doubt trying to find her cell. I spot a small book with a bookmark popping out of it.

"What are you reading?"

She looks confused for a moment, then her eyes reach the book lying upside down on the table. "*The Alchemist.*" She hands it to me. I like the cover. It looks like an exploding sun. "Have you read it?"

"Yeah. It's all about relentlessly pursuing your destiny. I think I like it most because my brother gave it to me. And my dad thinks it's scandalous somehow. Like it may stoke rebellious flames in me."

"Do you mind if I borrow it?" I slap a palm on the cover. "I'll need something to distract me from your absence over winter break."

"I'm about to finish it, then it's all yours." She smiles. "I've got something to tell you. I think it will brighten you a little."

I put down my fork. "What?" I'll take anything that will ease my bad mood.

"I told my parents that I wanted to do some prep work for next semester. You know, make sure I have everything in order. Do some pre-studying."

"Pre-studying?"

"I told them I wanted to come back from break a little early. Instead of Saturday, when everyone else is getting back to Alder, I'm getting back on Thursday." She grins. My mouth hangs open.

"Thursday?" I need confirmation before I let myself truly feel the excitement.

Noelle drops her voice. "Thursday. Do you think you want to get back a little early, too? It would mean two days and two nights alone. No roommates."

"No studying." I smile.

"None. Just you and me."

"I think I could be convinced." My mind floods with images of Noelle in my bed. I will do anything to get back to Alder early.

When it's time to say good-bye, Cassie gives me a bear hug, then slides into the back of Mr. Parker's BMW. He waits in the driver's seat, tapping on the steering wheel, seemingly uncomfortable with the outward affection displayed by his daughter and her friends.

"One second, Dad," Noelle tells Mr. Parker through the window, then steps over to me. Her eyes are clear and bright in the morning sun. "I'll call you every day," she promises.

I look at my feet. My winter boots are untied, and my jeans are halfway tucked into my socks like Priya told me not to do. "You don't have to," I mutter.

"Hey, it's going to fly by." She touches my arm. Only briefly. "Be careful. Please."

"I will."

She wraps her arms around me. Pulls me into a hug and turns her face into my neck so no one can see her kiss me there. She strides to the car. I let out a big breath, watch it hang in the air in front of me where she used to be.

Mr. Parker waves out the window. "All right, Bailey. It was nice to meet you. Have a safe trip home," he says.

"Thank you, Mr. Parker. Merry Christmas." I wave.

"Merry Christmas, dear." He rolls up the window. I stand in the shallow snow and watch them drive away, eyes glued to the shotgun window until they turn the corner down the drive. I trudge back up to Baker, feeling very alone. I try to fill the emptiness in my chest with images of my mom. I get to be with her and Dave soon. We'll have a peaceful Christmas without the threat of John blowing it all to hell with one of his explosions. We're still settling into life without him. I'm looking forward to that, at least.

CHAPTER TWELVE

"Right here is perfect," I tell Alex.
"You got it." He pulls up to the curb behind the Taylors' car and parks.

"Thank you so much for the ride."

"No problem. Text me if you want to ride back together, too. I was thinking of heading back on Saturday."

I grab my bag out of the trunk, then poke my head through the window. "I was actually hoping to get back on Thursday. Got some things I need to catch up on before classes start again. But I'll be in touch."

"Sounds good. Good night, Bailey."

"Happy Holidays, Alex. Tell your family hello for me."

He drives away from my house, and I send out thanks to the universe for sending me a quiet church buddy who is disinterested enough to drive me home and not pry during the long trip. I wrap Noelle's coat tighter against my chest and continue toward the warm glow of our home. Before I even open the door, I feel the music escaping our house any way it can: slipping through the door jamb, rapping on the windows, mating with the glow of candlelight to fall in pools over the lawn. Joy already fills John's absence. Joy already fills Noelle's absence. This break won't be so bad.

I shed my coat in John's old office. In the darkness, the big leather chairs and oak desk are daunting, and I see my younger self sitting there, sweaty thighs sticking to the leather, accepting punishment with shame and indignance, shame always winning out, but just barely. I follow the light to the kitchen where my mom dances alone in the corner.

"Babygirl." She's on me, quick as lightning. Kisses, kisses, kisses pelt my face. Familiar hands squeeze my cheeks. And the only thing keeping me upright through the ardent greeting is our embrace. I feel so warm and loved in her arms. So at home. For everything I've been through this year, it's like I never left.

"Mom, why are you dancing alone in here?"

"Oh, I was just grabbing another bottle of wine, but I got caught in the song." She points to the ceiling like "Guantanamera" emanates from the house itself. She grabs my hand. "Come on, baby, dance with me."

I start to shuffle my feet, snap my fingers, and sing along with the few words I know.

"No, no, no. What is this?" She holds my hand away from us to observe my lame attempt at dancing. "You know how to dance, Bails. Little feet, big hips. Little feet, big hips. *Little* feet. *Big* hips." Our hands join, and my little feet, big hips earns a smile and laugh from her. I've been so distracted lately that I forgot I missed my family so much.

We walk out to the backyard with another bottle of wine and a fresh bourbon for Mr. Taylor. Cigar smoke hangs in the air in its own atmospheric layer. The flames from the outdoor fireplace guide me through the haze to the stone patio that sits under the pergola, where Mr. and Mrs. Taylor laugh and puff on cigars.

I miss Baker, and I miss my friends, but I'm also home here. Maybe I have two homes, now. Two families. I'm rich.

❖

I open my eyes. It takes me a couple of moments to remember where I am: no Priya snoring, no coffee maker burping and bubbling. I yawn and roll over to grab my phone from my nightstand and grimace at the scent of stale smoke in my hair.

One unread message.

Noelle: *I miss you already. How was last night?*

I wipe my eyes as they adjust to the bright screen.

Me: *So good. The Taylors were over, and we spent the evening in the backyard, catching up.*

Noelle: *Catching up. You mean smoking and drinking and dancing?*

Me: *All of the above. How's it going over there?*

Noelle: *It's fine. Same old Parkers. We have a ton of leftover bbq from dinner last night.*

Me: *Oh yeah? Can I come over?*

Noelle: *Yes. I wish you were here.* She responds within the minute, and I imagine her lying in bed, just like me, doing nothing but texting and waiting for me to text her.

Me: *Me, too. What would we do?*

Noelle: *Community service, Mass, avoid being at my house. On second thought, maybe I should come to Savannah. Wanna know a secret?*

Me: *Always.*

Noelle: *I can't stop talking about you. I bring you up in super off topic conversations. I think I just like hearing your name out loud.*

Me: *I can relate. I can't stop rereading your name on my phone. It's the only name good enough for you.*

Noelle: *You kind of intoxicate me.*

Her words make me ache for her. I have to go distract myself.

I join my mom for a quick breakfast, then run outside into the subtropical winter day. Savannah winters mostly feel like spring, but occasionally, the oak trees wear a dusting of snow, doing their best impression of a Washington Spruce. Today is mild, though, and the sun warms my shoulders through my sweater as I hitch up my backpack and mount my bike. I head to my favorite café to start my typical Bailey weekend morning: coffee and croissant to-go, bike to Forsyth Park to people-watch, bike to Colonial Park Cemetery to look at headstones and read. Maybe catch a matinee. Bike home. Except, this Bailey morning isn't as sweet. Not even when I find the best headstone I've ever seen:

Jasper Funk
1740–1773
Dueled
Lost

The name alone puts it in my top ten, and there are so many gems to compete with in this cemetery, including countless Civil War graves and a signer of the Declaration of Independence. But it all kind of falls flat today because now I know Noelle exists, and now I know I'm without her.

I find the sunniest, driest patch of grass to lay my blanket on. I pull out my thermos and pour myself a cup of coffee, grab *The Alchemist*, and flop onto my belly, heels knocking in the air. I send gratitude to the strength of the sun, feeling its warmth pierce through the veil of icy wind. I sip my hot coffee. Read about Santiago. About Fatima.

As I read, I feel this presence in myself solidifying. Molecules shift, bond, gather force. With every page, I feel the words weigh me down. More. More. More. Like I'm a fat raincloud about to burst and flood the earth with all my water. All of these things I've been feeling all year, shifting and clicking. I feel a fire burning in me that I've never known. It's different than the fire I have for Noelle. This fire makes me want to harness it and use it to burn down the fucking patriarchy.

I shut the book. Think I hate it.

I flip onto my back and let the sun shine on my face.

Lesbian? Feminist? Queer?

Yes. This is what I am passionate about.

I pack up my bag and bike to the library, not sure I'll find anything useful, but I need help. I head straight to the computer bank and search *Feminism*. A slew of books pop up with similar titles and descriptions. I don't know which to trust, and all of a sudden, I feel very vulnerable. I scroll until I find one—*Feminism is for Everybody*. I scribble the call numbers on my hand and grab my bag.

I bike home as fast as I can. The book calls me, burns my flesh through my backpack. I yell a greeting to my mom and sprint upstairs to my room, close my door, and fall into bed. I prop up my pillows and pull out my new book.

My phone buzzes.

Noelle: *Hey you. What are you up to?*

So close. I close the book and unlock my phone.

Me: *Hey. Just been reading. Missing you a ton.*

Noelle: *How do you like* The Alchemist *so far?*

I stare at my phone. I shouldn't really get into this, with all my half-baked ideas and confusion, but I'm also not going to lie to my girlfriend.

Me: *Well, honestly, it's kinda breaking my heart.*

Noelle: *Don't worry. Santiago figures it out.*

Me: *I have no doubt of that. Hah. I meant more like...*

I send the text, start the next one, but opt to call her instead. Because at some point, texting is a little extra. I have a lot to say.

"Hey." Her voice is clear and bright.

"Hey, sorry, it was too much to type."

"It's okay. Tell me what you think."

"This is hard to explain, but I'm going to try. I know this book is about fulfilling yourself or your personal legend or whatever. But the message I'm receiving, reading it as a woman, is that I don't get a personal legend. I'm only supposed to be a part of a man's personal legend and take care of the home while he goes to pursue his dreams.

"Fatima is just someone's daughter, just a part of Santiago's legend. Even lead has a personal legend, to become gold. But she's nothing.

"I don't know. As women, we get that messaging pounded into our heads every day, and I guess I was hoping for something else," I finish. Take a deep breath. Wonder how crazy that sounded. This is one of the most popular books in the world. Am I just a crazy bitch who hates all good things? I bristle at my own harshness. Bristle at that word. *Bitch.* I mentally strike it from my vocabulary.

"Wow, I never noticed that."

"I don't think we're supposed to."

She's quiet for a beat. "Are you okay? You sound different. Like fired up or hurt. I can't tell."

"Both."

"I'm sorry about the book. I feel like an idiot."

"No. Don't be sorry. I'm going to finish it tonight. I think it may be the most influential part of my college education." I laugh, but I know it's true.

"Bailey?"

"Yeah?"

"I don't know. Nothing. I just miss you."

"I miss you so much, Noelle. Hey, can I tell you about my day?"

I want her to walk with me through Savannah. I tell her about Jasper Funk and how winter here is warm and strange. I tell her about my favorite coffee shop and the cobblestones by the river. I tell her I'm dying to see her, that all of my favorite things feel drab without her.

We hang up, and I grab my feminism book.

I think the words feed me. Pages raise me. Chapters discipline me. I can't stop. The validation is sweet as honeysuckle, and I keep pulling style after style, harvesting the little beads of nectar. What I've been feeling is okay, normal, expected even. Women have written volumes of validation. I make a quick list of other feminist books I want to read over break.

I want to learn about Hellen Keller. About Bell Hooks. Audre Lorde. About powerful women. Women who changed something. Built something.

I want to learn about the LGBTQ+ community. Learn about the feminist movement and the intense racial inequality within it. I feel robbed of this information in my education. Full of shame that I'm so ignorant of the disparity of representation between white women and women of color within the fight for gender equality.

Time passes as a wave of books rolling over my desk. Old books get returned. New books file into the available space. I keep notes. I'd like to highlight and underline and scribble in the margin of these books, but I can't. I write down the things that knock the wind out of me or that send me into flight. I write them with care and adoration, in my best handwriting, the words that I want to consume again, every night, so that they may germinate in me and grow into something wild, I hope.

❖

I close the book I'm reading. Push back against my desk and balance on the back legs of my chair. *Political Science.* I slam my chair down and pick up my phone.

"Hey, you." Noelle's voice is a little husky, like she just woke up. But I know she woke at half-past seven because she texted me. Still, the throatiness of it tickles me.

"Hey. Were you asleep?"

"Just lying in bed."

"I wanted to tell you something."

"What's up?" Her voice picks up a pitch of anxiety, and I wonder what she thinks I'm about to say.

"I think I figured it out. I want to change my major to Political Science."

"Whoa. What made you settle on that? Tell me everything."

"Well, you know I've been diving pretty deep into some feminist books, and I've been thinking a lot about what you said about majoring in me. And I think Political Science will give me the tools to do…well I don't know yet. But to do something."

"Oh my gosh, that's perfect, Bailey. I'm so happy for you."

"Thank you. It feels right."

"Like us."

I smile against my phone. "Yeah. Exactly."

"I'm very proud of you, Bails."

"Thank you."

CHAPTER THIRTEEN

M y mom sets a cup of coffee on my nightstand. "Merry Christmas, sweetie."

I rub my eyes and sit up. "Merry Christmas."

"Time to make breakfast. Dave will be here in about an hour."

"Ugh, why'd you invite that loser?" I'm kidding, though. I'm beyond excited to see my brother. Without John weighing us down, I know Dave will be present with me again. Like when we were little.

"Blood obligation." She winks. "I'm going to get started on the pancakes. When you're ready, come down and fry some eggs for us."

Once I'm up, I stand over the frying pan and crack six eggs into the popping oil, wiping the drowsiness from my eyes. My mom rearranges some gifts under our notoriously scruffy tree. "Looks like Santa came."

"Is it an obligation of every parent in the world to say that on Christmas morning?" I smile. It feels so good to be home. We're all healing together, joking like we don't have a care in the world.

"Mind the eggs."

I jump when our front door crashes open, and my mom rushes to greet Dave. He sweeps into the kitchen and wraps me up without giving me time to put down my spatula or turn to face him. "I'm going to get oil on you," I protest, but he just squeezes me tighter and lifts me off the ground.

He picks a mostly cooked pancake off the griddle and hot potatoes it to his mouth while my mom pours him a cup of coffee.

"Missed ya, Bails. How goes Alder? Any boys I need to beat the shit out of?"

The hairs on my neck prickle. I didn't even think to tell them about Noelle. Not yet. Everything feels so perfect right now, and I don't want to shake things up. I transfer the fried eggs to a plate.

"Nope. But I do have a little bit of news."

"Well?" Dave asks through half-chewed pancake.

"Breakfast is ready." I grin.

"Liar. There's something else," Mom says. We stand around the kitchen island and serve ourselves eggs, pancakes, and more coffee.

"Yeah. I, uh, think I'm going to change my major this spring."

"Oh yeah? To what?" Dave asks.

"Political Science."

"Why? Tell us more," my mom says.

I chew my pancakes and wash them down with a sip of coffee. "I think I've been noticing some things about our society that I'd like to learn more about and maybe one day help to change."

"Like?" Dave prods.

"Like gender issues. Like feminism. I want to learn more about gender equality."

My mom blinks. "Wow. I didn't know you were interested in that."

"It was kind of a slow build-up. But, yeah, I've been reading a lot, and I feel pretty strongly about it."

My mom walks around the island and wraps me in her arms. "I'm so happy for you, honey."

"What would you do with that? Be a lawyer or activist or something?" Dave asks.

"Something like that. I have a lot to learn before I know what route I want to take."

"You were always a little fireball in there." He pokes me in the chest. "'Bout time you crack open."

My phone buzzes, and I snatch it from my back pocket, hoping to see Noelle's name.

Alex: *Hey. Decided it'd be nice to get back early. Thursday works for me. Split gas and carpool again?*

Wow. It looks like Santa really did come through this year. I try not to grin like an idiot at my phone.

"Because of that, I was thinking about getting back a little early, like Thursday, so I can get my ducks in a row for next semester."

"Aw. We'll miss you. But if that's what you need to do, of course," my mom says.

Me: *Perfect. What time will you pick me up?*
Alex: *7.*
Me: *Great. Thanks, Alex.*

❖

I wait outside for Alex ten minutes before he said he'd be there, my wet hair cold in the morning breeze. This break has been incredible, but I'm bursting at the seam to get back to Alder and see Noelle.

"Why can't you wait inside?" my mom asks.

"Just want to be polite, Mom. It's a big favor, letting me carpool with him."

She sits next to me on our front steps, coffee in hand. "I'll miss you. You know you can call me for anything, Bailey. Anything." Those words bring my attention back to her. She looks like she's trying to tell me something with her eyes. "Don't forget that I know you. I've known you your entire life." She squeezes my knee as Alex's car becomes visible on our street. Her words make me want to hide, but more, they make me wish I'd come out to her over break. Is that what she's trying to tell me? It's too late now.

"Okay. I know, Mom. I love you. Tell Dave I said bye when he wakes up."

After we arrive at Alder, I walk through the front door of Baker and am hit with the familiar scent of old furniture and commercial grade cleaning products. Noelle should be here in about an hour, so I run upstairs and get ready. It feels like Christmas morning. There is nothing I could want more.

I pace in front of my dorm window and wonder if I resemble a ghost to the outside world. *I saw a weird girl in the window of*

Baker. I don't care; she'll be here any minute, and I have to see her arrive. The door to an old Grand Cherokee opens, and Noelle slides out of the driver's seat. This flabbergasts me. *Where's the beamer? Where's her dad? Is that her car? Wow, she looks so good.* I gape out the window and watch her shoulder her bag and disappear through the front door of Baker.

I wait, ears prickling as I try to pick up the sound of footsteps in the hallway.

My door flies open without a knock, and Noelle stands in its frame, cheeks rosy from the cold, a look on her face that tells me I'm in trouble. I set my coffee on my dresser and stare at her. She dumps her bag on my bed and crosses the room to me, cold hands on my face, warm mouth, Noelle. The whole world falls into place when she kisses me. As much as I wanted to put all of my faith in her, part of me worried she would back out of this plan. I let go of that fear now. She always boomerangs back through time and space.

She beams at me. "Hi." The dimples, the eyes, the golden hair. She's as incredible as I remember. More.

"I missed you so much," I finally say. "I can't believe you're here. Whose car is that?"

"My brother bought a new car, and his old one was technically my parents', so they gave it to me for Christmas." She grins. I know exactly why she's grinning that way, and I feel my own lips tugging up.

"Show me."

"Don't worry. You'll get to know my car pretty well this semester." She steps to me and plants a hand flat over my heart. "Particularly the back seat." She peeks at me, all mischief and want. Heat falls over me, and I can't believe this is my life. I can't believe that I get to be the one to tumble around with Noelle in her car. Me.

"Yeah. Well, safety first. You know, because…" I ramble, the heat from her palm on my chest, from her eyes boring into me, stirring my brain until I'm a bumbling unintelligible fool.

"Because the back seat," she fills in, "is the safest place to sit. Is that what you meant?"

I nod.

"Do you feel safe with me, Bailey?"

I nod.

She brushes her warm mouth over my neck. I wonder if she can feel how frantic and frenzied my blood is, how it pummels against the walls of my veins, under the blanket of my skin, trying to get to those lips.

Gone. Her lips are gone. I blink, cold in her absence, as my body trips on static, and Noelle closes the blinds. Her hand is back. It trails along the tops of my shoulders, leaving a pop of muscle spasms under each dragging finger as she crosses behind me to my door. Click. Locked.

That sound, *click*, snaps me into alertness, and I rock forward onto my toes. I am free and safe here. And I want to know what it feels likes to have a woman against the wall.

It's the smallest things that shift a moment. That shift the power. No, the word *power* doesn't belong here in my room with Noelle. Neither of us is more powerful or seeks to be. Neither of us needs to take the other someplace they may not want to go. We're equals in want. Regardless, when I cross the room and pin her against that locked door, her eyes widen, and her lungs release their breath in a puff.

"Do you feel safe with me, Noelle?"

I watch her lips part, watch the last bit of fleshy red pluck away from its thicker bottom partner. "Yes."

I drop my hand from the door to her cheek. Kiss her and step back.

She grips the bottom of her T-shirt and pulls it over her head, baring her purple bra and pale winter skin. My jaw clenches, releases. Clenches. Releases. Noelle nods to me, and I pull off my shirt.

I'm ice. Every muscle in my stomach, my arms, my legs freezes into rigid slabs of meat as she steps toward me. She wraps me up, pulls my head into the hollow of her neck, whispers something I can't hear into my hair.

All of my glacial planes pop and crack and slide into Noelle, my frozen muscles thawing into a chatter of kinetic energy. Another whisper stuck in my hair. I think it was my name.

"Baby, hey." This whisper burrows into my ear. *Baby* not *Bailey*. Noelle arches her head back to look at me, and I want to riot at the new distance. "You're shaking."

"I'm not cold."

"Okay."

"I'm not scared."

"I know." Her hand strokes my cheek.

"I'm sorry. I can't s…stop." My teeth chatter. "I'm just…I'm overwhelmed by you. And that apparently c…causes me to lose complete control of my body." So much for being sexy.

She grabs my hand and pulls me to my bed, guides me under my quilt, and settles her weight on top of me, her hair waterfalling over me, and holds me. My chattering explodes into her, her body absorbing every convulsion, and I focus on the warm weight of Noelle pressing me into the mattress, on the way her hair smells like violets and orange peel. I take a deep breath and wrap my arms around her, squeeze her to me, and ride out the last tremor before my wild fever breaks, and my body calms.

Noelle's mouth breaks into a smile against my ear. "Wow. That's what I do to you, huh?"

"Yes," I blow out.

"Is it weird that I'm super turned on by it?" She presses a kiss to my ear.

"No. I like that."

"Good. Because you're so sexy and adorable, and seeing what I do to you does things to me."

A knee settles between my legs, and her hips move slowly against me, rocking me into a steady building of pressure between my legs, one that I'm going to lose control over any second. She plants a kiss on my cheek that tells me she's going to break away, and she sits up, pulling off her bra and jeans and underwear. I follow suit and shimmy out of the rest of my clothes, trying to keep pace. After all of my hiding, I can't rip my clothes off fast enough. I am about to have sex for the first time with someone who adores me. There is not one doubt, not one fear, nagging at the back of my brain. It's pure joy. I wish it for the world.

We fall into my bed as a tangled pile of soft skin and tongues and fingers. Each of our crazed desires to touch and explore battling with the other's, a mad dash to everything that we promised each other. Every inch of my skin screams in need of her fingers, her hair, her mouth. We tussle and writhe and roll over, overwhelmed by the freedom, by the exploration.

I run a hand down between her thighs, shudder at the warm wetness and the small cry that emanates from her throat. Her incisor clamps down on her plump lower lip. I think I'd like to see a speck of blood there. She moves against my hand as I send kisses all over her, peppering her body with trails to where my mouth wants to go. I slide down, try to map every ridge, valley, and beauty mark, how the sweat glistens on her skin, the scent of her. The scent of *her*.

"Noelle?"

"Mmm?" she manages.

I gently spread her thighs and look at her, at her breasts rising and falling, quick breaths dragging through her parted lips.

"I love you." I lower my mouth to her center.

"I love—" She's cut off by her own whimper. She buries a hand in my hair, moves her hips against me as her body tenses and tightens, then dissolves.

She gathers me to her, my ear pressed to her breast so I can hear her heartbeat, strong and fast, as it comes back down to a normal pace.

"I was trying to say 'I love you' before you interrupted me." She strokes my arm that's draped over her stomach.

I close my eyes and listen to her heart.

Lub dub, lub dub, lub dub.

This. This is right.

"I know."

"Hmm?" Her fingers run lazy trails through my hair.

"I know you love me. I've known for a long time."

"Is that right? When did you know?"

"Well, I knew you *liked* me the night we met. I knew you *loved* me that night on the bench outside Starbucks. When you touched my scar. Held my hand."

She kisses the top of my head and rolls me underneath her. "I wanted you to be mine the moment I saw you walk into the dining hall. I didn't know why or what it meant or how, but I knew it was you. I love you, Bailey."

Her hand runs down my body, and I shut my eyes, focus on her fingers and her breath and my own heartbeat whooshing in my ears.

Lub dub, lub dub, lub dub.

We lie wrapped up together in my bed, clinging to this moment for as long as possible, until my stomach growls in the most obtrusive, embarrassing way. Noelle chuckles.

"I was literally about to say that I'm starving," she says.

I slide out of bed and jump into my jeans and a T-shirt.

"Boo, no clothes."

I lean over her and kiss her. "Come on, let's go eat dinner. The faster we do that, the faster we can come back here."

She pries herself from my bed and walks to my dresser, pulling out a pair of sweatpants and a long-sleeve T-shirt. No bra. No underwear. Just her naked body in my clothes.

"You're staring," she says.

"I really like this." I encompass her with a wave of my finger. Every time I wanted to let my gaze linger on her, I felt like she wasn't mine to look at. Now that I know it's all for me, I have a lot of staring to do.

She grabs my hand and pulls me to the door. Drops it when we get to the hallway. I don't let it bother me today. I push that little pang of disappointment deep, deep away to a place where I hope I can't find it again.

After shamelessly gorging ourselves on every carb in the dining hall, we steal Priya's Pop-Tarts from her junk food stash and enjoy dessert in my bed. Noelle plays some kind of folksy band I've never heard on my laptop.

She bites into her cinnamon sugar pastry. "So."

"So?"

"I know you've never had *sex*, well until..." She points a finger at both of us. "But what have you done?" She turns to face me, curls her legs under one another. I run a hand through my hair. "What is the sexual history of Bailey Sullivan?" she asks in her best commentator voice, raising the mic to my mouth. Rave night runs limping through my head like a crazed whack-a-mole that I just can't beat down. In my mind, I don't have a sexual history, not until Noelle. Those other times weren't sex; they were desperation and fear and denial of myself. They are no longer relevant to me or my sex life, but Noelle isn't asking about my definition of sex; she's asking about who has touched my body and when.

"Um. Not a lot, really. What do you want to know?"

"Everything. You are my entire history, and I want to know yours."

"Okay. Well, I had a boyfriend in high school. Greg. And we did..." I look to the ceiling, hoping to find more elegant words to use. "Hand stuff."

"Hand stuff? Like, you gave him a hand job, and he fingered you?"

I cringe at the crudeness. "Yeah. Only it was terrible. You know, first-time stuff. I'm sure I hurt him just as much as he hurt me. Neither of us knew what the hell we were doing. That was the nice part of it. But as you can guess, I wasn't that into him."

Noelle studies me as I speak. And I study her. The little vertical line between her brows deepens. "Hmm. And that was Greg."

"That was Greg."

"But he wasn't that guy you kissed at the Dylan concert?"

"No. There were a few random kisses in high school. None worth mentioning."

"What about college?"

My stomach drops. This is what she really wants to know. She wants to know about the gray area when I wasn't hers. With the people she knows. She wants to know about Luke and Hunter and how many times I tried to run away from her. Only, I'm not sure she'll see it for what it was. She ran away from me, too. My running was just a little uglier. I turn to her, mimicking her cross-legged posture, tuck my hands in my lap.

"College is a little different. There's also not much. But I'll tell you whatever you want to know."

"Tell me everything."

"Okay. But I just want to say, before I do, that it was a really confusing time for me because"—I look at my lap—"well, because I didn't know how to handle my feelings for you." I take a deep breath. Then I tell her everything and hope she understands.

I tell her about how attracted I was to her when we first met. About my initial intentions with Luke and the Wakeful Wednesday missed kiss. About how I just wanted to be *normal*. About rave night. How I gave Hunter a hand job in the middle of the dance floor, right after I'd had an intimate moment with her. How I went home with Hunter and tried to give him head. How he pushed his calloused fingers into me.

On paper, it's not much for a college girl. But for me, all of these things I did with guys are like holes in my atmosphere. They aren't me, and I hate that I have to confess these moments like they are. They are nothing. I just want to move forward.

"You were going to kiss him," she says, her gaze fixed on my quilt. "After you told me that you wanted to watch the sunrise with me."

"Yeah, almost. But I didn't. I thought of you."

Her fingers pick at my quilt. Some pilling, a piece of hair. "And rave night." She shoots her gaze up to meet mine, bites the raw spot on her lip. "We were already us then. We'd held hands, we basically kissed that night, and none of that even matters because you know as well as I do that we were something. We were *us*."

I let the air between us remain silent. I put my Pop-Tart on my desk and take Noelle's hand. "The fucked-up part is, I think that's why I did it. I remember pulling away from you at the frat house, and Matt stepped in. He put his hand on your hip. And I remember feeling foolish, like I was an idiot to ever think you'd feel the same—"

"But you knew I did, Bailey. You knew it. I mean, think of every moment we ever spent together before then. How we *touched* each other. What we *said* to each other. That's not how friends act with each other. I was yours. You should've known." She wipes at a quick traitor tear, clearly annoyed at its presence. I want to back away slowly with my hands up. There's no explaining this away. It just is. Now I need her to realize that she ran away from me, too. She ran after we kissed. Which is way worse.

"It's just—" She exhales through her nose. "It's just hard to swallow. You let someone who wasn't me touch you like that. And you touched someone who wasn't me like that."

"Noelle, I—"

"Look. I know I'm not being fair. I *know*, okay? I get it. But we were falling in love. How would you feel if I was sucking some random dude's dick and almost kissing Matt the whole time?"

"Noelle." She looks at me, the corner of her mouth pinched into an apologetic smile. "All of those experiences were painful to me. And they are moments that I try to forget. They are not a part of who I am. You have to trust me on that. After Halloween, you ran away from me. It's the same exact thing. It's not fair that we had to fight through all of that bullshit to be here together, but we did. We made it. That's all that matters. Let's show ourselves a little grace."

She throws herself on her back, looks at the ceiling. "Ugh. I'm so sorry. You're right." She drapes an arm over her eyes. "I know it's unfair for me to expect you to have honored this secret code that we never even talked about. You were single. And I know it was really hard for you. It was hard for me, too. It makes me sick to think of how I treated you after Halloween."

"Thank you. For the record, I would lose my damn mind if you had done that stuff with anyone else. I thought you and Matt might hook up that night—that was the boys' plan, at least—and when I couldn't find you, this terrible dread gathered in my gut. Pure dread, Noelle. And I'm sorry I made you feel that way."

"I'm sorry for being jealous." She throws a hand to my thigh. "I think I've always felt possessive of you. Like no one deserves you."

"I'm just me."

"Exactly."

"I've always felt so protected by you. And celebrated by you. I don't know." But I do know. She had unwavering faith in me even when I didn't have it in myself. When I was just a confused mess, she saw through everything. She saw me.

She presses a sweet Pop-Tart kiss to my lips. "I adore you, Bailey. I wish I could show you off."

That little pang pinches my heart. I drag a finger along her jawline, a strong jawline for a strong girl. Why doesn't she think she's strong enough to be public about us? She's the one who instilled this power and confidence in me, but she can't walk with me past this line in the sand. "You could, you know. There's nothing to be ashamed of here." The words tiptoe out of my mouth, creep through the air, and crawl into her ear.

"No. I can't. You know my family is fucking crazy. They wouldn't understand."

"So that's it?"

She shakes her head. "You make it sound so casual. Like it's nothing: *just tell your family*. But for me, that's everything. If they found out about us, they'd disown me. Like, literally throw me out. I'm not ready to think about that." She stares at her lap. It's not anger. It's sadness that slumps her shoulders, claws at her features.

"Hey. It's okay. We'll figure it out together."

Chapter Fourteen

She was right. I have become very familiar with the back seat of Noelle's Jeep. I slam the car door shut, wait for her to pull the keys out of the ignition and lock up. We're both a little high. Heads in the clouds, pat our bellies, kind of satisfied. I especially love the back seat. Love how Noelle goes crazy in it, hands gripping the leather headrest behind me while she finds a rhythm on my hand. It drives me insane. I look at her as she rounds her car. The little smile on her lips flickers in the streetlights. We'll be on the verge of maniacal giggling until we pass the chapel and yet again have to face our friends.

Noelle is scared of losing her family and her scholarship. She thinks that if someone saw us, we'd be reported to the dean, as if anyone would care enough to bother with that. She's not ready, and that shouldn't be hard for me to understand. But I am ready. I don't know how those two truths can continue to coexist.

For two weeks now, we've been sneaking around, stuck in the sugar-soaked honeymoon phase with little privacy and the threat of being caught always looming over us, like a jack-in-the-box always on the verge of popping, just keep turning the crank, bracing for the big one. I want to. I want to do anything in the world to make her happy, to make her feel safe and loved, but every time she drops my hand or looks through me to see if someone is watching, she adds another dagger to my heart.

It's like clockwork. We pass the first stained-glass window and put another six inches of space between us. We hit the quad, and we're at a foot. At the first bench, the wretchedness of it starts to annex my young love, pie in the sky, got laid vibe and replaces it with guilt, a little fear, and a sprinkling of shame. I feel the shift, feel my stomach sour, and stop walking. Two feet. Three feet.

Noelle doubles back to me, eyebrow raised. "What're you doing? Are you okay?"

"Don't you feel it?" A metallic rot coats my tongue, and I cringe, hand over belly. "Every time, we get back so giddy. Then we get here, and it's shit."

"Come here." She grabs my hand and directs me to the nearest bench, like she's embarrassed of my public display of displeasure. "Okay, what are you talking about?"

I lean my elbows on my knees and breathe. Tomorrow, I officially change my major to Political Science. I begin a journey on which I can learn about my passions, one of which is turning out to be women's and queer rights. And here I sit, in a clandestine relationship with a woman, a relationship that requires us to lie to our friends, deny who we are, and fuck in the woods like animals. The latter isn't so bad. But still. As much as I love Noelle, hiding our relationship is no longer aligning with who I am. I need to honor myself.

"Everyone asks where we're going when we leave. We lie. Everyone wants to know where we were when we come back. We lie. Our friends want to know about our lives. And we lie to them." I sigh and lean against the back of the bench. "And that's just one little part of it. I don't know what you feel, Noelle. But I'm gay. And I don't want to hide that. I'm proud of it. And I'm wildly proud to be dating you."

Noelle straightens, looks around for a recording crew, a boom hanging from a tree, maybe. "I'm not gay."

"Bi? Queer? Anything but straight?"

"No."

"How do you explain this, then?" I throw a thumb at my chest.

She turns to me, eyebrows tight. "I don't know. I don't know, Bailey. I mean. What do you want from me? I agreed to be in a relationship with you. That's what I can offer."

"*Agreed*?" I bore into her. "That's funny. That's not quite how I remember it."

"What's your problem? You seemed totally fine with it back then. *Oh, you're not ready to be public, that's okay, we'll figure it out together.*" Her face twists in the impersonation of me.

I slack my features, worried that my face looks that screwed up right now. "Look. I know it's a lot. It's scary as hell. But it's okay. Priya already knows about me, and she didn't bat an eye."

Noelle whips her head around to face me, eyes wide. "What? Did you tell her about us?"

One second, I'm fine, the next I'm boiling over: hot frothy water foaming out of my ears and nose and mouth. I clench my teeth.

"Bailey. Did you tell her about me?"

"No. Okay? No. I would never do that to you."

She lets out a breath, and her back hits the bench.

I feel it, like vomit. A slow building wave. A formation I can't stop. I have to come out. I can't betray myself. And if I can't do it with Noelle, I have to do it alone. Sneaking around with her is beginning to feel like trying to date boys. I want out. It hurts too much. "Noelle." I turn to face her. To plead with her. "Can you see any future where you and I are in a public relationship?"

She knows why I'm asking. "Don't," she whispers.

"I can't do this. I love you, and I want to be with you. But I can't do this."

She throws a hand out to grab mine. "Bailey. Please don't do this."

"Do it with me. We can do this together. Nothing bad can happen."

"Hah!" Her sadness cuts to anger. "Nothing bad can happen? You are so naive, Bailey. Look where we are." She scans the campus and displays it to me with an open palm. "Do you even know the laws in Georgia? Do you?" She shakes her head. "Do you know that Alder is a private college? *A Catholic private college.* They will have no problem throwing us out. There are no protections here. Hell! There are no protections in this state."

My head spins. I hadn't gotten that far yet. I stare at her, try to track with her, try to keep up with her words, with my thoughts, with my emotions.

"Look at you. You haven't even thought about this. Wake up, Bailey. The faculty here can still get fired for being gay. Totally legal. In fact, since you're so passionate and gung-ho about coming out at Alder, why don't you read Alder's policy on LGBTQ+ students."

"Noelle—"

"No. Then think about me having to go home to my family, to my *father*, and explain to them how I lost my scholarship, something you seem to care nothing about. And you have your mom. You have support and love. But I'd lose everything."

She's right. I don't care if I lose my scholarship and get kicked out. Sure, it wouldn't be ideal, but I know I will always have fierce support behind me, no matter what. I have my mom. Noelle has nobody. My heart breaks for her. But I can't relent.

"Noelle. That's enough for tonight. Please," I plead, wiping at my wet cheeks. I stand and shake myself off. Start toward Baker. I hear Noelle follow me, hear her catch up.

She grabs my arm. "Hey."

I shirk out of her grip.

"Hey." She doesn't bother grabbing my arm but wraps me into her. I feel my shoulders shake against her. I feel her hand run through my hair. "I'm sorry," she whispers. "I'm sorry." I push away. Her eyes are red-rimmed around the green. Like Christmas.

"Are we together?" she asks.

"Yeah. But I need some space. Please." I turn and walk away from her. *Why did I say yes?* I storm into our dorm room.

"Whoa. Who shit in your Cheerios?" Priya asks, mid-page-flip in her magazine.

"It's *pissed*. Who *pissed* in my Cheerios."

"No. Someone definitely *shit* in your Cheerios by the looks of it."

I collapse onto my plastic-y twin mattress. "Can we talk about it later?"

Priya walks across the room and sits on my bed next to me. "We could. But I already know everything, so why don't you let me take some of this off your shoulders?"

"I love you, but you don't know everything."

"I know about Noelle."

I shoot upright. "What?"

She examines her cuticles. "I know about you guys."

"Shh. What do you mean, you know about us? What do you know?"

"I know you sneak off in her car to hook up. I know you're together. Or maybe used to be, judging by how you look."

I just stare at her. "I want to come out. Need to come out. To everyone. But she can't. Won't even admit to me that she's gay or bi or queer or anything. She can't even tell me, the *girl* that she is in a romantic relationship with, that she's not straight. And I can't stand it anymore. I don't know how to meet both our needs. I only know how to meet mine."

"Hey. You need to do you. But before you judge Noelle for her fears, don't forget that it wasn't too long ago you were sucking dick trying to be straight."

I wince. "Jesus, Priya. A little harsh, don't you think?"

"It's the truth. And you know her family is crazy strict. Just think about it before you decide to do anything. Unless, did you just break up with her?"

"No. Not really. I said I needed some space."

"Well. Take some space, then. Think about her. Think about you. Maybe it doesn't have to be one or the other." She pats my knee and gets up. "Now come watch my trashy reality TV with me. I'm lonely. My roommate keeps ditching me for booty calls."

I walk to Decker Hall in the morning to meet with my counselor, not the therapeutic kind, which I should probably look into, but the *register you for class and make sure you get a degree* kind.

"Bailey Sullivan?"

"Yes, sir."

"Have a seat, please." I sit in the chair across from Mr. Clark's desk. His office is simple. One Alder University diploma, a sweaty plastic Lions thermos, a Braves hat, and a small sampling of family photos.

He studies his computer. "I see here on your request form that you are changing majors." The glow of the screen pops off his oily red skin and makes him look like a hologram. Mr. Clark is ushering me through one of the biggest moments of my life, but my gut still aches with the memory of last night.

"Yes. To Political Science."

He nods and scrolls. Scrolls and nods. "M'kay. Well. Good to make these changes early on. Most of your first semester was core classes anyways, so if you throw in one or two semesters of eighteen credits you should be just fine."

"Great. That's great."

"Now…" He trails off and continues to scroll and poke at his keyboard. "Right. There it is." He clicks a button, and the printer in the corner of his office spits out a paper. "Here is your schedule for this semester. You'll start your new classes tomorrow. All of your professors have been notified. Under that schedule is the contact information for your new advisor, Dr. Martin. Shoot him an email if you need anything. He's teaching your intro class, too. Here's the class info."

"Perfect. Thanks." I take the paper from him. A couple of clicks on his computer was all it took to change the course of my life. Excitement makes my fingertips twitch. It does. But changing my major also makes me feel further from Noelle. It feels like I'm taking a step toward myself and away from her.

"Is there anything else I can help you with today?"

"This is it." I wave the paper at him.

"Well. Congratulations." He reaches over the desk and shakes my hand. "Enjoy the rest of your afternoon."

"You, too."

❖

My crew is deep into a game of *Apples to Apples* in the common room. Matt has the most cards, with Priya trailing closely behind him. Noelle has her phone out, not paying attention to the card combinations that everyone else is laughing at.

"Bails," Cassie calls. "Is it official? Are you our new president?"

"One step closer, I suppose. Start my new schedule tomorrow."

Noelle puts down her phone and looks at me. I know she wants to run over and hug me, but I put her in a weird position. Like she's not sure if that's her role anymore because I'm the asshole who left her in the nebula between a breakup and a relationship.

"Big moves. We're so happy for you. Can't wait to see what you do with it," Luke says.

"I want to see at least five papers on why *Star Wars* is a disappointment to our society." Matt winks at me.

"I'll go write you one right now." I laugh. "I'm going to go shower and make sure I have everything in order for tomorrow. Y'all have fun." I've never tried my hardest in school, and now that I have something to try for, I'm scared I won't be good enough. But that's a better feeling than complete apathy.

The next morning is bright and cold. I fill a travel mug with coffee and swing my backpack over my shoulder, ready to go for my eight a.m. Intro to Political Science class. Priya is still asleep, but she wakes up just long enough to mutter, "Good luck," to me. I slip out of our room and close our door quietly, trying not to wake anyone up. As the door clicks shut, Noelle's opens. She walks out, hair disheveled, as if she rolled straight out of bed and into the hallway.

"Hey," she says, eyes swollen with sleep or lack of.

"Good morning."

We make our way to the staircase in silence. I sneak glances out of the corner of my eye. I did this to her. She is miserable because of me. Both of us turn right at the quad. "Where ya headed?" I ask her.

"Eaton Hall." Eaton is the building catty corner from Brown, where most of my new classes are, including my intro class this morning.

"Oh. Cool. Well, I'm heading that way, too. Brown." I clear my throat, squint into the morning sun. "Do you want to walk with me?"

"Sure."

Her melancholy tone jolts me awake. I suddenly feel the need to choose: relationship or no relationship. Anything is better than being suspended in relation-shit. Noelle is clearly suffering. And so am I.

"Noelle." I stop walking. She stops too and looks at me for the first time this morning. "I don't think it's fair to either of us to do this in-between thing. I'm sorry I put you in that position." I have to protect myself and my mental health. Lying about myself is stifling. I'm done with it. "I think it's best that we break up," I say, not prepared for the acrid bile creeping up my throat. My chest tightens, threatens to pulverize my lungs. My heart. I'm swaying.

"Really? You're breaking up with me ten minutes before my eight a.m. class? Cool, Bailey." She stares at me. I focus on breathing, scared that I may slip into my first bout of panic. "Jesus. Try not to pass out. You're the one who's ruining us, not me." She turns and walks away.

I sway. Breathe. People knock into me, hustle past me, try to sweep me away. I just broke up with Noelle. *Noelle.* She disappears into the concourse, and regret settles its weight on my chest. My heart is broken, but at least I'm free. At least I am honoring myself. Maybe one day, we can be free together.

Dr. Martin stands over his desk and sorts through some papers. "All right. Yes. Yes. Good morning everybody. Settle. Settle. I know it's sunny out, so we all want to flip our desks over and go crazy. I know." His glasses slip farther and farther down his nose as he looks at his mess. He pushes them back right before they fall, then looks at us.

"Yes. Okay. Class is about to begin." He picks up a stapled pack of papers, squints to read something on the top page. "Bailey Sullivan?" His eyes scan the sea of our class. I raise my hand. "Great. Great. Come up here, please." I walk to Dr. Martin. I feel tired eyes on me as I weave through the desks. This morning is supposed to be beautiful, the morning that welcomes me to my new life. But I'm fighting back tears when I reach his desk. Maybe I don't feel free at all.

He lowers his voice. "This is the syllabus for the semester. Also information about political science in general." He hands me the papers. The words all jumble together on the page, but I stare at it like I'm focused on this moment instead of drowning in pain and confusion.

"Thank you."

"And stop by my desk after class. Since we didn't have you from the beginning, I'd like to chat, get to know you a little better, see what you want out of this thing." He taps the stack of papers in my hands.

"Yes, sir."

He winces.

"Egh. Don't call me sir. Dr. Martin, please. Or Steve is even better." I snap back into focus.

"Steve Martin?"

He raises an eyebrow. "Yes. You're the only one to ever realize that. Go sit."

"Okay, Steve." I walk back to my desk and bite back a small smile. It feels wrong to have even a blip of happiness right now.

"Right. Class. Okay, did everyone complete the assigned reading from last week? Yes? Yes? Lovely." He lopes to the white board and starts scribbling. "As you all know, this is a pass-fail class, which means no real essays. But I want discussions. Participation is mandatory, don't forget." He yells over his shoulder. "I want to hear words coming from that hole in your face. This is political science. If you can't discuss an issue, you should probably just go home."

I scan through the papers in my hand, trying to find what reading he is talking about. I flip open my new notebook and get ready to write down anything and everything.

Steve steps back from the board. *Dissent* is written in messy, big blue letters. "There will always be tension between a government and its people. We as people want to grow and evolve. This will always happen faster than political change. And often, government will either drag its feet or oppose. What happens here?" he asks.

"Dissent," a guy from the third row calls out.

"Good. Robert, right?" Robert nods. "And Robert, what the hell is *dissent*?"

Robert clears his throat. "Opposition to what is traditionally held true by an authoritative body." I notice the green tips of his hair. A piercing in the cartilage of his ear.

"And what is the most basic ingredient of dissent? Bailey?"

Yep. That was definitely my name. "Sorry, Dr. Martin. I haven't read it yet." I swallow.

He stares at me. I'm too panicked to say anything. Wouldn't know what to say anyway. "You got the course materials yesterday. If you would've looked through the content, you could've seen that we started researching academic articles on the different manifestations of dissent." He waits for me. My lips are sealed. He turns back to the whiteboard. "Do better, Bailey. Robert, help her out please."

"Critical thinking."

The rest of the class period crashes like a wave. Swoops me up, higher, higher, higher, then pulls me under, spitting me out on the beach. Dr. Martin has seen me for exactly what I am: a slacker. And called me out in front of the whole class. Never again. For the first time in my life, I feel accountable to a professor. I care. I close my notebook, which looks like someone gave me one minute to write down my final wishes before execution and wait for most of the students to clear out before I walk to Dr. Martin's desk.

"Dr. Martin."

He closes a book and looks at me. "Bailey. You can't go back to *Dr. Martin* now. You already picked *Steve*. Commit to it."

"*Steve.* You wanted to see me after class."

"Mm-hmm. Look, Bailey. I don't know what your motives are for changing majors to poli sci, but it's going to be a lot different than education was." It feels like the first night in the dorms, transferring from anonymity to center stage. The lights are hot on my skin, and I have stage fright, but my gut shouts at me step up to the mic. I think I could be something big.

"Well, I hope so."

"Yes. And what are you hoping to gain from this degree?"

I tap a finger on his desk. Self-worth. Passion. A career that suits me. "I guess I want the skills to be able to…I don't know. Talk about and make changes in the things I'm passionate about." Those are words in sentence form, I think.

He walks to the white board and scribbles, *talk about and make changes in the things I'm passionate about.* He steps back and reads it under his breath. Cringes. "Yikes. Well, we'll certainly work on that." He walks back to me. "Okay. And what are you passionate about, Bailey?"

I realize Steve will be the third person I come out to. I feel sweat start to tickle at my pores. All of the familiar feelings of fear and doubt sweep over me. Those feelings are still muscle memory at this point. Clawing voices in my head tell me that Steve is old, and old people in the south are homophobic and bigoted. I shake my head. Those voices are lying. I look at his writing on the white board. At my words. This is what I'm here to do. *So do it.* I square my shoulders and look him in the eye. "Equity and rights for queer people and women, Steve."

A big smile breaks across his face. He slaps his desk. "Excellent. Excellent. I expect a lot from you, Bailey. Don't disappoint me."

"I won't."

"I know." He points to the door. "Now get out. This is my quiet time before next class."

I smile at him and turn to leave.

My sails are full, and the first thing I want to do when I get back to Baker is crash through Noelle's door to tell her everything. Tell her about my weirdo professor whom I adore. Tell her that I came out to an Alder staff member, and I haven't lost anything, just gained acceptance and courage. Tell her that I'm going to be a goddamn superstar in political science.

But I can't.

My high dissipates as quickly as it came. The aching is back. The panic creeps. I shoulder my bag and push through the flow of students back to Baker. I can't take it back now. It'd give us both whiplash. Besides, who'd want to be with someone so confused and flaky as I am right now?

I walk into the dorm, pass the common room, but turn when I hear someone call my name. Luke sits by the fire with his backpack. *Shit.* With so many things taking up my time and energy, I forgot to care about Luke. I forgot to be his friend.

I sit next to him on the couch. "Hey."

"How was your first class?"

"Really good. I think." I cross one leg over the other. "It was kind of a whirlwind."

"Do you want to get pizza with me tonight? Just you and me. Like we used to? I want to hear more about your class. And talk to you about other stuff, too."

"Yeah. Sure." I feel like I'm driving a tank at a hundred miles per hour down a winding mountain road. Losing control. About to crash and burn. Luke is just another curve in the road.

"Cool. I'll text ya later."

When I get back to our room, Priya is leaving for class. I want her to skip it. "Dude. Noelle looks like shit. What happened?" she asks me as she finishes throwing her hair in a topknot.

"I fucked up. I don't know what the hell I'm doing, Priya." I rip off my coat, too hot and panicky. Even if dumping her was the right choice, I should have been a decent human and done it in private.

She drops her hands on my shoulders and stares at me. "What did you do?"

"I broke up with her. On the way to class."

"You broke up with her. Before her first class of the day. So she had no privacy to process and be upset? Do I have all that right?"

"Yes."

She drops her hands and sighs. "Yeah, you fucked up."

"I know." Tears start to fill my eyes.

"I know you're in pain, too. Just—"

"I don't know if breaking up with her was the right thing to do. God, I'm so confused. I just want to be good and do the right thing, but what is the right thing?"

"You're doing your best. These big choices in life are never clear. It'd be too easy."

"I'm in love with her, Priya."

"You should be. I'd probably be, too, if I swung that way. Look. It's done now. You broke up. The best thing you can do is come out, focus on poli sci, and be a positive example of what it could be like for her, too. And be her friend. She needs you. Then, maybe, you guys can find a way to make it work."

"Yeah." We didn't break up because of a lack of anything between us. And if Noelle can ever come out, then there's at least a glimmer of hope for us. But for now, it's over.

I sleep away most of the day. Only wake for a blur of an hour when I zombie through a communications class. Then I crash back into darkness. I crash back into the world where I'm dying from my first heartbreak. I'm depressed, so I sleep. I slept for two days straight after I got my stitches. The realization of John's impact on my life and the sickness I felt from lying to Mom incapacitated me. That man tried to keep me locked away from my truth. And when he left, when my mom kicked him in the ass through our front door, I slept.

Sleep.

Sleep.

"Wake up." Priya shakes my shoulder. I crack open an eyelid. Grunt. "Wake up, Bailey."

"Why?"

"Because I know this play, and it's tired. Does not look good on you. Get up. Shower. And leave this dorm room."

I swing my legs over the edge of my bed. Wipe my eyes. "Ugh. I have to hang out with Luke tonight and explain everything." I run a hand down my face.

"Good. Clear it all up."

"I thought I had after Halloween."

"Bailey. I guess you couldn't see it because your head has been stuck between Noelle's legs, but he's been waiting for you. Ya didn't make it clear enough."

"That's ridiculous." It's not ridiculous. I've just chosen to ignore it because I don't have the capacity to deal with much else besides myself right now.

She shrugs. "Well, we shall see."

Luke and I borrow Matt's car to go pick up a pizza from town. We get three. It would be a cardinal sin to not bring home pizza for the rest of the crew. We text everyone that it's in the basement fridge, then grab ours and walk out into the night.

"Amphitheater?" he asks.

"Yeah." We walk in silence until we sit and become the only audience of the night.

Luke sets the box next to him and looks at me. "Can we talk first?"

My stomach drops because if he is delaying the pleasure of hot pizza, then this is serious. "Yeah. Of course."

"Okay cool." He turns toward me. "We never hang out anymore."

"What? Come on, that's not true."

"No. It's very true. Honestly, you spend all your time with Noelle. Which, I totally get. Y'all are super close and are suitemates, and maybe we'll never be as close as that, but it used to be you and me. You know? You and me running around together, getting pizza, roughhousing, whatever. And now, we're kinda just…well, not much of anything, really."

"Luke. I need to tell you something." I take his hand. This is the first time we've held hands, which is funny because I'm about to tell him I'm gay.

"You love her, don't you?" He squeezes my hand.

I let the words settle into my chest. They burrow there. I feel hot tears well and overflow. "Yes."

He throws his big arms around me and pulls me against him. His stubble scratches my forehead, and though it feels like it may leave a little raw patch of skin, it comforts me. "It's okay."

I don't want to leave his arms, but I also have a lot of explaining to do. He shouldn't have to comfort me. I sit up straight and wipe my eyes, try to snort the phlegm out of my nostrils to the back of my throat. Swallow it down. I want to be here for him, too. "I'm so sorry, Luke. For everything. God. I don't even know where to begin."

"Let's start with this, are you gay?"

Gets a little easier every time. "Yes."

"Okay. Before we get into all the other stuff, that's awesome. I'm so happy for you. And I love you."

"Thank you. I love you so much." I know that was the easy part. Now to the not so easy part.

"It's Noelle, huh?"

"Yeah. Except I just broke her heart. And mine."

"What happened?"

"I need to come out. I don't want to hide anymore. But she can't do it with me. Though it seems like everyone already knows anyway." He looks at me with his eyebrows raised. "Priya," I explain.

"Ah. Yeah. I thought I'd be the only one to think that."

"What do you mean?"

"From the moment I met you, I always thought it was going to be *us*. I was actually pretty damn sure it was going to be us. Until Halloween, I guess. But even after that, I saw us being together and getting married one day."

"Luke—"

"Then I noticed it. You know? How you look at her. How she looks at you. How half the time I tried to find you, you were off with her somewhere. But I thought I was being too sensitive about it. Like, I only saw it because I was jealous. I didn't want to see it, though. So I ignored it. Until now. And I'm really sorry. I should've been there for you earlier." I feel more loved by him than I ever have. And I love him more than I ever have.

"I'm so sorry, Luke. When we first met, you took me by storm. Your energy and light is so contagious, I just wanted to be around you all the time. And I think, back then, I really wanted it to work with someone, with a guy. And I met you. I wanted to be close to you." I take a breath and stare out into the darkness, wonder if I'm saying the right words. "I was really confused because I had also met Noelle. And I tried to ignore *that* for as long as I could. I know I sent you a lot of confusing signals. But I want you to know, every moment we had together was real. I love you. And I'm so sorry."

"I get it. All that makes sense. You just kinda forgot to be my friend." A knife to the gut. It's true.

"You're completely right. I'm sorry."

"I love you, Bails." He squeezes my hand, and I rest my head on his shoulder.

"I think you're incredible. When I'm reading all of my feminist stuff, I always think of you. You're the kindest, most loving man I know. You make me feel empowered and supported. Hell, I almost dated you." I laugh.

He snaps his fingers. "So close."

"You're going to make someone the luckiest girl."

He pops open the pizza box and hands me a slice. "Guess it's time for me to open back up to that possibility." He takes a bite of the greasy slice of pepperoni.

"Yep. Got anyone in mind?"

"Maybe."

I knock his knee. "Spill."

"Cassie."

Cassie? I try not to dribble grease down my chin. "Cassie? Whoa, you spilled way too easily. Cassie? What?" But then I see it. Luke and Cassie, two rocks. It actually makes sense.

"Yeah. I mean, now that I can put you out of my head—"

"Hey." He side-eyes me. I put up my hands. "Fair enough." The narcissist in me hesitates to give up my title of Luke's favorite, but I should have let him off my hook a long time ago.

"Now I can see other things. You know? She's incredible. Patient. Loving. Super sexy." I cover my ears at the last part. Luke laughs.

"Well, I wish you the best of luck. I think you guys would be great together."

"Thanks. What about you and Noelle? What happened? When did you guys get together?"

"First of all, she's not out. Maybe not even gay. And she really wants it to be a secret, so even though I didn't tell you, can you keep it between us? And Priya?"

"Of course."

I catch him up on the saga that is me and Noelle while we demolish the entire pizza. He listens and asks questions. We chew and chat and mend. My hands smell like pepperoni, and I feel like I may break out instantly from all the grease, but it's so delicious. We wipe our mouths and walk back to Baker, lighter. Luke and Priya have my back no matter what. Beyond supporting my sexuality, they support me through being nineteen and having no idea what I'm doing. I'm loved even when I'm fucking up.

I say good night to Luke and head back to my room, replaying the evening with him. I let the warmth fill me up. Everything is going to be oka—

"Oh my God, I'm so sorry!" I yell and slam the door shut. I look around the hallway to make sure I'm still on planet Earth. I hear a lot of thumping around, and *you said you locked it*. Then Priya flings the door open. Her T-shirt is on backward, and Matt hops into his socks, about to fall over.

"You are such an idiot," Priya says over her shoulder to Matt.

I stare at her. Flabbergasted. "What? What—"

"Matt. Out," she yells at him.

He finishes with his shoes and grabs his phone off my desk. He rushes past me. "Hey, Bails," he mumbles, cheeks flushed.

Priya grabs my arm and pulls me into our room.

I spin to face her. "Oh. My God. You and Matt were just fucking."

"Yes. This is not new."

"*What*?" Am I so self-absorbed that I've been ignorant to my best friend's entire life?

"Like I said earlier, your head has been firmly between Noelle's thighs for a month. It wasn't hard to sneak it by ya, Bails." Yes. The answer is yes, I am that self-absorbed.

"Why didn't you just tell me?"

She shrugs. "I dunno. It's just for fun right now. Didn't want to make things weird for everyone. I mean, look at you. You're kinda losing your mind over it."

I straighten up, pick my jaw off the ground. "I'm not freaking out."

She crosses her arms and stares me down. "*Psh.* Mm-hmm."

"Okay, okay. I'm freaking out. But I'm just so shocked. And now I have Matt's white ass burned into my mind." I touch my forehead.

Priya bites her bottom lip, and I know she's thinking about his white ass, too.

"Ugh. Gross, Priya, stop with the lip thing." I push her. "When did this start?"

"When we got back from break."

I guess I've been so distracted with my own love life that I forgot everyone else has their own stuff going on, too. "Well, I'm glad y'all are getting some."

"How'd it go with Luke?"

I fill her in on our conversation. Fill her in on my relief.

"Yay. See? One thing sorted itself out."

"I guess so. I'm going to go down to the basement to get my poli sci reading done."

She looks me up and down. "You're going to go do homework? Who are you?"

I'm a badass bitch. In training.

CHAPTER FIFTEEN

I have never worked so hard in my life. Not for anything school related, at least. I see now why I was lazy, why I didn't care. *I didn't care.* Not only do I now have a professor who stuck a fish hook in my gaping mouth, but I have a passion that burns at my heels. Sounds a bit torturous. It *is* a bit torturous. Someone wound me up, and now I can't stop.

Steve asked me to write him a paper on the history of LGBTQ+ rights in Georgia. Lately, I've been spending most of my time in the library or in the basement reading everything I can. Most of what I learn makes my fingers twitch with pain: Georgia was one of the last states to change their sodomy laws to stop discrimination against the LGBTQ+ community, for example. It took until 1998. But the hardest one to swallow, it took until June of 2020 for queer people to be protected from discrimination in the workplace. We could literally be fired for no other reason than being gay.

This blows my mind. We're really just beginning.

But I am also learning about all the people, specifically in Atlanta, who played a part in this wave of change: journalists, lawyers, neighbors. I want to be that. The defamed music festival flyer hangs above my desk, spurring me on. I've passed twenty more just like it, the queerness torn from it. Just like me.

"I never thought I'd have to say this to you," Luke says from the doorway. I finish reading the paragraph I'm on, like an asshole, then look at him.

"Thought you'd never have to say what to me?"

"You gotta take a break. Let's go play FIFA or something."

I look down at the next paragraph. The letters bleed into one another, blurring into swirls. I shut it. "You're right. One game."

Luke sets up the PS4 and hands me a controller. We pick our teams and set our lineups.

"It's cool to see you like that. I mean, a little scary because I feel like it means the end of the world is coming or something but mostly cool," he says, eyes on the TV.

"Thanks, I think." Luke always demolishes me in this game, so my attention is on setting my lineup. I'm too competitive.

"Now I see why you had to break up with her. There's no stopping you."

I abandon my team and turn to Luke. "What do you mean?"

"I mean, you jumped in. You can't put the toothpaste back in the tube, ya know?"

I shrug. "I guess."

"You know because toothpaste—"

"How is she? She's avoiding me."

"Well, that's not hard to do right now. You're hardly here."

I ignore his annoying little jab. "Luke."

"Hard to say. She's been hanging with Cassie mostly. Lying low."

I nod. Put down my controller. "I gotta go."

"What? *No.*"

"Sorry. We can play tonight. I promise." I head downstairs to my floor, not sure if I'm headed to my room or Noelle's. I stop at her door. Raise a fist to knock but can't. I drop my head. I want to bust down the door, swoop her up, bring her with me to take on the world together. I want her to—

"Creep," Noelle says. She walks down the hall toward our rooms. "Do you do this a lot? Just stand outside my door with your head bowed?"

I haven't been this close to her in weeks. I would give almost anything to touch her. Almost anything. "Sometimes," is all I can think to say.

She reaches past me to her doorknob. "Excuse me."

"Wait."

She stops, considers me. "Wait? For you?" A smile forms on her lips that sickens me.

"I was hoping—"

"Wait for you? Is this a joke? You couldn't wait a single day for me."

"That's not fair."

"You don't care, Bailey. You're never around anymore. You haven't even tried to talk to me. I'm just here. Alone." Her eyes water. "So, no, I can't wait for you."

I step back to let her into her room. Think I've done enough damage for one day. I'm going to be late for Steve's office hours if I don't leave now anyway.

❖

I serve myself a slice of pizza and sit at one of the giant tables while I wait for Priya. I spot her paying for a salad.

She hurries across the dining hall and sits next to me. "How was Dr. Martin's?"

"It was good. He likes my paper so far and said he's excited to see what I do here at Alder."

"What's that mean? You're going to get your degree *here at Alder*." She pours the Italian dressing over her salad and mixes it with her fork and knife.

"Yeah, I guess. I don't really know. Getting a couple A's would be nice. Have you talked to Noelle lately?" I want to know. But I also just need to say her name to somebody. The past two weeks have only been extreme highs and extreme lows. It's exhausting to be heartbroken and amped up. No rest.

"Yeah." She chomps on her salad. I look at her, waiting for more. "Not about you."

"She hates me."

"Well, you kinda broke her heart."

I put down my pizza and wipe my hands on my napkin. "It's not like I'm over here *not* heartbroken."

"Two things here, Bails. One, you did the dumping. Two, you have something to distract you: poli sci."

"It's just a major. She has one, too."

"Don't downplay it. You have this super exciting life change happening. It makes it easier for you. Meanwhile, Noelle's life is totally the same. Except for you."

"I miss her so much." It makes me sick to think of how I've hurt her and that I can't be the one to comfort her. She has no one to comfort her.

"You guys have to figure out how to be friends."

"I don't want to be friends. I want to be with her."

"Well, you don't get to right now. Figure something else out."

We dump our trash and walk out into the sunshine. *You don't get to.* Priya's words ring in my head, but I don't know how to let Noelle go. I don't want to.

The beginning of spring has made the air sag with humidity. I sneeze when the sunlight hits my eyes. Try to blink it out, gain my vision back before I run into anyone on the concourse.

The zealots are posted up on the stone ledge lining the concourse. "It's an abomination! An abomination!" My eyes are still adjusting, but their yelling registers in my brain just fine and ignites every little synapse.

Priya throws her hands up. "Not these assholes again. Why are they even allowed on campus?"

"Wouldn't look good for a Catholic college to kick them out. Alder probably accepts donations from their church or something."

Priya takes my arm and tries to drag me away. I don't budge. "What are you doing?" she asks.

I take a step toward the yelling. I can't ignore this. Not anymore. "Let's check it out." I'm already several paces ahead of Priya before she catches me. A boy hops onto the ledge about ten feet from the zealots, and I notice the green tips of his hair. His piercing. "That guy is in my poli sci class."

"Is he one of the crazies?"

"No. Definitely not."

"What is he doing up there?"

Robert sheds his backpack. His chest rises and falls a couple of times. Then he shouts, "I'm Catholic! I'm gay! I'm proud!" He thumps his chest with his fist. "Catholic. Gay. Proud." Our small audience looks between Robert and the zealots.

The older men and women of the original group look confused and raise the volume of their own shouting. "God hates your sin! Repent!"

"Catholic. Gay. Proud."

Louder. Louder.

I grab Priya's hand and pull her out of the zealot's crowd and post up in front of Robert. He smiles at us in between yells. I feel my stomach tighten. The wave builds. I can't stop it. I drop Priya's hand and jump onto the ledge next to him.

"Robert," he says to me and extends his hand. I shake it.

"Bailey."

"Catholic. Gay. Proud," we yell together. Over and over. And it makes me want to laugh that "Catholic" is the only thing I'm questioning out of the three words we're yelling. Priya watches us for a couple minutes, a smile across her lips. She reaches a hand, and I grab it to pull her up with us. Three voices now. And all of the attention from the group next to us.

We continue our shouts, throats scratchy. A modest group of students forms in front of us, and I recognize another person from our poli sci class, a girl that usually sits a couple of seats to my left. *Ashley*, I think. She pulls out her phone and starts recording us, a smile on her face. I feel fear blaze through me. Then calm. Because I don't give a fuck who sees this. I want the world to see this.

❖

We're all scattered around a table in the basement of Baker chatting and studying.

"Y'all should've seen our girl up there," Priya brags to our crew and paints the whole picture for them.

"It was all Robert. He started everything. I just joined."

Matt looks up from his book like he's just now tuning in. "Wait. Are you saying...are you gay?"

I look around the table. Noelle looks away from me.

"Yeah, I am."

"Awesome," Matt says.

"Wait. What? I thought you were just helping Robert. You're gay?" Cassie asks.

"Yeah."

She looks at Priya and Luke and Noelle. "Y'all know?" Then to me. "They know?" I nod. "Why didn't I know?"

"It's recent. Well, the coming-out is recent. And it just hadn't come up. I wasn't trying to keep it from you. You too, Matt." Noelle doesn't engage, but I hope she internalizes this moment.

"Wow. Huh. I'm kinda shocked," Cassie says. "I thought..." She points to Luke.

"Me and her? No way." He laughs. I punch him in the shoulder. "She's like my sister."

"I'm really happy for you, Bails. And really proud of you and Priya," she says. Then she cocks her head at Priya. "Are you gay, too?"

"Nope. Not that I'm aware of at least."

Everyone is busy with homework and studying, so the conversation soon peters out, to my relief. Turns out, being queer just isn't that big of a deal to my friends. The university needs to catch up. I'm going to make them.

The next morning in poli sci, I stop at Robert's desk. "Thanks for yesterday."

He looks at me from under the green tips of his hair. Smiles. "Hey, Bailey. Thank yourself. You did it, too," he says, words raspy. His voice has suffered a little more than mine.

"Do you want to hang out sometime after class?"

"Yeah. Definitely."

"Cool." I smile and walk to my regular seat.

Ashley walks into class, takes the seat right next to mine, and pulls out her binder and books. I watch her from out of the corner of my eye. I'd never seen her tattoo up close. It's some kind of branch and flower, different shades of gray, crawling into her sleeve.

"It's magnolia."

I avert my eyes. "Sorry. I didn't mean to…It's beautiful."

She turns in her seat to face me. "Bailey, is it?"

"Yes."

She holds out a hand for me to shake. "I'm Ashley."

"Nice to meet you."

"You and Robert were awesome yesterday. I got it all on my phone. What's your number? I'll send it to you." She hands me her phone so I can add my number. She tucks her blond hair behind her ear, exposing all of her piercings. Too many to count without getting caught again.

"There are seven in that ear."

Shit.

Steve makes his way to the front of the class.

"I'm an idiot," I finally say to her.

She smiles and shakes her head. "You're cute. Not an idiot. Can I take you out sometime?"

I stare at her. I almost forgot being a lesbian doesn't just mean wanting Noelle.

Steve's voice fills the room. "Robert and Bailey, can you come see me, please?"

My eyes are on Ashley. She smiles, and it hits me how pretty she is. She tilts her head toward the front of the room.

"Head in the sky as always," Steve says.

I snap my attention to him. He said my name before. I think. "Sorry?" I say.

"Come see me," he repeats. I get up and follow Robert to Steve's desk. "Ashley showed me the video of you two from yesterday.

An administrator emailed me this morning. There have been a few complaints about you. But fuck 'em. I'm really proud of you guys. This is exactly what political science is all about. Making moves."

Robert and I stand there, shoulder to shoulder, mutter our thanks.

"Okay, back to your seats. Time to get this show on the road."

I walk through the mess of old desks. Feel Ashley's eyes on me. I don't listen to Steve for the rest of class. I sneak peeks at the magnolia flexing as Ashley scribbles notes. I stare at my own blank notebook, then at Ashley again. I've spent so long trying to hide, for myself, then for Noelle, and one day, a woman just asks me out. Out of nowhere. Like it's nothing. That's how it should be: easy. And though I'm becoming more attracted to Ashley every time I look at her. She's just not Noelle. I could be attracted to a million women, but I'm only in love with one.

Noelle.

She doesn't want me anymore. She wanted the old me. The me that had nothing to look forward to except for her. But things have shifted now, and I've changed. I have to stay true to that. Even if it breaks both our hearts, which it has, I can't go back.

I notice the class shuffling through their things, packing up, so I stand and start to slide my books into my backpack. Ashley hikes her bag onto her shoulders and waits for me to do the same. I try to give myself every last second to come up with an answer for her. I slip my bag onto my shoulders and smile at her.

"Do you have a girlfriend? Boyfriend? Gender nonconforming friend?" Ashley asks.

I glance out the window, blink back an image of Noelle. "No."

Ashley smiles. No dimples. "Cool. Well, what do you say? Friday?"

"Yeah. Okay. Friday."

"Great. I'll text ya." She smiles, then rushes past me to her next class. If I go out with Ashley, that would be it for me and Noelle. Time to put my money where my mouth is.

I stop by the dining hall for a cup of coffee and a quick bite. There are a few less winter coats scattered across the benches and a few more rain jackets. I nibble at my cranberry scone and think about Ashley. Think about Noelle. I have to tell Noelle. It will probably be the nail in our coffin, but I tried. She chose. Just like I did. I pull my phone from my back pocket. I have a text from a number I haven't saved, but I know it's Ashley.

Ashley: *Hey, you. 7 on Friday?*

Me: *Sounds good. Where should I meet you?*

Ashley: *I'll pick you up. Where you live?*

Me: *Baker*

Ashley: *I'll call you when I get there*

I close out of that message and find Noelle's name in the lists of conversations. Our whole texting history pops up. My chest tightens. *Love you* is the last text she sent me. When I text her, she'll see that too.

Me: *Hey. I don't mean to bother you.*

Me: *I just thought I should tell you that I'm going out with a girl from my poli sci class this Friday.*

I sound like a tool. Definitely sounds like I'm trying to hurt her.

Me: *I'm not trying to hurt you. Just wanted you to hear it from me. I miss you.*

That was terrible. What the hell am I doing? Why couldn't it be us? It was supposed to be us.

"Moving right along, aren't we?" Noelle sits on the bench next to me. I blink at her, mouth dry. "Bet you wish you would have waited to send that text." I feel her thigh pressed against mine. For a second, I want to cave. I want to turn back time and take it all back. Anything. Anything to have her back.

"Huh. You had so much more to say over text," she says.

I can't take the edge in her voice. The hate in her eyes. I feel mine begin to fill with tears.

"Bailey. Don't. Not here, okay?" she whispers, then looks around to assess the observers.

I wipe an eye, find my words. "That's the problem. Right there," I tell her and mimic her surveying the people in earshot. "You chose them over me."

"What are you talking about?"

"I mean right now. Right now, your priority isn't our conversation. Your eyes break contact every five seconds to look over my shoulder. You care more about other people's opinions than you do about mine. It's that simple. And that's why we're not together."

She makes a point to hold my eye contact. Reminds me of when we first met. Always daring me to look away. "You knew how I felt before you agreed to this relationship. You fucked me, then ten minutes later, basically dumped me. Then actually dumped me right before I had to go to class." She bites her lip, looks away.

"Look. I get it," she adds. "You're like an avalanche right now, and there's no stopping you. I'm just not ready, Bailey. *It's that simple.* And if you can't wait, you can't wait. But neither will I. I don't hate you. This is just really hard."

"I miss you so much, Noelle. I miss us."

"It didn't have to be like this."

That's exactly what I want to tell her. *It didn't have to be like this, Noelle.* But it is. I can't go back in time. I can't just wallow here and second-guess everything. It's done.

I crack open a beer and toss one to Priya, who is currently raiding my closet. She pauses to take a sip. "Where is she taking you?"

"Just some dive bar in town, I think."

"Hmm. That's not romantic."

"It's our first date. She's basically a stranger. Wouldn't want to do much else besides that, anyway."

Priya sits next to me on my bed and puts a hand on my knee. "I know she's not Noelle. But she seems cool. And obviously has great taste in women. Try to give her a chance, okay?"

"Yeah. You're right."

Priya walks back over to my closet. "Casual, then." She slides hangers down the crossbar. "Let's just do jeans, a cute T-shirt, and your coat." She pulls Noelle's old coat off the hanger, and my stomach drops.

"I can't wear that. I can't wear that out with another girl."

Priya puts it back on a hanger. "Okay, okay. No worries. I get it."

"Can I just wear my sweater?" I want the cozy comfort of it. Of him.

"Yeah. A sweater. That's perfect."

My phone buzzes, and Priya wishes me luck before I go to meet Ashley in the parking lot. I open the door and slide into the passenger seat of her old Camry. My first official date. The nerves make me a little dizzy.

"Hey. I would've come to your door, but you know, can't get in."

"No worries. It's the thought that counts."

Ashley finds some old-school country on the radio to ease the awkwardness of the drive to town. We comment on the mountain roads, on Steve and Robert, on dorm life. Then she pulls into a gravel lot and parks. A half-lit sign that reads *Nan's* hangs above the door.

Nan's is indeed a dive bar. Well, technically, a dive pub. The air is heavy with grease and the cigarette smoke that's stuck in people's clothes, and peanut shells crunch underfoot. The lights must be tinted because it feels like we're in a pulsing blood vessel, dark and red. We approach the tail end of the L-shaped oak bar and grab two stools, cozy and tucked away, just private enough. The bartender approaches us, a buff guy, black hair, dirty V-neck T-shirt. I'm surprised there's not a cigarette dangling from his cracked lips. He winks at Ashley and throws a coaster in front of each of us.

"Ladies," he greets us, then looks at Ashley. "Been a while since you've come to see me."

"You know I'm busy, Sam, can't drink away every weekend with you."

He throws a hand over his heart. "You wound me, dahlin."

"Yeah, yeah."

"What're we having?" he asks.

"Gin and tonic for me," she says.

"I'll, uh, I'll do a High Life, please," I say.

"And an order of fries. Extra crispy," she adds.

"I know, I know," Sam says and walks to the register to type in our order. I scan the bar. There is a mix of Alder U folks—students and professors—but also a good amount of locals crowded into Nan's. Sam is back in an instant with our drinks, then off just as quickly to take another order.

"I couldn't help but notice that we weren't carded. How do you know Sam?" The red light plays tricks in her hair, turning it pink, setting it on fire.

"He's my cousin. Graduated from Alder a couple years ago and never left. Been hiding here ever since."

"What's he hiding from?"

"Responsibility? Who knows?"

Sam drops off the fries, and I can tell that they're the best kind. Dark golden brown, well-seasoned, and crispy. Beer and fries. I love this date. Ashley is gorgeous and nice, and she likes me. Maybe life goes on.

I pop a fry in my mouth. "This is perfect. Thanks for bringing me here."

"They're good, right?"

"The best."

"You can get real food, too, if you want."

I shake my head. "Honestly, this is great."

"The company ain't too shabby, either." She winks.

We go back and forth, chatting about poli sci, about where we're from. She's an Atlanta girl, wants to be a civil rights lawyer. I tell her about Savannah and how it's haunted and strange and beautiful. Tell her she has to visit. It's just a thing people say. I don't actually mean it. I want to go at a snail's pace with this girl. We order another round of drinks. Another gin and tonic for her and a Manhattan for me.

"Since you came on this date with me, is it safe to assume you're into women?" she asks.

"Yes. Since you asked me on this date, is it safe to assume the same thing about you?"

"Yeah. Well, I like both men and women. I'm pan."

"Oh. Cool. I'm just gay." I smile.

"No ladies in your life, then?"

"Nope."

She puts a hand on my knee, and it feels foreign to me. Not quite right. But she bites her bottom lip, and I think I can be convinced.

"You're in so much trouble," she says.

"Trouble?"

"Girls are going to be coming out of the woodwork for you. Just wait."

I'm not sure I'm ready for that. I'm barely ready for Ashley. "You're the only girl I've met that's interested in me."

She leans into my ear. "I'm glad I found you first."

And that's when I feel it, that little tug low in my stomach. I can do this. I smile and raise my drink. "Cheers to that."

She knocks my glass, and the red glow of the bar pulses a little more with every sip. Ashley drops a coaster on top of our drinks and hops off her barstool. "Come to the bathroom with me?"

If I had a dollar for every time Priya has dragged me to the bathroom with her when I didn't need to go, I'd be rich. I'm not sure why women do this. I hop off my stool, and she takes my hand like it's the obvious thing to do and leads me through the whooshing blood vessel to the bathrooms. There are only two stalls, and both their doors are wide open. I take a step toward the smaller stall. She heads for the handicap stall and pulls me in with her.

"What—" I start to ask, but she turns me, and my back hits the wall of the stall with a thud.

She plants a hand next to my head, trapping me. Her mouth finds mine and smashes a hard kiss on my lips. I'm too taken off guard to process what is happening, much less if I love it or hate it. My body finally springs into action, and I move my lips against hers, accept her tongue into my mouth. We're both tipsy at this point, and our teeth knock and gnash in our sloppy make-out session. I'm overwhelmed, so I put myself on autopilot and make my mind go blank.

"Come home with me," she breathes, then covers my mouth again with hers, not allowing me to answer. The door to the women's room swings open and cracks into the commercial-grade doorjamb. I gasp and stiffen from months of almost getting caught with Noelle. Ashley just groans in annoyance and pushes off me, takes my hand, and pulls me out of the bathroom. She doesn't even make sure the coast is clear. I put a finger to my lip, sensitive from her teeth.

Ashley pulls the coaster off her drink and takes the last ice-thunking pull from it, then produces a pack of American Spirits from her back pocket. "Wanna join?"

"Um, no, thanks. I'm going to finish my drink."

She shrugs. "Order me another, will ya? I'll be right back."

I grip the edges of my stool and start to swivel, left, right, left, right. Take a sip of my Manhattan. The cold booze makes my lips tingle, eases them a bit. Making out with Ashley was fun, right? Why do I feel so on edge?

"'Nother round?" Sam asks.

I stop swiveling, hoping I didn't give up my age with the childish mannerism. "Yes, please. And more fries. Thanks."

Sam winks like the second order of fries is silly. I polish off my drink before the next round comes. I look around at all the strangers and realize that this is the first time I've been off campus without one of my friends. The thought hits me hard, and I feel very alone. Vulnerable. A little off.

"Ah, nice. More fries."

I jump at Ashley's voice. I hadn't even noticed Sam deliver the food and drink.

We chat about nothing. Mostly what I would call *first date stuff*: logistics of how we each wound up at Alder University, what we plan to do with our degrees, likes, dislikes, etc. I pop the last fry in my mouth and cut the grease with my last sip of whiskey. Ashley pays Sam and slides off her stool.

I pull out my phone. "What's your Venmo?"

She waves me off. "Don't be confused. This is a date. Plus, Sam always gives me his employee discount."

We walk outside to her car, and my eyes relax with the lack of red, and I realize I'm a little drunk from three drinks and no real dinner. She unlocks the car and opens her door.

"You, uh, good to drive?" I hate the hesitation in my voice, hate that I'm embarrassed to question our safety on these mountain roads at night.

"Yeah." Her answer is in a higher pitch. She ducks into the driver's seat, and I slide into the passenger.

"You sure? Because my friend Matt can come grab us. We can take you back in the—"

She cranks the engine to life. "Bailey, I'm good. Promise."

I buckle up as she pulls out of the gravel lot and onto the road. I stare out the window, struggling to swallow the fact that I'm letting someone drive me home who's probably too drunk to drive these roads, all because I didn't want to bruise her ego. I grip the *oh shit* bar with every curve she takes. She accelerates into them and brakes out of them. Totally wrong. Wonder how strong those guard rails actually are.

I'm uncomfortable. That's what it is. This whole night. When Ashley threw me against the wall, it was uncomfortable. Her teeth knocked into mine too many times, and she hurt my lips and tasted like ash. She kinda scares me. I close my eyes because I can't watch the road anymore; it's too terrifying. I wonder if my mom will see us on the morning news. *Underage. Alcohol in their system. Wrapped around a tree.* I open my eyes when I feel us turn right and start climbing Alder's steep drive. Relief loosens my muscles, and I drop my sweaty hand from the bar above the window.

"Do you want to come over?" she asks.

All I want to do is crawl into Priya's bed and make her hold me. "Another night. The fries aren't sitting well in my stomach."

"Totally. I get it." Ashley stops her car in the lot of Baker and turns to me. "I had a really nice time with you tonight."

"Yeah. Me, too. Thanks for the drinks and fries."

She leans over the center console and kisses me. Softer this time, to my relief. I pop open the door and swing myself out. "Let's hang out again soon," she says through the downed window.

"Yeah, for sure."

"Night, Bailey."

"Night."

I jog to my dorm room and am about to fling open the door when Matt's ass flashes in my brain. I take my hand off the doorknob and knock instead. "Come in," Priya calls. I bust through the threshold and fall into her bed.

She starts gentle strokes through my hair. "Okay. I know you saw Matt's ass, but you're not allowed to knock. This is your room, too."

"Can you blame me?"

"He forgot to lock the door. If it's locked, then you know what's up."

"I almost died tonight," I mumble into her shoulder.

"What?"

I tell her every detail of the evening while she runs her fingers through my hair. Brings me home.

"Hmm," she says when I finish.

"Yeah. Maybe she's too much for me. I dunno. I'd like to give her another chance, though."

"Really?" She pinches my arm.

"*Ouch.* What the?"

"That's for endangering yourself, you idiot. What? You're too independent and honest with yourself to date Noelle, but you can't put your foot down with drunk driving? You don't get to be a world-saving lesbian if you're dead."

I know better than to say anything. I rub my arm where she pinched me and accept my scolding.

"I'm serious, Bailey. That was really fucked-up. I mean, who knows if she was fine or not? Doesn't matter. You weren't comfortable with it, and you should've called us."

I sit up in her bed. "I know. I know. I fucked up."

"You did. Okay. That's enough of that. Wanna watch *The Bachelor* with me?"

"I'm gonna shower. Start without me."

I strip and think about why I let Ashley drive. It didn't feel much different than coming out, except I failed. I guess it takes a lot of exercising those muscles before standing apart from the crowd becomes easier. I could curse myself, feel ashamed, and play my cowardice on repeat in my head, but I'm not going to do any of that. Tonight, I will be gentle with myself. And tomorrow, I will do better.

CHAPTER SIXTEEN

Robert leans over my shoulder and squints at the computer screen. I take a sip of coffee and wince when I find it's gone cold. I scroll through the student organization section of Alder's website. Robert points at the third paragraph. "There."

I scan the rest of the second paragraph to catch up with him. "'Forming a student organization or club requires a faculty sponsor, an approved mission statement by an administrator, and a completed and approved application. You can find more resources at the bottom of this page,'" I read. "Well, that sounds easy."

Robert sits at the table behind me. The library is at its typical Tuesday night capacity. Each floor holds a low buzz of constant activity. Never too loud, just enough hustle and bustle to make you feel like you're not alone.

"Yeah. *Sounds* easy." He flips through our rough drafts.

"The approved mission statement?"

"Yeah. That's the catch. An administrator is going to have to personally approve something with the letters LGBTQ+ on it. Fat chance here at Alder. I don't blame them either."

"Yeah. A school like this depends on donors, and they're probably all Catholic. It'd be like signing away their job."

I print the page from the website and a student organization application and sit next to Robert. We read over it. My eyes are drawn to little carved letters on the edge of the table. I lean closer to read them.

Julie is a cumdumpster

Seems a little harsh. I point it out to Robert.

"Lucky girl," he says, then turns his attention back to our task. "We could just call ourselves the equality club."

"Mmm. Yeah, but that would only work for so long. They'd catch wind and shut us down."

"You're probably right."

"Plus, the point is recognition. You know? They need to be faced with the fact that there's a queer presence in their school. And they need to accept us," I say.

Robert sighs and pushes himself onto the back legs of his chair. "It's never gonna happen."

"Seriously? This coming from the guy who started a queer chant on the concourse? We'll figure it out." We *have* to figure it out. Allowing hate groups to accost our student body is not an option. If we do nothing, we are complicit.

"*I know*," he scoffs. "I just like the drama."

I shove him in the shoulder and start gathering our papers into our respective folders. I shoulder my backpack and throw away my coffee. "I gotta get going. Wanna meet again next Tuesday?"

"Yeah. Should we talk to Steve about being our sponsor?"

"I know he'll do it, but I want to present him with a solid plan. Let him know that we're serious. Maybe after we meet next? We can really hammer down our mission statement."

"Totally. You're right."

We shake hands for some reason, then head our separate ways. I go back to my room and splay all the different versions of our mission statement across my desk. I leave them there while I make another pot of coffee, hoping the papers will marinate with the wood of my desk and somehow make the perfect mission statement evident to me. This is the most important thing I've ever done. It has to be perfect. My coffee maker spits and gurgles, and I sit at my desk, knee bouncing.

The mission of...

Shit. We haven't even picked a name yet. How are we supposed to write a mission statement without an identity? I text Robert: *Can't stop thinking about the mission. We need a name first.*

I stare at the ceiling, trying to come up with something. Queer or LGBTQ+? Which one, which one, which one?

Robert: *Yeah, you're right. How about the cockpit and lickety split?*

I reread his text until I finally get it. *Hah. I just got it.*

Robert: *Oh Bails.*

Me: *What about Alder Queer Fellowship? Or Alder LGBTQ+ committee?*

Robert: *Well, those aren't fun at all. Alder Queer Fellowship. For sure*

I send him a heart emoji, grab a Sharpie from Priya's desk, and write *Alder Queer Fellowship* across my folder in big bold letters. It's perfect. I like the word queer, and fellowship is used a lot in Christianity. There are, no doubt, a lot of queer Christians out there. I trace the letters with my finger. I pull out a fresh piece of paper and take another stab at the mission statement, now that we have an identity.

The mission of the Alder Queer Fellowship is to promote equity and unity through service and celebration.

Celebration?

I close the folder. Need to take a break and come back to this later. Alder Queer Fellowship. It's a good name. But I can't finish the mission statement until I finish something else. I look out my window over the quad. The tulips have bloomed, always the early bird. A frost will kill them soon. I pace back and forth. My phone sits heavy in my pocket. I know what I need to do next.

My mom is on the top of my recently called list. All I have to do is hit the green button.

Just hit the button. As cool as my mom is, I'm fucking terrified. She has never openly hated on gay people, but that's *other people.* Tons of homophobic folks don't care much about other people being gay, but if their kid turns out to be gay...

I shake the thought out of my head. My mom is not homophobic. She's not.

One step at a time. Easy. My vision blurs at the edges, and a nervous flutter settles deep in my stomach. Not a nervous flutter like I'm about to kiss Noelle, a nervous flutter like I may shit my pants. More of a nervous crunch. I try counting down from ten. *Ten, nine, eight, seven, ah fuck it.* I hit the green button before I can wimp out. The ringing makes me jump. Is it always so loud? *Don't answer, don't answer.* The ringing stops, and a robot tells me to leave a message. No, thank you. Right when I hang up, my phone buzzes in my hand. I swallow down my hesitation.

Mom. Here we go.

"Hey, Mom."

"Ay, Bailey. You won't believe it. I was just getting out of the shower when you called." My mom feels the need to shout when she's on the phone, like she thinks that's the only way for her voice to travel to North Georgia. I hold the phone away from my ear to avoid any damage to my eardrum.

"Great timing," I say.

"I've spent all day airing out the house. The Taylors came over last night, and of course, Mr. Taylor smoked half a humidor. *Dios mio.* But the birds are chirp, chirp, chirping. I'm going to have lunch with my teacher friend, Susan, today."

I have to cut her off. My adrenaline is going to make me pass out if I don't interrupt her soon. With every word she yells through the phone, my body falls further into the deep end of hot anxiety. My heart kicks into overdrive and pounds in my ears. My tongue feels like a beached whale in my desert mouth. My eyeballs prickle.

"Mom, how many times do I have to tell you that I know who Susan is? I've known her for fifteen years. You don't have to say 'my teacher friend' every time you reference her. Just Susan."

"Okay, Ms. Saucy Pants."

"Listen, Mom, I called to talk to you about something."

"Is everything okay?" Her playful tone takes a hard one-eighty into "worried mom" tone.

"Yes. Everything's okay. All good, I just have to tell you something." *Say it, say it, God, just spit it out before you pass out.*

"Bailey, you know you can tell me anything. It's okay. I can hear your breathing, all quick and scared. Deep breaths. In through the nose, hold it in your belly. There you go. Out through the mouth."

I focus on the deep breathing and feel hot tears pooling in my eyelids, about to hit a critical mass.

My mom's soft voice starts again. "Now, take ten more seconds. Keep belly breathing."

"Mom." My voice cracks. I sniffle through the mucus in my nose, which instantly formed when the first tear rolled over my eyelid. *Go.* "I'm gay." My heart skips a beat, and my blubbering stops. I stay silent, waiting for her voice.

"Well, yeah."

"What?"

"I've had an inkling since you were little."

"What? How did you? I don't understand."

"You've been my little girl your whole life. I know you. I see what you do and where you invest your intimacy. And not to mention that one time when you were six."

My head spins. "What? What one time when I was six?"

"Well, you know how we caught you naked with the neighbor boy, Tommy Wilkerson?"

"Yes, I remember. But wouldn't that give me points in the 'Bailey is straight' category?"

"It would have, but I never told you what you said to us. You were so incensed that you were getting in trouble for stripping with the neighbor boy, you said 'What's the big deal? I don't even like Tommy. I like Lisa.' So that, combined with just knowing you, made it pretty damn clear to me. And guess what, I don't care. It's part of what makes you, you."

My mouth hangs open. All these years of trying to hide, trying to trick everyone, and the person I was most concerned about already knew. She already knew because I told her when I was six. Part of me is angry at my six-year-old self. I'd worked so hard to try to convince everyone I was straight, to try to convince myself I was straight.

"Bailey? Are you okay?"

"Why didn't you tell me? Obviously, you must have known I was struggling. John didn't exactly make it easy on me with his commentary on my 'queer snowflake generation.' Why didn't you help?" I can't tell if I'm asking out of curiosity or if I'm upset. Upset that I could've lived without the constant fear and lying. But that was my decision. I did that to myself.

"Sweetie, it's your life. You know I'm always here for you, but you had to figure it out for yourself. Yes, John didn't make anything easy on anyone. Allowing him to stay for as long as I did was a mistake. I am sorry for that. But that's life. It can be hard. Now figure it out. Don't you try to play like you felt you couldn't talk to me."

"I know, you're right." I sigh. Internalized homophobia is no joke. I locked myself in that prison and pretended I couldn't get out. All I had to do was open the door. "I feel so light." And I do. Telling my mom was the last big hurdle of coming out. I'm getting back to being my bold six-year-old self. I don't know when I slipped out of that.

"I'm so excited for you. You're just beginning. Stop wasting your precious time now. You hear?"

"Yes, ma'am."

"Who knows?"

"I told my friends." I'll explain the Noelle thing another day.

"Good. I'm proud of you, Bailey. Hey, maybe one day you can call me just to shoot the breeze, you know?"

I smile against my phone. "I'm sorry. You're right. I keep crying every time I talk to you."

"Just a thought."

"I love you so much. I'll call you soon for a regular chat."

"Love you, sweetie."

And that's that. I can't believe I haven't told her earlier. I could have saved so much time and so much stress. I sit on the edge of my bed and let my blood come down, let my muscles relax. I'm out. Done. Now I can move on and actually *be*. I'm so lucky to have a mom like mine. I just had a loving experience that not everyone is lucky enough to have. I consider trying to find my stepdad to tell him, but I don't know why. Don't even know if he wants to see me. Time and space do a lot to heal things, and I probably haven't had enough of either.

Noelle knocks on the bathroom door and walks into my room. The strobes of sunlight from my window catch in her hair. I exhale slowly through my nose as she meanders over to my desk and runs a hand over my folders and scrap papers. I feel like I've spotted a deer and don't want to scare it away, anything to stay in its beautiful presence. She looks at me for the first time, hand still on my desk.

"I overheard your call." She looks back down at my Sharpied folder. I stay still, stay quiet. Don't startle her. She flips open the folder, reads my draft mission statement, closes it. Her eyes meet mine again. "I wouldn't say celebration. The admin will probably think y'all are drinking and doing drugs in your club." She sits next to me on my bed and folds her hands in her lap. Clears her throat. I want to grab her hand and show her the way, but I have no idea what to say to her. "Anyway. Like I said, I could hear your phone call. And I just wanted to say that I'm sorry I wasn't sitting next to you while you did it. I'm sorry for both of us."

I say the most obvious thing that pops into my head. "You're sitting next to me now."

She looks up and smiles. "I also wanted to tell you…" She stares at Priya's side of the room, then back at her lap, then back at me. "I'm really proud of you."

If she's proud of me for coming out, that has to mean she's warming up to the idea at least a little bit. My heart stutters with hope. "I—"

"Listen. This is everything I want for you. When I met you, you were a steady glow like an ember. Now you're a full out bonfire. And I know there's no putting that out. I don't want to. I'm so proud of you and Robert for trying to start this club."

"Please." I wave. "No more." I smile at her, and she lets out a small chuckle, shakes her head. I harness all my confidence and take her hand into my lap. "You're the one who saw me. When I felt like nothing compared to all of you. When I had no clue what to do. You were the one. You're the one," I whisper.

She strokes my hand with her thumb. I wonder if she'll ever smooth my brow again. "We're going to figure this out. You know how much I care about you, Bailey."

"I know." I don't know which way the chips will fall for us, but for the first time, I know that we'll be okay. Whether it's as just friends or as a couple, we will be okay.

❖

Luke throws the football to me from across the quad. Since the weather started to warm, playing catch in the quad has become higher stakes, with more and more students reading on blankets in the grass. I catch it and spin the ball in my hands. Luke has had the same football for at least a decade. Maybe from dropping it in the ocean too many times or leaving it out in the sun, but *something* has turned its leather rock-solid. It's like playing with a petrified artifact. He throws it to me again, and I jam my finger against the rock. I mutter a slew of profanities and try to shake it out.

Luke jogs over to me. "You okay?"

"You know your football puts true meaning to *toting the rock*." I grimace.

"You know, if you catch it properly, it doesn't hurt."

"Get a new football." I shove the old one against his chest.

We sit on a sunny bench, and Luke takes my finger. "Take a deep breath on three. One, two—"

Pop.

"Fuck," I yell. "What'd you do?"

"I unjammed it. It hurts now, but it will save you a lot of swelling and pain in the next couple of days."

I cradle my finger and sway back and forth. "I don't think that's real." I breathe.

"We'll see." He shrugs. "How are things with Noelle?"

"I think we're friends. She stopped by my room the other day and said she was proud of me for trying to start the club." Things may be looking up, but I have never been more confused about where we stand. When she was mad, things were clear. When she was scared of being with me, things were sort of clear. But now? I can't say.

"Nice. Any chance of being more than friends?"

"I don't know. Not right now, I don't think."

"Well, I guess you got Ashley now anyway."

"I don't *got* anything. Or anyone."

"Mm-hmm. Didn't you say you're going to her party this weekend?"

"Well, yeah. But we're friends."

"Friends who make out."

"Only once. We've been on one date." One weird date. My lips hurt just thinking about it.

"Well, we'll see after this weekend."

"I guess."

After our last meeting in the library, Robert and I decide that it's time to talk to Steve about our club. I try to focus on Steve's lecture, but I keep rereading the notes Robert and I have prepared for him. Not only do I want him to say yes, but I want his help, and most of all, I want to make him proud. Ashley lays a folded piece of paper on my desk. My eyes flash to the front of the classroom to make sure Steve didn't see it. I unfold the paper, annoyed at its presence in my space.

Are you coming tomorrow?

Really? That couldn't have waited until after class? I catch her eye and raise a thumbs-up. She nods and tears another bit of paper off her notebook. I try not to groan, not sure why I want to explode at her.

Be my date?

To her own party? Sure. Another thumbs-up. Her smile pulls down just a bit at the corner, and I feel the guilt start to pool in my chest. She's just being nice. I tear a bit of paper and scribble her a note.

Yeah. I'll be there, and I'll be your date.

Class can't end quickly enough. I gather all my things into my bag and zip it. Ashley watches me, waiting to leave together.

"Robert and I have to talk to Steve about this club we want to start."

Ashley's brows furrow.

"I'll tell you about it tomorrow. You'll love it."

"Okay. Well, I'll see you tomorrow, then. I'll text you the address."

"Okay, cool. Let me know what I can bring."

"Just yourself. My date drinks for free." She smiles and walks past me toward the door. That girl is aggressive. I shake her out of my mind for now.

Robert waits for me to join him by his desk. I pull out our presentation folder while the rest of the students clear out. "You and Ashley, huh?" He knocks his shoulder against mine.

"It's nothing serious."

"Does she know that?"

"I haven't given her reason to believe otherwise."

"She called you her *date* when she invited me to her party." He winks at me.

"People bring dates to formal balls, doesn't mean anything serious is happening. Or even that they're dating." I refuse to be put into a relationship with this girl. I did not agree to it.

Robert throws up his hands. "Okay. Okay." He picks up the folder and slaps it against his hand. "You ready to do this?"

I take a deep breath. If we don't get Steve, we're done. "Yeah. Let's do this."

Steve opens our folder and flips through the papers. He pauses briefly on the mission statement, then continues to thumb through all of it. We even included some research about how a club can help LGBTQ+ youth feel safer on campus. Steve scratches his whiskers, then looks at us. "You guys basically want to form a LGBTQ+ club, that would…what, exactly?"

Robert and I look at each other, then I hop into action. "Think of it as Alder's Young Democrats or Republicans clubs. We have common interests and goals. One of those goals is getting added to the school's anti-discrimination policy."

Steve nods. "Mm-hmm, mm-hmm."

"It's what has to be done. I'm tired of walking to class and feeling personally attacked by sponsored religious crazies. It grates me. It grates *me*. Can you imagine how some other kid may feel walking by those people? Some other kid who isn't out? Some other kid who's *at risk*?" Robert says.

"We're just asking for a platform. And for the school to recognize us," I say.

"You know I'll be your sponsor," Steve says. Robert and I exchange a quick smile. This at least gives us a fighting chance. We at least get to make someone besides Steve read our concerns. "But how are you going to get an admin to sign off?"

"We were hoping you could help us with that," I say.

A smile breaks across his face. "Oh God, I knew you'd be trouble, Bailey. You're going to get my liberal ass fired. I'm sure they're just waiting for me to do something like this. Fuck 'em. I miss the beach anyway, sick of these damn mountains."

"How should we do it?" Robert asks.

Steve leans back in his chair and closes his eyes. He rests a hand on the slight curve of his belly. "I think, for the big guys of this school, money is obviously king. Therefore, *liability* is also king. If you present them with a concern for student safety—use this research but also get more—and pitch your club as a solution, you'll at least get them to listen. Once they have your argument in their hands, it would be hard to ignore that liability."

I scribble in my notebook, trying to keep up with everything Steve tells us to do. When he finishes, I pull out the sponsorship form for him to sign. We've hurdled the first obstacle. The easy obstacle. Now for the fun part.

I hand him the paper. "Let's make this official."

"Welcome to the Alder Queer Fellowship, Steve," Robert says.

"Ah geez. Okay, okay." He takes the form and scribbles his signature in the two signing blocks. "Bring me your admin proposal on Monday. I want to look at it before you submit it. I'll think about which administrator we should go for over the weekend."

Robert and I take a moment to celebrate our small win before we head to the rest of our Friday classes. "Are you going to Ashley's?" I ask.

"No, got another thing going on."

"Shit. You're making me go alone?"

"You're a big girl. Meet Sunday?"

"Yeah. See ya Sunday." I thought I'd at least have Robert to share the social burden of the party with. But Ashley will be the only person I know. A nervous flutter stirs in my stomach.

CHAPTER SEVENTEEN

"Thanks for the ride," I say to Matt.
"No problem. Just call me when you wanna come home."
I shut his car door and watch him pull out of the small driveway.
Cars already line Ashley's street, and people spill from them to the
house for the party. I take a deep breath and look around before I go
inside. The neighborhood is nice, homey. Hedges outline her home,
and flowerpots hang from her awning. A coffee can full of rainwater
and cigarette butts sits on a small table next to the door. I reach for
the doorbell, but the loud music and voices remind me that it's a
party.

I walk into the house. The Grateful Dead rattles the windows
and shakes the furniture. I squint to try to see through the dim
haziness of cigarette smoke and weed. There must be a hundred
houseplants, all different sizes and shapes, hanging, sitting, and
crawling around the house. Like they were the original owners and
Ashley just happened to move in. For a split second, I wonder if
they're suffocating in all this smoke and body heat. I make my way
to the sliding doors at the back of the kitchen and step out onto the
deck, already relieved to be out of the suffocating house. I consider
calling Matt to come get me, but I see the keg and stack of Solo
cups.

That'll do. At least I get to have a cold beer.

I fill my cup with mostly foam, wait in the cool night breeze,
then get some beer to flow into my red goblet. I chug it. First one is

for the nerves. Second one is for drinking. A couple of partiers step out on the deck with me, eyes almost squinted shut, crooked smiles slapped on their faces. *Strange creatures.* I decide the second one is for nerves, too. Start pouring my third. I take my beer and slide past the people on the deck and back into the house. I crinkle my nose when I'm hit with the smell of sweat, dead skunk, and incense. Ashley spots me from the living room and walks over.

She loops her arm through mine. "There you are. I was expecting you a little earlier." Looking around at all of her patrons, tattooed and half-clothed, I wonder how Ashley got to be attracted to me.

"Sorry about that, I was kind of at the will of my friend, Matt," I shout over the music, thankful that the beer is starting to buzz on my lips. She pulls me down to kiss me.

"No worries. Is that beer? Nuh-uh. Come here." She drags me to the kitchen and orders her ghostly friend to mix me a drink. "She wants a Manhattan," Ashley commands. I drain my beer and toss my Solo cup in the bin, wondering what quality of drink I'm about to receive. Wonder if this guy even knows what a Manhattan is. He hands me a new cup with a handful of ice in it, then pours me bourbon from the handle of Jim Beam. I wait for a second with my cup out, thinking he'll produce vermouth next but quickly realize I'm an idiot. I sip my bourbon, pleased. A southern girl can't go wrong with bourbon on the rocks.

"Good?" Ashley asks.

"Perfect. Thanks."

She pulls me back into the living room where the couches have been pushed against the walls, and people dance in front of the fireplace. She picks up what looks like a Coke bottle that's been cut in half and takes a hit, coughs.

"Do you partake?" She holds up the device.

"Um, I honestly have no idea what that thing is," I say, noticing my slight slur.

"It's a good time, that's what it is. Come here." She lights something and pulls one of the plastic bottles up, then guides my mouth over the opening. "Just relax, here it comes." She pushes the bottle back down, and smoke bellows into my mouth and lungs. I choke. Can't stop coughing, so Ashley ushers me out onto the deck for some fresh air. She pours a beer and hands it to me. I drink the rest of my bourbon in between coughing fits and start on the cold beer.

"That'll help to ease it. Could've been worse for your first time."

"Worse?" I cough like I'm hacking up a lung. This is not fun. As it turns out, I do not perform well without my friends. I register this as an issue that needs further evaluation before I fall deeper into this strange haze.

"You're fine, Bailey. It'll pass. Just finish your beer."

I feel the sway in my body, the jelly in my limbs, the fire in my lungs. It doesn't feel like I'm fine. And she can't force me to be.

My empty cup is suddenly heavy again.

Drink.

The cool liquid is helping on multiple levels. I care less about the fire in my throat and my discomfort. I feel a hand at the base of my throat.

"Better, right?" A whisper in my ear. The hand tightens. Plays at choking me. Loosens.

I nod. A static comes over me. A white noise. I'm dry wood in a fire. Crackle and pop. Am I high?

"I know something else that will make it better," another whisper.

A warm tongue in my mouth.

"Follow me."

Ashley takes my hand and leads me through the familiar Twilight Zone to the back hallway of the house. I think I see a bathroom and some bedrooms. I take the right turn too sharply and smash my shoulder into the door frame. Drink. Hands on my shoulders. Ashley sits me on the edge of her bed. There are lights strung above me somewhere. Somehow. A dragon lamp. I'm not scared of her. Just apathetic.

"Stay right here." And Ashley's gone.

Okay. My back hits her soft bed, and when I open my eyes, I'm an axis. Walls spin around me. I shoot upright again, hot nausea brewing in my stomach.

"Hey, you." Ashley is in lingerie. All black. Drink. I look at her body. Her breasts. The lace. I kinda want her. She looks soft. I bet her skin is soft under there. Her thighs, full. She steps toward me, and I flinch. Realize it's me. I'm the target audience. She takes another step into my space. Thumbs a strap. "Pull it off me. I want you to rip it," she whispers. She puts my cup on the nightstand.

Knuckles against her hip, black lace in my hand. She's sexy, but I don't like her very much.

"Do it," she moans against my ear.

Her walls spin, spin, spin. *Okay.* Pop. Pop. I drop the fabric on the floor. Ashley is on top of me. Grinds into me. My clothes are on the floor. Thigh's wet from her straddling me. We flip. On my knees, her ass in my hands.

"Fuck me. Just fuck me."

My fingers twitch. Tighten. I do. A sting pierces my eyes. I'm here. My tongue inside her. I pull up. I don't want to do this anymore.

"Bathroom," I mutter.

"Out to the left," Ashley tells me between breaths.

No clothes. Quick left. Cold tile. Splash.

Vomit.

Rinse. I'm too fucked-up for this. I need to go home.

I stand at the foot of Ashley's bed. "Mmm. Come back here."

"I don't feel so good."

"You're okay, come finish up." She opens her legs. Her wetness glints in the candlelight from her nightstand. I settle into her, hope the bile on my tongue stings her. *Hope the bile on my tongue stings her. What the fuck? Just leave.*

I stand, wipe my mouth. "I gotta go."

I throw on my clothes.

"What, why? Just stay here tonight."

"Can't. Sorry." Shoes on, I reach for the door. Turn back. "Thank you for having me." Leave.

The cool air fills my sore lungs. I take greedy breaths, walk to the end of the street, and call Matt. Sit in the grass and listen to the phone ring, waiting to be rescued. Not *rescued.* Picked up. Waiting to be *picked up.*

"Bailey. Are you okay? It's two in the morning," Matt says. Sleep and panic are in his voice.

"It is? Can you come get me? Please."

"Of course. Be there in fifteen."

"I'm sorry, Matt."

"It's okay. You're okay, Bails. I'll be there soon. Want me to stay on the line until I get there?"

"No. No, I'm okay."

I sit on the curb with my back propped against the post of a stop sign, thankful for the bougie wood design instead of the standard skinny steel pole. The spinning isn't so bad out here in the fresh air. I'm less of an axis and more of an ass. I push my palms into my eyes. What am I doing? What did I just do? I have a feeling that I've had before. I have a simmer of nausea in my stomach, an aching at my temple, and shame trying to strangle me dead.

It's rave night.

Headlights flash over the hill and follow the road up to my corner. I stand slowly to not spill my pot of boiling nausea and wave down Matt's car. He opens the door to the back seat for me, and I crouch into it.

"Priya," I say, announcing her obvious presence.

"Bailey. Are you okay?" She slides to the center of the bench seat and puts an arm over my shoulders.

"Yeah. What're you doing here?" I was hoping to slip into our room in secret, but maybe it's better this way. She is all-knowing.

Matt puts the car in gear and turns. I roll down my window, need fresh air.

"Matt said you sounded a little fucked-up, so I came, too."

"Ah, because you were together. Gross." I grin.

"You're the gross one. You smell like vomit, and your sweater is on backward. Why don't you tell us what happened?"

"Ugh. Tomorrow? I don't feel good." And as if to prove my point, I roll the window down the rest of the way, lean my head out, and vomit all over the side of Matt's car.

"Jesus, Bailey, you coulda asked me to pull over."

"I'll clean it tomorrow, I promise." I groan.

Priya scrunches her face and waves in front of her nose. "Wow, you are a mess. Plus, your sweater tells me everything I need to know for now."

I lean forward and try to tuck my head between my knees, try to find any position that relieves the nausea or the headache. I'd take either. Priya drops her *stern mother* act and rubs my back in concentric circles. I focus on the pressure of her fingers, the small circles, then the bigger ones. I imagine my vertebra is the axis now, and Noelle's fingers circle around my bone, forever in my orbit. I feel her thumb on my brow, her arms around me, her—

"Bailey," Priya whispers. I open my eyes and sit up straight. Look around. "You fell asleep, boo. We're home. Come on." I hear two car doors and take the hint that I should open mine, too. Priya takes my hand and guides me out of the back seat.

I shut the door and grimace at the sight of my vomit stuck to the silver paint. "God. I bet you're glad you picked *me* up tonight," I say in the most sarcastic tone I can muster at the moment.

Matt steps next to me and puts a hand on my shoulder. "I am. Don't worry about this right now. It's all good. I'm going to go park in the deck. You and Priya get in there."

I turn into him and hug him. Mutter a *thank you* into his jacket. I'm embarrassed of my behavior. But I'm living fast right now. I'm bound to run off the tracks a couple times.

I start the water in the shower.

"What're you doing? It's almost three, just go to sleep," Priya says from the doorway.

"I can't. I need to shower first. I'm…" The word that pops into my mind is "disgusting," but I've used this as a descriptor for myself too many times. No more. It's time to be gentler with myself. I'm not disgusting. I'm a nineteen-year-old human girl who drank way too much and got way too high. "I'm not the freshest." I point to a stain on my sweater that is the unmistakable reddish orange of vomit.

Priya cringes like I could be contagious. "Fair enough."

The steam cradles me in its warm embrace. My head no longer feels like it's about to crack open at my temples and ooze brain everywhere. I scrub at my skin and think about the shame I've felt. How ashamed I was after rave night. Why I let myself feel shame tonight. So much shame. For what? I could have made better decisions.

But at the end of the day, I'm single, Ashley's single, and we had sex. When it felt wrong to me, I bailed. And that's all I can do. It's okay.

I'm okay.

I'm allowed to have sex with people. And I'm allowed to not like it.

I dry myself and put on a fresh pair of sweatpants and a clean white T-shirt. I thank the gods above that I washed my bedding yesterday. I slide into my clean bed, in my clean clothes, with my clean body. *I'm okay.* Priya's light snoring is like the steam, a warm embrace. I close my eyes.

I wake just before noon, an hour before I'm supposed to meet Robert at the library. I peek out the window. The day is clear and bright, and students already litter the grass to claim their spot of sunshine. I pull on jeans and a sweatshirt, then head to the dining hall for breakfast.

I pile my plate with pancakes and eggs and hash browns and place it on a nearby table, then hit the coffee bar.

"No food?" Noelle asks. Instead of a taunting tone, I think I hear something of concern in her voice.

I secure the lid over my coffee cup and smile at her. "I've got my plate on the table already. Are you eating? I mean, you want to join me?"

"Yeah." She smiles and runs a hand through her wavy hair. "I'm going to grab some lunch and meet you over there."

I settle onto the bench and take a sip of coffee before I dive into my mountain of food. I've eaten all of my eggs by the time Noelle sits next to me. She looks at my plate of yellow goo and pancake mush.

"I'm glad to see some things don't change," she says, and stabs at her salad with a fork. I nod, not able to respond through my mouthful. "I, uh, heard the shower running this morning. At like three something."

I wipe yolk from the corner of my mouth. "Did I wake you? I'm so sorry. I was trying to be quiet."

She digs at her salad, never taking a bite. "You slept with her, didn't you?"

I can tell she's not angry. Maybe tired. I push my messy plate away, feeling it's out of place. "I have to meet Robert at the library." I check my watch. "Like, now. Will you meet me there after?"

She's quiet.

"I really want to talk to you. Alone."

"Okay."

"Okay. Great. I'll text you when we're finishing up." I stand to start clearing my area. "I like how often I run into you here." She doesn't respond, but I know she's listening. She's been listening the whole time. Something about this day makes me feel hopeful. Hopeful for me and Noelle, hopeful for AQF, hopeful for myself.

Robert waits for me on the front steps of the library, visibly overflowing with energy. He hops down the stairs when he spots me, his movements jerky and caffeinated. I take a breath to steady myself before he reaches me, not sure if I can handle whatever he's got going on right now.

He falls into stride with me. "You're late."

"By five minutes. Can we stop for a coffee before we start?" I slow my pace when we reach the café.

Robert crosses his arms and arches an eyebrow. "Fine. But hurry up."

"Okay. Geez." I order myself a dark roast with cream and walk out of the café to meet Robert again. "That wasn't so bad, was it?"

"Come on." He grabs my arm to pull me to our usual table. Before I can relax into my chair, Robert starts. "I've been waiting all morning to tell you this." He smiles.

"Tell me."

"Being the good gay boy I am, I reached out to some of my friends in Atlanta." He smirks.

I sip my coffee and lean my elbows on the table. "And?"

"And I have a connection to a writer for the *Atlanta Sun*. It's not a huge publication, but it's big enough." His grin stretches to the limits of his lips.

The pieces start to form a picture in my mind, bells ring. I catch up to where Robert is running. "Oh, wow."

"Yeah, *wow*. I've been emailing Will, the journalist, all morning. He's going to write an article about the formation of the club. A *will they or won't they* about the Alder administration."

"It's perfect. Put the spotlight on their decision." I knew this day was magic.

"Exactly. They have a ton of conservative religious pressure on them. They do. But that is a microcosm of the world, not a reality. I mean, it's 2022. If they deny us recognition and this article goes out, they're totally fucked."

I start scribbling on a blank piece of paper in my folder. I don't want to forget any of the ideas that race through my head. "It can't be a threat, though. We need to approach them like, look, this newspaper is going to do an article on this awesome moment for the university. Like we think it's obvious they'll approve us."

"Yes. Exactly."

"Okay. Catch me up on your conversations with Will. Tell me everything."

We sit for hours, formulating our application and cover letter to send to the administration. We argue about verbiage and length and tone, both of us so sure of what would be most convincing. We write about how the *Atlanta Sun* will cover this momentous decision and that we look forward to being a part of Alder's rich history of inclusion. Vomit.

I've never felt surer of anything. I'm not who I used to be. I can feel it. I'm the kind of girl who knows exactly what she wants. And I'm going to get it. I won't stop until I do. "We need to have an event," I say.

"What do you mean?"

I pull out a fresh piece of paper and push the application to one side of the table. "I mean, if this thing gets approved, we need to have an inaugural meeting and celebration. Which brings me to my next subject: we've been so busy applying, we forgot to get members."

"Can't get members for a club that doesn't exist."

"We at least need a sign-up sheet. So if it goes through, we have people to attend the first meeting or party or whatever. I know my friends will join." I stop and look to the ceiling. "Well, most of them, I think. And there's Ashley and most of our class."

"You're right. We can get at least fifteen people signed up."

"And for the party?"

"Inaugural meeting in Steve's classroom. A *short* meeting. Then we can take over my house. I have some awesome stereo equipment and can make it pretty epic."

"Done." I smile and pull out my phone to text Noelle.

Me: *Done here in ten. Meet me on the steps?*

I pack away all of our application and cover letter drafts, saving the winners to put on top in the folder. I watch Robert as he packs his own bag. His blond green hair skims just above his eyes. His shoulders are broad, and he always holds them back and straight, a manifestation of his easy confidence.

He catches me. "Thought you were gay."

"Feel like experimenting?" I wink.

He straightens and looks me up and down. Shrugs. "I've done worse."

I push him in the shoulder. "Jerk. I was just admiring you. Feeling thankful for you."

My phone buzzes. Noelle: *Be there soon.* I smile at the screen.

"Ashley?" Robert asks.

I tuck my phone away and start walking with him to the café. "No. That's over." I slow when we run into the aroma of coffee. "I'm meeting another friend to study for history."

He pops a brow. "Mm-hmm."

I pull him into a quick hug. "I'll submit these tomorrow."

When Robert clears the library, I go back into the café and order a coffee for Noelle and another for me. I take the two cups and sit on the top step outside. The breeze is warm, thickening with pollen. Soon, we'll all be covered in a green snow. The early azaleas are in bloom, and pouty irises spot the common grounds. I close my eyes against the sun, anxious about how quickly this semester has changed from frost to flower. The light permeating my eyelids shifts to black, and I know she's standing in front of me before she even speaks.

"Hey, loser."

My eyes flutter open, try to adjust. All I see is a black form of Noelle, backlit and empty. I blink in rapid spurts, overwhelmed with the need to see her in color. I scramble to my feet and step to her side, relieved to see her gold and green form in front of me.

I hand her a coffee. "You have a way of sneaking up on me." We walk together through the library doors.

"Not hard to do when you have your eyes closed."

We take the elevator to the third floor, the perfect floor for a private conversation. The fourth floor is the quiet floor, so any whispering would draw attention to us. But the third floor doesn't have a computer lab, doesn't have a coffee spot, and isn't the main floor, so it is pretty desolate.

I sit on the carpet. "This is perfect."

Noelle sits next to me, our backs against a small section of books about the Australian Outback, menacing spiders and snakes try to crawl off the covers and down our backs. Our legs stretch across the aisle but don't quite make it to the rack of books across from us. The air is tired from so many old books oozing history and dust into the atmosphere.

I sip my coffee and gather my thoughts. Noelle sits quietly next to me.

"Noelle, I am so sorry," I finally say. Then, a couple seconds of silence because I instantly forget everything I'd planned to say to her. To her, Noelle, this girl who changed my life. She watches me struggle for words, and her mouth twitches at the corners in a struggle not to smile.

"I...So, what I mean is, I just—"

Noelle's resolve shatters. "Oh geez, Bails, please stop. It is literally painful to watch you flail like this. I know you had sex with her." Her fingers tap the lid of her coffee cup. She bites her lip and lets her head fall back against the animals of the outback. "I won't lie. It fucking shatters me. But I guess you're single and can do what you want. Go date or whatever." Her throat twitches, a swallow, some choice words, pain.

"I had sex with her. And in the middle of going down on her, I ran naked through her hallway—during a raging party—and threw up, like, five times. When I came back in the room, I told her I felt sick. But she spread her legs and asked me to finish. And for some fucked-up, demented reason, I tried. And I had a thought. I thought, I hope the bile from my vomit burns her. Then I got up and left."

Noelle stays quiet.

"I know. It's gross. And it doesn't change anything. I had sex with someone who wasn't you. But you should know what it was like." I lean against the bookshelf and look at the dirty carpet between my knees. Why did I ever get involved with Ashley? I'd be heartbroken if Noelle so much as kissed someone else. Maybe she has.

"George asked me out."

"George?"

"From history, remember?"

"All I remember from that class is you." I see the corner of her lip twitch, like it wants to smile. "What'd you tell him?"

"Yes."

I run my hand through my hair. Try to breathe in through my nose, out through my mouth.

"I mean, what do you expect? You're clearly moving on."

"So this is how it feels." She's right. What did I expect? I want to explode. I wring my hands in my lap, knock my head against the books behind me but accidently hit the metal crossbar. "Fuck." I rub at the back of my head.

"I can't believe you're just now realizing that. I haven't even been out with the guy. Imagine how you've made me feel this last month. You've had your head so far in the sky, you couldn't even see me anymore."

I turn to her. "Are you crazy? You're all I fucking see, Noelle." Tears gather force. "I can't run away from you, you're always there. I try to drown you with alcohol, I try other people, I try to bury myself in school, but you're always there. You think I broke your heart. You're right. But you broke mine, too."

We sit in silence. My breathing is loud and fast, so I focus on slowing it down, evening it out. It grows louder, faster. My heart pumps like it didn't get the memo that we canceled windsprints.

"I believe I'm doing the right thing. Or I wouldn't have done it," I say between my loud breaths. My hands shake. I have no control over my body and wonder if a nineteen-year-old can die of a heart attack. "I wouldn't have given you up. You..." Breathe. Breathe. Breathe. "I think you may be the love of my life. And all of a sudden, this road just appears, and I have to take it. And you won't come with me, and it's like, you led me here. You were my scaffolding, but you won't come to the top with me. And I—" I gasp for air.

"Breathe, Bailey," Noelle whispers, "just breathe." But I can't breathe without her. I know now that I could've had it all. Dumping her was a mistake. Nothing can change who I am now, not even having a girlfriend who's not ready to come out. That doesn't make me weak. It has nothing to do with me. If I'd respected her...

I feel like the deeper I breathe, the faster my heart beats. Skips beats. And my lungs can't suck in enough oxygen. My vision blurs, and I cover my eyes, falling into a light-headed buzz. Noelle pulls me into her. Her arms hold my head against her chest. Fingers pass through my hair. Her whispers sound far away, like I'm underwater, and she's on land, calling to me.

"It's a panic attack. They're super common. You're okay."

I shiver against her body, focus on the whooshing of her heart instead of mine.

She gathers me against her. "Breathe, love. Breathe. It's all okay." I feel her lips in my hair. I wrap an arm around her waist to pull us even closer together, feeling like she's my lifeline right now. I hear her breath hitch. I breathe and listen to her heartbeat. Breathe and listen. Breathe. Listen. I feel my body start to relax. Muscles I didn't even know were clenched, loosen. I release the fistful of Noelle's shirt and stretch my fingers.

"That's it, baby," she whispers, sending a different kind of shiver through my bones. I straighten up, smooth my hair, rub my hands over my knees.

I breathe out, eyes wide, hand over heart. "Holy shit. I've never experienced that before."

"That was a classic panic attack. It's okay. You're okay." She pats my knee, and I grab her hand, hold it in my lap.

I look at her. "It felt like I was dying. Like I was literally fading."

"Yeah. A lot of people feel that when they panic."

I squeeze her wrist. "You called me *baby*." I run a hand up and down her forearm, reveling in her soft skin. Her breathing quickens.

"You misheard. I said *Bailey*, not *baby*."

I turn into her, place a hand on her cheek, put my mouth against her ear like it's a necessity in order for her to hear me. "You called me *baby*." And now I know for sure. She still loves me, and I want her back.

She grips my wrist. I brush my mouth from her ear down to her neck, press my lips against her there. "Come here," she says. She leans in to me, her approach opening up the storm clouds of us. Every memory, every familiar kiss pours over me in a million little drops. Just one more drop for us.

I lean in to meet her and close my eyes when my lips touch hers. It feels like the end and the beginning. I have no idea which it actually is, so I try to memorize this moment. Memorize how soft her cheek feels against mine. How my lower back aches from the awkward angle. How her warm breath tastes like coffee and a little bit like vanilla from her ChapStick. How her fingers firm around the back of my neck, as if I'm something special. And how the second our lips break contact, Noelle's turn up at the corners, and her eyes fill with wonder or maybe disbelief, as if that was the best thing that could have ever happened to her.

She's the best thing that could have ever happened to me.

Our foreheads stay pressed together, both of us unwilling to let the moment go. Low, warm chuckles fill the space between our mouths.

"I love you, Noelle."

"I love you, Bailey."

I lean back against the shelf, sighing with the pain and relief of changing positions. "What does this mean?"

"Let's just see what happens. Okay? I think we both need to think about it for a while."

I take a deep breath and struggle to my feet with a groan. I wipe my hands on my jeans, then offer Noelle a helping hand. "I can assure you, this is all I'll be thinking about for weeks."

She puts her hands on my shoulders, smooths out my shirt. My hands find her hips.

"One more kiss?" I ask.

She answers with her lips on mine. Nothing tentative about it. Our tongues brush over one another, and I press myself against her. Just as quickly, she breaks off and pushes me away, holds me at arm's length.

I lean into her hand pressed against my chest. "I just want you to find it, too, you know?"

"Find what?"

"Your treasure." I wink.

"I'm trying. You need to know that I'm trying." She drops her hand and wraps me into a hug. "Now, enough of this. Let's get out of here before you have another panic attack."

I feel like I am finally seeing clearly. The last pieces of me are falling into place, and I know exactly what I want. I want it all.

CHAPTER EIGHTEEN

A pril in Alder: everyone walks around slightly underdressed and goose bumped, optimism and eagerness winning out over reality. I feel my own flesh push into bumps when I pass under a big shady oak. I could swear the temperature drops ten degrees in the shade. My shoes grow soggy from traversing the dewy grass, but I want to get to Brown Hall ASAP, and that means taking shortcuts, not paths. A constant humming noise accompanies the mornings now, filling the air with the smell of fresh cut grass. I wonder how they can cut it when it's so wet.

Robert waits on the bench in the entryway of Brown.

I smooth down my hair and clothes. "Hey."

"Hey. You got everything?"

I know I do. I have everything. Priya, Cassie, and Noelle helped me put the finishing touches on our proposal. We stayed up until one in the morning practicing my pitch, and Cassie gave me a special clear folder to bind my proposal, though she assured me it wasn't fancy. I know I have it in my backpack, but a seed of doubt grows into a redwood. I sling my bag off my shoulder and unzip it. Pull out the crisp folder and hand it to Robert. I've never been prouder of anything or more nervous.

"Got it."

He looks over the title page, flips through the seven pages of mission statement, officers, members, meeting locations, etc. "Awesome. Looks great."

"*You* look great."

Robert is wearing black pants and a nice button-down. His hair is combed and parted to the side, most of the green has faded out, giving him more of a *spent too much time in a chlorinated pool* look. "You, too. We basically wore the same thing." He looks me up and down. "Lesbians." He sighs.

"You should be flattered. Do you have the tape recorder?"

"Yep." He produces a sleek little recording device from his pocket. It's not a *tape* recorder, but it still has that classic recorder shape; there's no mistaking what it is. Of course, our phones can record conversations, but we decided it would be a better visualization tool for Dr. Lymer.

"It's perfect. And Will is ready to receive a phone call from Dr. Lymer?" I ask.

"Yep, he's prepared to verify he's writing a story about this."

I pace in front of him. Check my watch twice more, compare it to the clock on the wall. Five minutes till blast off. "Why do I feel like we're about to rob a bank?" I ask.

Robert steps toward me and grabs my arm, halting my pacing. "Hey. Relax. This is a win-win for us. If they approve it, great. If they don't, well, we have a big project ahead of us."

"Yeah. Yeah, you're right. Nothing to lose."

"Everything to gain."

I jump at the front doors slamming open. Steve rushes in and beelines to me and Robert. "Made it just in time." He smiles, one hand gripping each of our shoulders as if we're his misbehaving kids. He looks down at both of us, his hair disheveled, smelling like cigarettes. No, not cigarettes. He smells like cigars. "Now remember, I'll fail both of you if you mess this up."

I laugh a nervous laugh, not because I believe him but because I think he's nervous, too.

"No, in all seriousness, no matter what happens, I'm really proud of you two. Just try not to get me fired." He winks.

The seriousness of what we're about to do hits me. We could actually get Steve fired. I could lose my scholarship. I breathe through the anxiety.

A rotund, balding man rounds the corner, and I know from my internet stalking that this is Dr. Lymer. "Bailey and Robert?"

We affirm in unison.

"Great. Follow me, please."

"Good luck," Steve calls to us as he sits on the bench to wait. Robert and I follow a couple paces behind Dr. Lymer until we reach his office door and are ushered inside. We sit in the two chairs in front of his desk. I hand him our official proposal and pull out two copies for Robert and I to follow along with. Heat floods my cheeks, and I fall into fight or flight mode. Time to fight.

"All right, so what do we have here?"

Robert clears his throat and explains our formation of the Alder Queer Fellowship.

Dr. Lymer quickly cuts him off with one chubby pointer finger held in the air. "I'm sorry. Let me make sure I understand. You want to make a gay club at Alder University?"

"Yes." Robert's affirmative is clear and strong.

I pull the tape recorder from his bag and place it on the table. Dr. Lymer's eyes flash to it. "To keep the minutes," I explain.

"Listen, why would we have a gay club? Do we have a straight club? No. I don't understand why we should be starting clubs based on sexual orientation."

I jump into action. "Sir, the Alder Queer Fellowship is not a club about sexual orientation. It's a club made to protect our queer students. Did you know that forty percent of transgender adults report having tried to commit suicide? Did you know that LGBTQ+ youth attempt suicide at a rate five times higher than their heterosexual peers?"

Dr. Lymer shakes his jowls.

"I believe that knowing these statistics is particularly helpful when trying to understand this final one. For each occurrence of abuse or verbal harassment—such as the harassment Robert and I face almost every week from the religious protestors allowed on our campus—the likelihood of self-harm for queer youth is increased by 2.5 times. Words *matter*. The messaging that you allow on your campus *matters*. This is a life-or-death situation for too many of us. The Alder Queer Fellowship strives to work with university leaders to form a more inclusive, and therefore safer, campus for all students, ultimately bringing us closer to our mission as Catholics." I stop talking, hope I didn't do the thing when I'm nervous and talk extremely fast.

But I'm not nervous. I'm angry.

Dr. Lymer steeples his fingers and looks at Robert. "Do you have anything to add?"

He drops his eyes to the recorder. "We've been in contact with a reporter for the *Atlanta Sun*. We're extremely excited for Alder University to turn the corner on these critical issues."

I close my notes and wait for Dr. Lymer to say something.

He drops his thick hands to the folder of information we provided him. "Thank you. I will consider this." He holds up the folder, then shoots his gaze toward the closed office door. It takes me a second to realize what he's trying to say. *Get the fuck out.*

I stand and pack away our copies of the proposal, reach a hand out to Dr. Lymer. For a moment, I think he won't shake it. Because I'm gay? No, I know it's because of the terrible position we just put him in. He reaches out and gives me a dead fish handshake. "Thank you for taking the time, Dr. Lymer. We look forward to hearing from you."

Robert shakes Dr. Lymer's dead fish and clicks his recorder off. We bound down the hallway. I feel like we've escaped with bags full of money. At least it's done. Steve waits for us on the bench.

He jumps to his feet when he sees us turn the corner. "How was it? Are we starting a club, or are we burning down the university?"

"They are considering our offer," Robert tells him.

"Well, the deadline is next Friday, so we should hear back soon," Steve says.

"I think it went well. He definitely took us seriously. Seems like he knows what kind of damage the article would do," I say.

Steve envelops us both into a hug. "I'm so proud of you." I allow myself to feel that pride in myself. And I didn't lose my scholarship. Not yet, at least. He releases us and looks at the clock.

"Okay, I got a baseball game to go watch. See you guys in class." He turns and leaves.

I extend my hand to Robert. "How about a real handshake?"

He smiles and shakes my hand with a firmness that reflects respect and determination. "Great job in there," he says.

"Really? I think I blacked out."

"No. You killed it."

"Thank you. We're a good team."

"Ashley said we could use Nan's if we want. May be nice instead of my dingy house. We could actually dance and have a party." I must bristle at her name because Robert pops an eyebrow at me again. "What? Things not go so well at her party?"

"No, it's fine. I'm just not really interested. But it would be awesome to have the party at Nan's." I need to text Ashley. "Let's plan for that. Email our members?"

"All fifteen of 'em. On it. See you at class tomorrow?"

"Yep."

After Robert leaves, I sit outside on the front steps of the building, the concrete clawing at my pants. I should have talked to Ashley earlier. We've just been ignoring each other. I don't want her to feel uncomfortable around me. I think she's a good enough person, just not my person. That position is filled.

Me: *Hey. I think I owe you an apology. I'm sorry I bailed so abruptly at your party.* Send. That was the lamest text. I stand and stretch my arms over my head, untuck my shirt, start walking back to Baker. *Buzz.*

Ashley: *It's all good. I mean, pretty weird, but whatever.*

Me: *Well, you're pretty weird, but whatever.* Delete. Delete. Delete. Jesus. Me: *Robert mentioned we could use Nan's for our first meeting-party. I wanted to make sure that was still okay with you.*

Ashley: *Well, yeah. I am a part of the club, too.*

Me: *Yeah, of course.*

Ashley: *So how'd it go? Are we a club?*

Me: *We are under consideration. Should have an answer soon.*

Ashley never responds to my last text, which I understand. I should have been honest with her sooner about not being interested.

It would have saved us both some trouble. If she were someone closer to me, I'd need an apology from her, too. But, as it turns out, I just don't care. I walk home and smile, thinking about my friends. Thinking about Cassie and Noelle and Priya staying up to help me. About Noelle. How she smiles at me. How she looks at me. Like she used to. Things are starting to come together. I never could have imagined that this would be my life.

"Hey." A chorus greets me from the common room.

"Hello, everybody." I fall into the open seat next to Noelle. "Hey, you."

"Well, how'd it go?" Luke asks.

I fill them in on the meeting, on the dead fish handshake, on the trembling jowls and the "tape" recorder. How I wish I could tell them more details, but I'm pretty sure I blacked out.

"Whoa. You and Robert are badasses," Matt says.

"Thank you." I blush, taken by his rough compliment. I look around at everyone. "What're y'all doing down here, anyway? Did Luke drag you guys into some Luke game or something? What're we playing?" I rub my palms together at the idea of a fun game.

Noelle's hand finds my knee. "No games. We just wanted to be here when you got home."

"Noelle rallied the troops," Matt adds.

I stare at her. She squeezes my knee, smiles.

"Well, thanks. Means a lot."

"You know, it is super nice out," Luke says, and everyone cranes their neck to peek out the window.

"This is true," I say.

"Game of touch in the quad?"

Definitely.

We play touch football for almost three hours, drunk on spring sunshine and each other. We decide we're satiated once the grass stains take up more surface area than not on our T-shirts. After everyone washes up, we walk to the dining hall together and eat like the hungry horde of teenagers we are. For once, I don't have a care in the world. I am completely seen and completely happy.

❖

I toss and turn under my quilt. My calf muscles are drawn tight and ache with a need to be stretched. Priya isn't asleep yet, either. There's no soft snoring coming from her bed. I slide out of my sheets and sit in the middle of our floor, stretch one leg out, curl one leg in. Reach.

"We do midnight yoga now?" she mumbles.

"Sorry. I have such restless legs. Can't sleep."

Priya rolls on her side to watch my floor routine. She surrenders to being awake and sits up, resting her head in her palm.

"When are you guys going to get back together?"

My initial reaction is to ask *who*. But who the hell else would she be talking about? "I don't really know."

"What? You guys are back to how it was before. Drooling all over each other."

"You can tell a difference?"

"Yes. One-thousand-percent."

I think about how Noelle made sure everyone was in the common room when I got back today. How she brought me down from my panic attack. How she kissed me in the library. I push off the floor and tell Priya to scoot over and crawl into her warm bed. She waits for me to say something. But I let my thoughts race, one trying to outrun another. Ashley, Noelle, Luke, Hunter. I sigh and rub a palm against my closed eyes.

"Tell me," Priya whispers.

I stare at the dark ceiling, trying to define my thoughts as well as the orange glow defines itself against the black night.

"It's like, every time I've had a confusing problem, I try to punish myself. Except 'punish' isn't the right word. I don't know how to say it. In my mind, Ashley is the same as Hunter, you know? It's weird. What is that about?" It's like a very bad coping mechanism. I think I've corrected the behavior, but it's worth reflecting on.

Priya stays quiet but starts soft long strokes down my forearm. Her long nails drag across my skin and teeter between tickling me and soothing me. It's soothing for now.

"I guess what I'm afraid to see is, I don't know, a pattern in the way I face my personal problems. I just steamroll into a different problem. Or a different person."

"Bailey. You, more than anyone I know, don't run from your problems."

"But—"

"No. Listen. You are passionate, and you don't let anything push you off your path. That's who you are." She takes a moment. I know she's trying to find the best way to phrase what she wants to tell me, something that she thinks may offend me. I steel myself.

"Seems like, maybe, all of those *problems* you referred to are really just Noelle. Like, with the Ashley thing, you were never into it. I think you're right. You got with Ashley for the same reason you got with Hunter, just trying to run away from her." She nods to the room next door. "You can't stay in some nebulous gray area. It's not fair to you or her. And if I'm honest, you're being an idiot about it. I know something happened between you two. It's written all over y'all's faces." She takes a deep breath, and I know the big one is coming. I wait.

"Bailey, I love you and think you're incredible, but you're being selfish. She loves you. She *loves* you. You can't just take that love without giving yourself to her, too."

All of my familiar arguments swirl in my head. *She chose fear, she wants me to lie, she's denying me.* But I breathe, trying to see past them. Breathe. *Breathe, love. That's it, baby.* I feel like a petulant child while Noelle is the steady parent, waiting me out, waiting for my tantrum to end.

"You're right. I have been selfish. I am selfish. She is…she's…"

"I know. I know, boo."

"Ugh, God. I'm sorry I'm such an ass."

"It's okay."

"I love you guys."

"We think you're all right."

"Shut up."

I shimmy out of her bed and back into mine, under my faded quilt. I wanted so badly to do what was right, but I didn't even know what *right* was. It's being me. Being queer and strong. It's being a feminist. It's Noelle. It's all of those things together. *I want it all.* My eyelids grow heavy as I think about her.

❖

Ashley, Robert, and I wait for all the students to file out of Steve's class. We hung a clipboard with a sign-up list for the Alder Queer Fellowship on the wall by the door. I walk over to check it. Run my finger down the email addresses I already know, find two new ones at the bottom of the list. That puts us at twenty-one members. Well, twenty-one *potential* members. Steve received the decision via email this morning. I've been trying to read his face all class. I want to know so badly, but I also relish these last moments of not knowing. Because if the answer is no, I'll be heartbroken.

The last outsider disappears through the doorway. "All right, guys. Ya ready?" I glance at Robert, trying to judge if he's feeling what I'm feeling. It's just a club. It's *not* just a club. We've worked so hard on the Alder Queer Fellowship, and regardless of which decision the administration made, it will be monumental for the university.

Steve hands us each a printout of the email. "I want you all to read it. Keep it."

My heart skips. He wants us to keep it.

Dr. Martin,

After much deliberation, myself and the rest of the Alder University administration feel that the Alder Queer Fellowship does not align with our school values and our own Catholic fellowship. While we welcome all students and strive to provide safe and equal accommodations for all, Alder University, as a devout Catholic institution, simply cannot sponsor this kind of club.

We have noticed most of the potential members of this club are enrolled in either your Intro to Political Science class or your Political Science Research Methods class. There is a concern among the administration about how you are using your influence over these young minds. We would be much obliged if you could stop by the offices after your final class today to help us better understand your involvement.

    God Bless,

    Phillip Lymer

    Alder University Board of Trustees

I feel the blood drain from my face. I stare at the tiny black letters until they begin to fuzz and blend and liquify and—

"What the fuck?" Robert's voice snaps me out of my ink trance. *They rejected us.* "What the? They're going to try to fire you, Steve. They're gonna try to fire you."

"Hang on, Robert, we don't know that. Everything is going to be okay. I want you guys to focus on your next steps here, not on me. This is important, and it's far from over." Steve runs a hand through his scraggly hair and looks past us somewhere. "I mean, you can change this place. That's what all of you want to do one day, change something for the better. This shitty email is just the beginning."

I stare at him. He must not understand. I can't let him lose his job over something I did. "What about you? You're the best damn thing about this school. Without you, we wouldn't even have the tools or support to try this. You can't get fired," I protest. *I'm only a freshman.* Selfish.

"Don't tell the admin that," he chuckles.

"This is so fucked-up," Ashley says. I almost forgot she was here.

All of the next steps race through my mind. "Robert, we need to contact Will ASAP."

"Let's go to the library," he says.

We all look to Steve for something he just can't give us. We want him to tell us he won't get fired. He can't.

Instead, he shoos us out of his classroom. "Go. Go get these assholes."

We have no choice but to channel all of our anger into this. We at least need to have enough of an impact in the press to save Steve's job.

❖

We sit at the first open table we see, the printed-out email still in each of our hands.

"We should make an outline for Will. Make sure he knows what points we want to make. I mean, I know it's his article. Just suggestions. I'll scan this to send him with our recordings and club information," I say.

Robert and Ashley nod. "I just can't believe it." Robert sighs.

"I was thinking on the walk over here that we picked the perfect name. Alder Queer Fellowship. Alder is the name of our city, so our club doesn't have to be an Alder University club. It can just be a club in the city of Alder, Georgia," I tell them.

"Hmm. Good point," Robert says.

Ashley brightens. "Yeah, okay."

"We can still do everything we want to do. We can form this fellowship. Reach out to our members and have meetings and parties. We just didn't get the recognition we need from the university. Which will be at the top of our agenda for next year." *Nothing to lose. Everything to gain.* Maybe this was meant to be because now the three of us are more revved up than ever.

"I love it," Robert says.

We draft an email to Will with everything he will need to write the article. Hit the send button and pray to God that he is as good of a journalist as Robert claims. We need a calm, solid article full of facts and details, not a fanatic pile of shit.

We plan the details of our party at Nan's. Once our collective energy begins to fade, we pack up and call it a day. I'm about to walk away when Ashley grabs my arm. "Bailey, wait. Can we talk?"

My initial reaction is *no*. "Sure."

Robert looks at both of us and shrugs. "Well, I'll leave you guys to whatever this is. See ya at Nan's."

Ashley and I sit back down at the table, and I prepare for whatever this conversation is going to be. "You could have just told me," she says.

Bullseye. That's my one regret. Not getting too drunk or high or acting foolish. I regret lying to her. I told her I was available. And even though I wasn't technically in a relationship, I was the farthest thing from available. "You're right. I'm really sorry that I wasn't up-front with you."

She nods. "It's not too late to be. Although you haven't used your words to tell me, I know now nothing is going to happen between us. And if you would have used your words like an adult, then maybe I wouldn't have felt like you were really into me and wanted to have sex with me. Which you clearly didn't. Instead, you made me feel terrible and used."

I listen to her words with care. Everything she says is spot-on. If I had been honest and shared any of my feelings with her, we would have never gotten to the point of having weirdly bad sex and both feeling bad and used. It wasn't her fault. It was mine. Time to woman up. "I wasn't ready to date anybody. I'd just gotten my heart broken and am still in love with the girl. I was attracted to you, but I wasn't truly open to the possibility of moving on with someone else. But I used you to avoid dealing with her. And didn't tell you when I knew things wouldn't progress with us. You are completely right, and I'm sorry."

She nods along with my words until I finish. "Thank you. We don't have to date. I never wanted you to feel forced into that. You're queer and cool, so I just want to know you regardless. Friends?"

"Wait. There's one more thing I want to be honest about. When we were having sex in your room, I didn't like it when you asked me to finish you off after I'd thrown up in your bathroom. I hated it. It upset me."

Her eyebrows shoot up to her forehead. "You threw up? Oh my God."

"Well, yeah. I told you I didn't feel good."

She shakes her head. "I thought you were just a little high. I didn't know you were throwing up in there, Bailey. Fuck. I'm so sorry."

Wow. I'm shocked at how much a little miscommunication can mess with a relationship. Ashley isn't as bad as I thought she was. "I'm an idiot."

"Me, too. I really appreciate you talking to me. Can we officially start our friendship, now?"

One more puzzle piece snaps into place. One that I didn't even realize belonged in my puzzle, but I'm so thankful that it does. I want Ashley on my team. "Yes, please." I wrap her up in a hug, and she walks me back to Baker.

CHAPTER NINETEEN

"D id you see the article?" I ask Steve when he makes his way past the little dance floor. He cocks his head, points his ear at me, cups a hand over it. The music is a little louder than I was hoping, but Robert decided we had everything to celebrate, so he and his boyfriend went all out with the DJ stand.

I hold up a printout of the article, one of fifty that are scattered throughout Nan's tonight: "Alder University Falters: Says No to LGBTQ+ Club, Remains Firmly Planted in a History of Discrimination." Will did a great job. The article is clear and concise, outlining the very real consequences the university will face without coming across as a diatribe.

"The article. Did you read it?" I shout.

He nods, then catches the wave of the baseline and starts to dance along with his affirmative. I put a hand on his shoulder, trying to tamp down my mounting frustration with everyone tonight. Am I the only one who realizes how much work there is to do? This article is just the beginning.

Steve stops dancing and leans into me. "Bailey, I am wildly proud of you. And I can see you squirming in your skin, not ready to put down this project until the Fall. But look around, the school year is over. You go back to Savannah tomorrow. What can you do until then? Enjoy tonight. Enjoy your success. And tomorrow, when summer vacation starts, get to work. But not tonight. Don't let tonight pass you by." His words are shockingly clear for all of the tang of bourbon each of them carries to my nostrils.

"Did you get fired?"

"Got a paddle to the ass and ten Hail Marys."

"What do—"

"Oh Christ, Bailey. It's a damn joke. I didn't get fired. Just probation for the summer, which basically means I don't have to teach my summer classes but still get paid. Thank you kindly."

I smile wide and take a sip of my Coke. Forming AQF could have taken our scholarships and Steve's job. But it didn't. It gave us purpose and community. And it gave Steve the summer off to go do whatever Steve Martin does in his free time. I don't want to know. He's right, though—tonight is for celebrating.

"I need a beer." He thumps his fist against my shoulder before he turns to find the bar.

The turnout tonight surpassed any estimate I could have hoped for. With the help of Sam, Robert's older friends, and Steve's friends in town, we've grown our club membership by almost one hundred percent, pushing forty people now. It's thanks to the university, really; now our membership isn't restricted to just the student body. I look around Nan's. The place is packed. I sip my Coke before heading back into the masses to introduce myself to more of our new members.

Robert grabs my arm and pulls me toward him. "Hey, sexy."

"Not into guys. Sorry."

"Oh please, don't flatter yourself. Listen. We need to get onstage and say something. Like, now."

"Stage" is generous. The DJ equipment stands on a tiny platform that not even one person could fit on.

"You're right, we should say something." Part of what made coming out so scary to me was standing out. I never wanted to stand out. But now, not even speaking in front of fifty people can scare me.

"Come on." He pulls me to the front of the crowded dance floor and grabs the solo mic off the speaker. The crowd retreats a couple of feet, allowing us just enough space to command attention.

"Jules, kill the music for a sec," he says to his boyfriend, who is manning the sound system. The music dies, and all the drunk dancers look around, feeling the abruptness of being out of place. Then eyes fall on us. Robert turns on the mic and taps the top, sending an electric *thump-thump* through the bar. He hands it to me and winks.

I squint against the glowing red and try to will away my nerves, feel the tickle in my blood that tells me I'm about to speak way too fast. But just like in Dr. Lymer's office, I'm not scared. I'm excited. I take a deep breath, and on my exhale, I see Luke and Cassie, and they're holding hands. I smile against the mic. *They're here.* I should say something.

"Thank you all so much for showing up tonight," I say, and for some reason, people applaud. I take the moment to lower the volume on my mic and search the crowd. Priya and Matt are at the bar, smiling and waving at me. Scan. Scan.

And there she is. Noelle.

I knew she would come. I knew it. But at the same time, I'm floored. She showed up to the Alder *Queer* Fellowship party. Which means she had to sign her name on a piece of paper that aligns her with the LGBTQ+ community. I start to sweat under the red lightbulbs. I want to run to her and kiss her. The applause tapers out.

Shit. I need to refocus. I need to speak.

"We have much to celebrate tonight. Thanks to Dr. Martin, Will Harper from the *Atlanta Sun*, and my co-founder Robert Olson, we have established a very public base on which we can build our agenda for next year. We all love Alder. We all love Alder University. Together, the Alder Queer Fellowship will fight to make campus a space where *all* of us feel welcome to succeed. A place where student safety is prioritized. And that means a place where we don't have to get harassed between classes and a place where we are protected by anti-discrimination laws and school policies. These protections are past due. Again, thank you everyone for your support. I'm going to hand it over to my more charming counterpart, Mr. Olson."

I hand the mic to Robert and make my way through the cheering crowd. People pull at me, shake my hand, congratulate me. And it all feels very big and special. The support for AQF that floods this old dive bar in the Blue Ridge mountains makes me want to happy cry. Only one thing can trump that thought right now. Only one person. I need to find—

"Bailey. Bailey Sullivan?" A woman in a black pantsuit calls to me as I reach the edge of the crowd.

"Yes. I'm Bailey." I shake her hand.

"My name is Sarah Webster. I'm the hiring coordinator for the Atlanta Equality Foundation." She pulls a business card from her suit pocket. "Steve is a good friend of mine and said you were someone we should have our eye on. Are you familiar with our organization?"

"No, I'm sorry, I'm not." I turn her card over, the first business card anyone's given to me.

"The Atlanta Equality Foundation is a nonprofit formed by people like you, created to tackle the wide variety of inequalities faced by Georgians today."

"Wow. That sounds incredible and important. Incredibly important."

She laughs. "Well, we think you would be an excellent fit for our summer internship. You can continue working on the Alder Queer Fellowship but also reach out to other colleges that leave LGBTQ+ students out of their anti-discrimination policies. We can give you the support and tools you need."

"Thank you so much, Ms. Webster. I'd be honored." I can't keep the stupid grin off my face. I am going to make a difference in Georgia. I started this year afraid of everything. Afraid of myself. My mom told me freshman year is like throwing yourself in a blender to see what flavor smoothie you make. There were times when I thought I wouldn't make it through. Times when I thought I hated myself. But I fought hard to make it. Everything is almost perfect. There's just one thing I still need to do.

"Great. Email a summary of the work you've done with the Alder Queer Fellowship to the address on my card, and we'll go from there. I won't keep you any longer. Time to celebrate." She squeezes my shoulder and heads to the bar where Steve is chatting with Sam.

"Hey."

I whip around at the sound of her voice. The crowd yells and laughs at whatever joke Robert just cracked. But we're at the edge of it all, a satellite. "Hey."

She borrowed Priya's black dress again. The one from rave night. I grin because after all of this, after this whole shit show of freshman year, now I look at rave night, and I see her. I don't see Hunter. I see her. And I see us. "Who was that?"

"A lady who works for this equity project in Atlanta. She offered me a summer internship."

A grin breaks across Noelle's lips, and her dimples cut to frame it. Her eyes water. "I can't even express how fucking proud I am of you. That's incredible. You deserve it. You deserve everything."

"Thank you. And thanks for believing in me."

"Bailey." She grabs my hand. I look around, feeling the familiar fear of *getting caught*. "Hey." She tugs on my arm. "Don't worry about any of them. Look at me." She squeezes my hand, and I look at *her*. My stomach churns, and that little vertical line between her brows deepens. Then her dimples. Her eyes meet mine again.

"Noelle, I want—"

Her hands find my face, and her lips crash into mine. A smothering kiss meant to shut me up.

I wrap my arms around her waist. "Easy," I whisper.

When she pulls back, her cheeks are a deep scarlet. "I didn't mean to crash into you like that. I just wanted to be the one to say—"

"Wait." I grab her hand and pull her through the crowd to the back door by the bathrooms. We walk outside into the night. The early summer crickets fill the quiet night with their chorus of chirps. This moment between Noelle and I deserves quiet and privacy. Ironic, I know. All I ever wanted was to be public, and her kissing me in front of all those people slayed me, but this moment is just for us. We need to talk.

I turn to her and grab her hands. The pale yellow floodlight above the door casts her in a warm golden glow. Her lips begin to form words, but I cut her off. I can't hold it in anymore. "Noelle, I am so madly in love with you. I'd do anything to be with you again. We belong together. It's that simple."

She pulls her hands from mine and shoves me in the chest. I stumble backward a couple steps. "Goddamit, Bailey. You stole my big moment. I told you that *I* wanted to be the one to say it."

I double over and bellow laughter loud enough to compete with the crickets. Tears form in my eyes, and I lose my breath to the joy that is flooding from me. I can't stop. Noelle laughs and shakes her head at my crazed antics. "Easy with the goddamits," I say between laughing fits. "I hear they have a dungeon full of students who use the big guy's name in vain."

She takes a step toward me. "I can't believe I'm risking it all for you. You're the worst," she says, but she's chuckling.

"No," I say, still laughing. "I'm the fucking best. And so are you."

"Will you shut up and kiss me already?"

My laughter vanishes. I close the small distance between us and scoop her up like it's nothing. She wraps her legs around my waist, and we make out with pure abandon. No fear. Just two normal teenagers doing normal teenager stuff. Falling in love. Making out outside of a bar. Anything we want. I walk her back until we're braced against the door. If I didn't have an entire party waiting for me inside, I'd be tempted to pull her into the shadows and do what we haven't done since January. Her hands find my breasts, and I know she's thinking the same exact thing.

It takes all of my willpower to break away from our kiss. "I want you so badly right now. I'm dying for you."

She nods along with my words as I back us away from the wall and let her down. "But I want to talk," I say and slide down the wall to sit on the ground.

She sits next to me and grabs my hand. "Can I speak now?" she asks. I nod. "Will you be my girlfriend?"

"Yes, Noelle. Obviously." I kiss her knuckles. "Can I ask what changed for you?"

"Don't you know? Nothing. Nothing has changed about how I feel about you since the day I met you. I told you I just needed more time. I wasn't ready, but now I am. You've been really busy lately, so Priya and I have been hanging out a lot. About a week after our kiss in the library, we were taking a walk together, and she basically told me she knew that I was gay, but she said it in a super coded way that gave me an out if I needed it. But I didn't. The moment felt right, so I took the opportunity she gave me. I think I just needed someone outside of us to see me for what I am and still show me love. That was the first step. Kind of like how you came out in stages, I needed to go slow in my coming out process, too. But I've built up to this moment. I'm here. I'm ready. I'm yours."

I lean over and kiss her. I am complete. I pull away when I remember she has a crazy family. "Have you told them?"

"Not yet." She doesn't even have to ask who I'm talking about. "I need to do that in person."

"I can help. I can be there with you."

"It's okay. Priya is going to come home with me to 'visit.' And if things go terribly, then I'll go home with her and figure it out from there."

Holy shit. This is real. She's actually doing this. I'm excited, but I'm also terrified for her. I had it easy compared to this. "Will you be safe?"

"Yes. I will. The worst they'd do is kick me out. And that's what Priya is for. She's already talked to her mom about it, and we're all prepared for the worst. I'd live with them if it came to that."

I close my eyes and shake my head.

"What's wrong?" she asks.

"That was supposed to be me. I deserted you when you needed me. I should have been there to support you through this. I mean, I'm so glad Priya has your back—and it's probably best you stay with her because I don't think couples are supposed to move in together this early in a relationship—but damn, I'm so sorry, Noelle."

She rubs my knee. "Hey. It's okay. I think we can both attest to the fact that coming out is really hard and confusing. You once said to me that we should show each other a little grace. Let's do that now. I forgive you. Do you forgive me?"

"Yes."

"Look at me."

I meet her eyes. I found myself in those eyes. I found myself in her love. She brushes her thumb over my scar, and I find myself again in her touch.

"You can't stay out here all night with me. You have responsibilities to attend to inside. People want to talk to you. We have our whole lives for this." She leans into me and kisses me one more time before we return to the party.

❖

After a couple of hours, the celebration dies down, and Robert and my friends and I help clean up. Once all of the guests clear out of the pub and Sam locks the front door, he pours us a round of drinks while we work. We take stacks of empty pint glasses to the bar and return tables to their regular locations. Robert and Jules pack away the DJ equipment and bid their farewells.

My friends and I finish cleaning and hit the bar for one last round. Matt sticks to Coke. I sip my bourbon and smile. "God, I'm gonna miss the hell out of you guys. Can't believe I gotta be away from you all summer," I say.

Luke pats me on the back. "Ah, it'll fly by. Plus, it sounds like you'll be busy with a new fancy job."

With everything that happened outside with Noelle, I almost forgot about the badass internship I scored tonight. I can't wait to see my mom and tell her everything. Noelle and I have to plan to have her visit Savannah so she can meet my family.

Cassie points her tequila sunrise at me and Noelle. "I, uh, saw you guys kissing. Why am I always the last to know everything?"

I pull Noelle against me and plant a kiss on her cheek. "Don't worry, Cass, I'll catch you up on everything. I promise," Noelle says.

"By the way, Bailey, I want to apply for a leadership position in the Alder Queer Fellowship," Cassie announces.

I dribble bourbon down my chin, and Noelle wipes at it with her thumb. "Sorry, what?"

"Yeah. Alder is a *Catholic* college, and we probably have a population of students that are religious and gay. And no offense, Bails, but you're not the most devout."

"I'm literally trying to feel offended." I scrunch my brows at her then give up. "Yeah, nothing."

"Which is fine. But I think if this club takes off, we need to provide resources for that community. The church has done a lot of harm to the LGBTQ+ population, and we need to start healing that. Robert and I can work together. I feel like I have a lot to offer."

"You're right. Okay, yeah. Robert has a lot on his plate this summer. He's spending most of it with his uncle in New York. I bet he'd love the help." And I'd love to have my friends involved. AQF isn't a club solely for the queer community; it's a club for all of us. When we heal one part of our community, we all grow stronger together.

Noelle squeezes my waist and raises her beer. "Well, here's to the Alder Queer Fellowship, to Bailey"—she gives me a quick peck on the cheek—"and to freshman year."

We hoot and holler and clink glasses.

"You know, we aren't really bar folk. And it's a beautiful night out. Our last night of being freshmen at Alder. Anyone in the mood for some flashlight tag?" Luke asks.

We all look around and find the affirmatives in our upturned lips.

"Matt, take us home," Priya says.

We pile into Matt's car. Priya, his co-pilot. Me and Noelle in the middle bench seat, and Cassie and Luke in the back.

Matt plugs his phone into the auxiliary input and searches through a playlist. "Everyone buckled up?"

We roll down the windows, and the sound of crickets is drowned out when Matt turns up Sylvan Esso on the stereo. He pulls out of Nan's, crunching through the gravel lot.

He slows going into the curves and accelerates out of them.

Noelle slips her hand in mine, and I watch the dark pines blur into a streak of black green.

I pull out my phone and text my mom.

Me: I didn't turn out to be a smoothie at all. I'm vanilla ice cream with rainbow sprinkles.

About the Author

Ana Reichardt is the debut author of *Changing Majors*. She worked in the Pacific Northwest wine industry for seven years and now lives in her hometown of Roswell, Georgia, with her wife, their fluffy German shepherd, and their mildly evil cat. She loves all things fermented or distilled, walking through the local trails, and eating pastries. So many pastries. She is currently working on her second novel and dreaming of her next beach trip.

Books Available from Bold Strokes Books

A Fairer Tomorrow by Kathleen Knowles. For Maddie Weeks and Gerry Stern, the Second World War brought them together, but the end of the war might rip them apart. (978-1-63555-874-6)

Holiday Hearts by Diana Day-Admire and Lyn Cole. Opposites attract during Christmastime chaos in Kansas City. (978-1-63679-128-9)

Changing Majors by Ana Hartnett Reichardt. Beyond a love, beyond a coming-out, Bailey Sullivan discovers what lies beyond the shame and self-doubt imposed on her by traditional Southern ideals. (978-1-63679-081-7)

Fresh Grave in Grand Canyon by Lee Patton. The age-old Grand Canyon becomes more and more ominous as a group of volunteers fight to survive alone in nature and uncover a murderer among them. (978-1-63679-047-3)

Highland Whirl by Anna Larner. Opposites attract in the Scottish Highlands, when feisty Alice Campbell falls for city-girl-about-town Roxanne Barns. (978-1-63555-892-0)

Humbug by Amanda Radley. With the corporate Christmas party in jeopardy, CEO Rosalind Caldwell hires Christmas Girl Ellie Pearce as her personal assistant. The only problem is, Ellie isn't a PA, has never planned a party, and develops a ridiculous crush on her totally intimidating new boss. (978-1-63555-965-1)

On the Rocks by Georgia Beers. Schoolteacher Vanessa Martini makes no apologies for her dating checklist, and newly single mom Grace Chapman ticks all Vanessa's Do Not Date boxes. Of course, they're never going to fall in love. (978-1-63555-989-7)

Song of Serenity by Brey Willows. Arguing with the muse of music and justice is complicated, falling in love with her even more so. (978-1-63679-015-2)

The Christmas Proposal by Lisa Moreau. Stranded together in a Christmas village on a snowy mountain, Grace and Bridget face their past and question their dreams for the future. (978-1-63555-648-3)

The Infinite Summer by Morgan Lee Miller. While spending the summer with her dad in a small beach town, Remi Brenner falls for Harper Hebert and accidentally finds herself tangled up in an intense restaurant rivalry between her famous stepmom and her first love. (978-1-63555-969-9)

Wisdom by Jesse J. Thoma. When Sophia and Reggie are chosen for the governor's new community design team and tasked with tackling substance abuse and mental health issues, battle lines are drawn even as sparks fly. (978-1-63555-886-9)

A Convenient Arrangement by Aurora Rey and Jaime Clevenger. Cuffing season has come for lesbians, and for Jess Archer and Cody Dawson, their convenient arrangement becomes anything but. (978-1-63555-818-0)

An Alaskan Wedding by Nance Sparks. The last thing either Andrea or Riley expects is to bump into the one who broke her heart fifteen years ago, but when they meet at the welcome party, their feelings come rushing back. (978-1-63679-053-4)

Beulah Lodge by Cathy Dunnell. It's 1874, and newly engaged Ruth Mallowes is set on marriage and life as a missionary...until she falls in love with the housemaid at Beulah Lodge. (978-1-63679-007-7)

Gia's Gems by Toni Logan. When Lindsey Speyer discovers that popular travel columnist Gia Williams is a complete fake and threatens to expose her, blackmail has never been so sexy. (978-1-63555-917-0)

Holiday Wishes & Mistletoe Kisses by M. Ullrich. Four holidays, four couples, four chances to make their wishes come true. (978-1-63555-760-2)

Love By Proxy by Dena Blake. Tess has a secret crush on her best friend, Sophie, so the last thing she wants is to help Sophie fall in love with someone else, but how can she stand in the way of her happiness? (978-1-63555-973-6)

Loyalty, Love, & Vermouth by Eric Peterson. A comic valentine to a gay man's family of choice, including the ones with cold noses and four paws. (978-1-63555-997-2)

Marry Me by Melissa Brayden. Allison Hale attempts to plan the wedding of the century to a man who could save her family's business, if only she wasn't falling for her wedding planner, Megan Kinkaid. (978-1-63555-932-3)

Pathway to Love by Radclyffe. Courtney Valentine is looking for a woman exactly like Ben—smart, sexy, and not in the market for anything serious. All she has to do is convince Ben that sex-without-strings is the perfect pathway to pleasure. (978-1-63679-110-4)

Sweet Surprise by Jenny Frame. Flora and Mac never thought they'd ever see each other again, but when Mac opens up her barber shop right next to Flora's sweet shop, their connection comes roaring back. (978-1-63679-001-5)

The Edge of Yesterday by CJ Birch. Easton Gray is sent from the future to save humanity from technological disaster. When she's forced to target the woman she's falling in love with, can Easton do what's needed to save humanity? (978-1-63679-025-1)

The Scout and the Scoundrel by Barbara Ann Wright. With unexpected danger surrounding them, Zara and Roni are stuck between duty and survival, with little room for exploring their feelings, especially love. (978-1-63555-978-1)

Bury Me in Shadows by Greg Herren. College student Jake Chapman is forced to spend the summer at his dying grandmother's home and soon finds danger from long-buried family secrets. (978-1-63555-993-4)

Can't Leave Love by Kimberly Cooper Griffin. Sophia and Pru have no intention of falling in love, but sometimes love happens when and where you least expect it. (978-1-636790041-1)

Free Fall at Angel Creek by Julie Tizard. Detective Dee Rawlings and aircraft accident investigator Dr. River Dawson use conflicting methods to find answers when a plane goes missing, while overcoming surprising threats, and discovering an unlikely chance at love. (978-1-63555-884-5)

Love's Compromise by Cass Sellars. For Piper Holthaus and Brook Myers, will professional dreams and past baggage stop two hearts from realizing they are meant for each other? (978-1-63555-942-2)

Not All a Dream by Sophia Kell Hagin. Hester has lost the woman she loved and the world has descended into relentless dark and cold. But giving up will have to wait when she stumbles upon people who help her survive. (978-1-63679-067-1)

Protecting the Lady by Amanda Radley. If Eve Webb had known she'd be protecting royalty, she'd never have taken the job as bodyguard, but as the threat to Lady Katherine's life draws closer, she'll do whatever it takes to save her, and may just lose her heart in the process. (978-1-63679-003-9)

The Secrets of Willowra by Kadyan. A family saga of three women, their homestead called Willowra in the Australian outback, and the secrets that link them all. (978-1-63679-064-0)

Trial by Fire by Carsen Taite. When prosecutor Lennox Roy and public defender Wren Bishop become fierce adversaries in a headline-grabbing arson case, their attraction ignites a passion that leads them both to question their assumptions about the law, the truth, and each other. (978-1-63555-860-9)

Turbulent Waves by Ali Vali. Kai Merlin and Vivien Palmer plan their future together as hostile forces make their own plans to destroy what they have, as well as all those they love. (978-1-63679-011-4)

Unbreakable by Cari Hunter. When Dr. Grace Kendal is forced at gunpoint to help an injured woman, she is dragged into a nightmare where nothing is quite as it seems, and their lives aren't the only ones on the line. (978-1-63555-961-3)

Veterinary Surgeon by Nancy Wheelton. When dangerous drugs are stolen from the veterinary clinic, Mitch investigates and Kay becomes a suspect. As pride and professions clash, love seems impossible. (978-1-63679-043-5)

A Different Man by Andrew L. Huerta. This diverse collection of stories chronicling the challenges of gay life at various ages shines a light on the progress made and the progress still to come. (978-1-63555-977-4)

All That Remains by Sheri Lewis Wohl. Johnnie and Shantel might have to risk their lives—and their love—to stop a werewolf intent on killing. (978-1-63555-949-1)

Beginner's Bet by Fiona Riley. Phenom luxury Realtor Ellison Gamble has everything, except a family to share it with, so when a mix-up brings youthful Katie Crawford into her life, she bets the house on love. (978-1-63555-733-6)

Dangerous Without You by Lexus Grey. Throughout their senior year in high school, Aspen, Remington, Denna, and Raleigh face challenges in life and romance that they never expect. (978-1-63555-947-7)

Desiring More by Raven Sky. In this collection of steamy stories, a rich variety of lovers find themselves desiring more, more from a lover, more from themselves, and more from life. (978-1-63679-037-4)

Jordan's Kiss by Nanisi Barrett D'Arnuck. After losing everything in a fire, Jordan Phelps joins a small lounge band and meets pianist Morgan Sparks, who lights another blaze, this time in Jordan's heart. (978-1-63555-980-4)

Late City Summer by Jeanette Bears. Forced together for her wedding, Emily Stanton and Kate Alessi navigate their lingering passion for one another against the backdrop of New York City and World War II, and a summer romance they left behind. (978-1-63555-968-2)

Love and Lotus Blossoms by Anne Shade. On her path to self-acceptance and true passion, Janesse will risk everything—and possibly everyone—she loves. (978-1-63555-985-9)

Love in the Limelight by Ashley Moore. Marion Hargreaves, the finest actress of her generation, and Jessica Carmichael, the world's biggest pop star, rediscover each other twenty years after an ill-fated affair. (978-1-63679-051-0)

Suspecting Her by Mary P. Burns. Complications ensue when Erin O'Connor falls for top real estate saleswoman Catherine Williams while investigating racism in the real estate industry; the fallout could end their chance at happiness. (978-1-63555-960-6)

Two Winters by Lauren Emily Whalen. A modern YA retelling of Shakespeare's *The Winter's Tale* about birth, death, Catholic school, improv comedy, and the healing nature of time. (978-1-63679-019-0)

Busy Ain't the Half of It by Frederick Smith and Chaz Lamar Cruz. Elijah and Justin seek happily-ever-afters in LA, but are they too busy to notice happiness when it's there? (978-1-63555-944-6)

Calumet by Ali Vali. Jaxon Lavigne and Iris Long had a forbidden small-town romance that didn't last, and the consequences of that love will be uncovered fifteen years later at their high school reunion. (978-1-63555-900-2)

Her Countess to Cherish by Jane Walsh. London Society's material girl realizes there is more to life than diamonds when she falls in love with a non-binary bluestocking. (978-1-63555-902-6)

Hot Days, Heated Nights by Renee Roman. When Cole and Lee meet, instant attraction quickly flares into uncontrollable passion, but their connection might be short lived as Lee's identity is tied to her life in the city. (978-1-63555-888-3)

Never Be the Same by MA Binfield. Casey meets Olivia and sparks fly in this opposites attract romance that proves love can be found in the unlikeliest places. (978-1-63555-938-5)

Quiet Village by Eden Darry. Something not quite human is stalking Collie and her niece, and she'll be forced to work with undercover reporter Emily Lassiter if they want to get out of Hyam alive. (978-1-63555-898-2)

Shaken or Stirred by Georgia Beers. Bar owner Julia Martini and home health aide Savannah McNally attempt to weather the storms brought on by a mysterious blogger trashing the bar, family feuds they knew nothing about, and way too much advice from way too many relatives. (978-1-63555-928-6)

The Fiend in the Fog by Jess Faraday. Can four people on different trajectories work together to save the vulnerable residents of East London from the terrifying fiend in the fog before it's too late? (978-1-63555-514-1)

The Marriage Masquerade by Toni Logan. A no strings attached marriage scheme to inherit a Maui B&B uncovers unexpected attractions and a dark family secret. (978-1-63555-914-9)

POLITICAL
GOSPEL

POLITICAL

GOSPEL

PUBLIC
WITNESS
IN A
POLITICALLY
CRAZY
WORLD

PATRICK SCHREINER

PUBLISHING
NASHVILLE, TENNESSEE